MORE WOMEN THAN MEN

MORE WOMEN THAN MEN

by

I. COMPTON-BURNETT

LONDON
VICTOR GOLLANCZ LTD
1974

ISBN O 575 01959 X

Printed in Great Britain by
The Camelot Press Ltd, Southampton

CHAPTER I

"IT IS WITH an especial feeling that I welcome you back to-day," said Josephine Napier, rising from her desk and advancing across her study to greet the woman who had entered it. "I do not forget that you are embarking upon your eighth year on my staff. Believe me, I have not been unmindful of my growing debt. May I say that I think no one has lived a more useful seven years? You will allow me to say just that to you?"

Josephine Napier, the head of a large girls' school in a prosperous English town, was a tall, spare woman of fifty-four, with greying auburn hair, full hazel eyes, an impressive, high-featured, but simply modelled face, a conscious sincerity and simplicity of mien, rather surprisingly jewelled hands, and hair and dress arranged to set off rather than disguise experience.

Miss Theodora Luke, a mistress in her school, was an erect, pale woman of thirty-eight, with a simply straightforward and resolute face, smooth, coiled hair, grey eyes with a glance of interest and appreciation, and an oddity of dress displayed in the manner of the university woman of Victorian days, as the outward sign of the unsuspected inner truth.

"Indeed I will allow you to say it, Mrs. Napier," she said in a quick, deep voice, with a quick, deep laugh. "It definitely smoothes my path towards decrepitude."

"I think that maturity has very few disadvantages inherent in itself," said Josephine, speaking as if simply from her own experience, and adding by way of putting the full gulf of years between her companion and herself: "Did you have a pleasant journey, my dear?"

"Yes, very pleasant, thank you. The train was rather

5

crowded. But I see no reason myself for objecting to the presence of my fellow creatures." Miss Luke looked full at Josephine as she set forth her individual view. "It is extraordinary how seldom we meet unpleasant people, or see an unpleasant face. Have you ever met a repulsive person, Mrs. Napier? I think I have not."

"No, I think all faces I have met have had their human dignity and charm. But then I have spent my life amongst educated and intelligent people. I would not say that some faces might not show signs of—shall we say a different history? I hope"—Josephine bent towards her companion with a humorously guilty smile—"that you had none of those in your carriage?"

Miss Luke yielded for a moment to laughter.

"Well, what I always feel, Mrs. Napier, in meeting such people, is simply respect for their harder experience. I pay the rightful homage of the highly civilised—yes, that is what I choose to call myself—to those whose lives are spent at the base of the civilisation. Surely no other view should be admissible?"

"No, indeed it should not. I think you have given more thought to the matter than I have; to the equality of all kinds of usefulness. Possibly I have been too busy with the practical observance of it. Now, if I may claim your attention for a humdrum matter not within your province, I have to tell you that your room is changed." Josephine took up some slips of paper. "Yes, it is on the left side of the second corridor, with the south facing. You remember that the doctor said you were to have sun? I hope you will not mind making the adjustment?" She raised her eyes with her pencil on her lips, concerned simply with her programme.

"Mind? What a question, Mrs. Napier! I hope the change did not involve too much trouble. I am most grateful."

"Grateful?" said Josephine, in a faintly perplexed tone, still preoccupied. "And I have put Miss Rosetti next door.

I like to feel that intimate friends are together. In a case of sudden sickness that may mean a good deal. It is good of you all to make my task of general so light."

"Ah, I hardly think it can be that," said Miss Luke.

"Well, so pleasant then. And that would be my choice. I have no desire for any lessening of my labour. I hope you are happy to come back to yours?"

"Well, yes, the ayes have it," said Miss Luke.

"I am glad that there is a pull on the other side," said Josephine, looking at her with searching kindness. "That means at once more for you, and for other people. And now you must want your tea, and anyhow I want it for you. Crowded railway carriages need an antidote. So go and do your duty to yourself and to me."

Josephine rose for a moment as her companion rose, and then sat down at her desk and took up her pen, but in a minute rose again to welcome the successor. This was a grey-haired, foreign-looking woman, taller and frailer and some years older than Miss Luke, with finely chiselled features, pale, dreamy eyes, with a cynical look that came as a surprise, and openly languid movements, whom Josephine greeted in a manner which showed her less assured of her own impression.

"Well, you have followed close upon Miss Luke. I remembered that your trains were near together. I hope you have escaped her experience of a crowded carriage?"

"No, I have not escaped it. I have been sitting upright in the middle of one row of people, and opposite another," said the newcomer, in a deep, dragging voice, a movement of her shoulders implying that the posture she mentioned was unnatural.

"Well, I suppose we have no reason for objecting to the presence of our fellow creatures," said Josephine, continuing in Miss Luke's line.

"I had reasons for objecting to the presence of these creatures. And I don't know why they were my fellows: I saw no basis of fellowship."

7

"I confess it does not always strike the eye," said Josephine, giving a full smile. "Though we should not dare to say so to Miss Luke. At least, I should not. Perhaps you, as one admitted to greater intimacy, would have more courage."

Maria Rosetti had been born of Italian parents and brought up in France, and was qualified by these means, and by others in herself which Josephine recognised, as an exponent of modern languages.

"Well, I trust your holiday has been pleasanter than your journey back to us?"

"I have not had a holiday; I have been in a holiday post. It is wise for me to earn what I can, while I can. I have been happy and well."

"Well, I hope you will have a pleasant term. We must see that your work is not too much. Or rather I must see to it; for I do not believe I can trust you." Josephine considered a time-table fastened to her desk. "Could we cut out your afternoon conversation classes? Yes, I think we might do that." She drew her pencil through them. "Then I shall feel that your afternoons are your own."

"My holiday work has nothing to do with my work in the term, Mrs. Napier."

"Has it not?" said Josephine, on a musical note. "But it has to do with my opinion of your fitness for it. I am glad you have told me: I quite see that that was a piece of luck."

"I am quite fit for my work, Mrs. Napier."

"You need not tell me that," said Josephine gravely. "It is easy, indeed, for you to be fit for work so well within your powers. I often wish I had duties for you more up to them. But failing that, I must feel that the daily round is not enough to be a burden."

"My work is hardly up to me," said Miss Rosetti, in a level voice. "I do not give it the whole of myself, as it does not claim it. I have been waiting to say that, if you ever have an opening for a partner, I should be grateful for

8

it. I am in a position to meet the material demand; or why should I not say, pay for it?"

"Now, I hope I do not seem to you self-sufficient," said Josephine after a pause, leaning over her desk with an open expression. "Believe me, I am only hard-working, and un-used to having anyone to take the work off my hands. And at the moment I am grateful, for your giving me this mark of your confidence early enough for it to have its meaning. I will bear it in mind for the future; and bear it in mind for the present for my own encouragement. And we must see that the common task is not a tax upon capacities too rare for it. I think a little lightening of it will secure that."

"You are very kind, Mrs. Napier."

"No. Why am I kind?" said Josephine, seeming to speak in an aside from jotting something down. "You have always done all you can for me."

"I will certainly do it, Mrs. Napier," said Miss Rosetti, her eyes just resting on Josephine's empty page, as she left the room.

She was succeeded in course by a short, rather ponder-ous woman of faintly comical aspect, who advanced to-wards Josephine with an expression that suggested an appreciation of her own ambling gait. She had a fresh, round face, nondescript features, unmarked for her fifty years, drab-coloured hair arranged at the least expense of effort, and prominent, vague, bright eyes, that roved and suddenly withdrew as if their owner were informed.

"How do you do, Mrs. Napier? I have come back to-day because the term begins to-morrow."

Having uttered this greeting, Miss Emmeline Munday stood at ease and in silence.

"That is very considerate. I hoped we should see you to-day. Miss Luke and Miss Rosetti have arrived, and will be waiting in your common room. I hope you are one of those people who find holidays agreeable? Which do your find the more enjoyable, the holidays or the term?"

9

"The holidays," said Miss Munday, looking steadily at Josephine.

"I should rather ask, which gives you the more satisfaction?"

Josephine paused for the corresponding amendment.

"The holidays," said Miss Munday, her lip twitching.

"Well, that is healthy," said Josephine, not prone to be dissatisfied. "Have you any suggestion to make to me before you join your friends?"

"No," said Miss Munday, blinking her eyes.

"Nothing about your hours, your classes, your number of pupils; anything? You know you are my senior mistress; you have been with me longer than any member of my staff; and I have nothing to ask of you, but that you will consult yourself in any matter that arises. You know that that could be my only wish for you?"

"Yes," said Miss Munday, and upon her corroboration turned and left the room.

The fourth arrival was the only married member of Josephine's staff, a small, harried-looking woman of forty-five, with a small, brown, untidily-featured face, small, brown, flurried hands, unkempt, noticeable clothes, and the alert, enquiring, engaging aspect of some little woodland beast. Her husband had been blamed for leaving her without provision, but with some injustice, as she was qualified for teaching English literature, by being the widow of a man who wrote. The senior branch of this subject Miss Munday conducted, by virtue of a degree, thus indicating the place of her colleague's equipment in the scale. Mrs. Chattaway seldom referred to her wedded life, and her companions, in spite of their sincere deprecation of the married state, assigned her reticence to her sense of loss; whereas the truth was, as they might consistently have guessed, that the memory was uncongenial.

"Oh, I am sure I am later than all the others; I am so ashamed. But I have had a dreadful journey. My train was late, and while I was waiting for it, it went on without me.

I did not notice it; it was my own fault. So I had to wait for the next."

"Well, I am glad that that one did not go on without you," said Josephine, smiling and retaining the speaker's hand. "It is not at all the duty of trains to us, to go on while we are waiting. We cannot be expected to do more than arrive and wait. I am afraid you must be very tired?"

"I am not so much tired as flustered and vexed with myself. And I feel so hopelessly untidy; I cannot guess how I must look." Mrs. Chattaway remedied this inability by glancing in the mirror, but seemed to take advantage of her distraught condition to pass over what she saw. "I am so very sorry to begin again by being late; I know you like us to be here for tea."

"Well, if I like that, it is for your own sake. And if you are going to arrive as troubled as this, I feel I am right. But you are mistaken in thinking that you are so late; the others have only just arrived. And if you were, fresh tea could be sent up to you. Though I admit that I do not care for you to run your meals too close, as nothing is more prejudicial to appetite. Now, may I depend on you to take the rest you need to-morrow, whether in working hours or out of them? You will serve me in that matter?" Josephine's manner was held in lighter check with this member of her house.

"You are too kind, Mrs. Napier. It is quite like coming home to come back to work here."

"Well, I should hope it is. You give me two-thirds of your life; and it would be a pretty thing if my house did not seem like home to you. There would be something very wrong with me if that could be so. If there is ever any little thing that would make it seem more homelike, you will tell me of it? May I trust you?"

"Indeed I will; indeed you may, Mrs. Napier. Not that there ever is anything; it is all thought of before we can imagine it. We do appreciate your kindness. I think you do a great work in making a self-supporting life so pleasant for the women who have to lead it."

"I am sorry you feel that about your life. May I congratulate you on hiding it so well? For it must need courage."

"Oh no, Mrs. Napier; indeed it does not. There is nothing to hide. I don't know what I meant by saying it. And of course I should not foster a feeling that might unfit me for my work."

"A feeling of that kind, even if not fostered, does unfit you for your work," said Josephine in a serious tone. "But may I pay you a compliment, and say that I do not think you can have it? I have watched you—No, no! No more and no less than it has been my duty to watch you—and I think that the feeling was a part of the disturbance of your life, when you first joined us—Believe me, I saw it with great sympathy—and that it has since vanished. Am I not right?"

"Yes, indeed you are, Mrs. Napier; I had not realised it myself. I am glad to be shown how happy I am in my life. I should be most ungrateful if I were anything else."

"You would be most unfortunate. Not to be contented in a life of useful work, that is within our power, is indeed to be unfortunate. I can imagine no lot more satisfying, and I am speaking from my own experience. I am not a person to speak lightly from a position that is not my own. And now I have preached at you long enough; I will not keep you from your tea another moment. And here is your new colleague, Miss Keats, arrived in time to share it with you! Run away, and if you will do me a kindness, ring for fresh tea for yourself and for her. Thank you very much."

Mrs. Chattaway literally ran away, and a tall, thin girl of twenty-three advanced towards Josephine, lifting her pale grey eyes from her small, pale, lively face, alert to turn to the ends of her own tongue whatever might be said.

"I am glad indeed to see you safely under this roof after

your long journey. You have been in my thoughts more than once today. I hope you found it a good one?"

"I must shatter that hope," said Miss Helen Keats, in her soft, staccato voice, meeting Josephine's eyes with her expression unsteady. "I found it a bad one. A girls' school was returning; and as this school returns to-morrow, I knew that they were returning on the wrong day. I did not say to them: 'This is the mistresses' day.' I realised that the time for controlling myself with girls was at hand."

Josephine stood smiling into her face, looking as if she would bend her head, if the face were not on a level with her own.

"You must be tired, and ready for tea and rest."

"Yes, I find that girls in numbers have that effect. It augurs well for my appetite here, if not for my work."

"I hope the appetite will not wait until tomorrow for the numbers. The tea is ready now. And you will not see much of the numbers, my dear. Nothing except in school hours; and then your classes will be small. I do not make it difficult for people to use their gifts."

"It sounds as if I had brought with me a healthy aversion from the class of beings I am concerned with. I may see the better how to improve them."

"My dear, you have brought with you a brave spirit, or you could not have joined us at all. Believe me, I am not thinking little of it, your first plunge into professional life. My own memories are not so blunt. Will you remember that a woman older than your mother is waiting here for you, if you can put her to any of the uses that youth has for middle age? And now go and make some use of that appetite you were boasting of. If you remain so pale and slender, I shall think it was an empty boast. Your common room, the senior mistresses', is on the upper floor to the right. You are very young to belong to it, but people must be in their own place. No, I will not come up with you. The room is yours, not mine. You will hear the voices through the door."

Helen went upstairs and knocked at the door described. "Is this where I am to be?" she said.

"Yes, it is, though I don't wonder that it strikes you as improbable," said Miss Luke, coming cordially forward. "So you are the glimpse of youth promised to our failing eyes; and we—there is nothing stranger than truth—are your future companions! Did Mrs. Napier warn you that you would find us all in the sere and yellow leaf?"

"Yes, I believe she did just warn me," said Helen.

Miss Luke showed amusement at finding her surmise correct, and recovered herself to introduce Miss Munday.

"I am the eldest, the senior mistress," said Miss Munday, lifting herself from the sofa to offer her hand, and sinking down again with her eyes on the floor.

"It is thoughtful of you to arrive after the rest of us, so that we are assembled to look at you," said Miss Rosetti, in the mellow tones of some of her moods, her eyes roving over Helen's form.

"You look so fresh and charming after your journey, that I can hardly believe it," said Mrs. Chattaway. "I dare not think how I must look beside you. I hardly liked to appear before Mrs. Napier, kind though she is. I think she was especially kind to-day."

"I noticed that her standard was high," said Helen.

"It is wonderful how she enters into the lives of all the people about her. If I had known it when I first came, I should have had a happier beginning."

"I suppose she forgot to tell you," said Helen. "She cannot remember with everybody."

Miss Rosetti laughed, and Miss Luke a little dubiously did the same.

"She may think that self-praise is no recommendation," said Mrs. Chattaway.

"I think she meant it for a recommendation," said Helen. "I don't see what other purpose it could serve."

"I think it often is a recommendation," said Miss Luke, standing rather squarely. "A little self-praise may augur a

14

good deal of quality. We none of us like to praise ourselves as much as we deserve." She laughed.

"I think Mrs. Napier would like it. But I admit that she only hinted at the whole."

"Ah, she is a large person, our principal," said Miss Luke, looking round. "You should all support me when I say a thing like that. You make me feel I have been fulsome."

"I support you most warmly," said Mrs. Chattaway.

Miss Rosetti raised her eyebrows, and Mrs. Chattaway at once turned towards her.

"You are too clever and cynical, Miss Rosetti, to see the ordinary good qualities the rest of us see in people," she said, intending no disparagement of anyone involved.

"I see a great many qualities in Mrs. Napier, some of them good, and very few of them ordinary."

"We have a remarkable employer, head mistress," said Mrs. Chattaway.

"We have both," said Miss Luke, gently and frankly.

"It must be trying to be the head of a school," said Mrs. Chattaway.

"It is surely the least undesirable position in it," said Miss Rosetti.

"Let me get you all some more tea," said Mrs. Chattaway. "It is too humble a duty for any of you."

"We must wait on our qualified women," said Miss Rosetti, coming to her aid.

"They say that more and more women are qualifying every year," said Mrs. Chattaway, her sequences of thought vague.

Miss Luke fell into open mirth.

"I did not mean that you were not unusual. I meant that more women were struggling to your level, who did not find it so easy."

"Oh, it was not done so easily," said Miss Luke.

"Even Mrs. Napier is not qualified, is she?" said Mrs. Chattaway.

"No," said Miss Luke, in a colourless tone.

"It is a privilege for me to have your friendship, your companionship."

"Oh, don't grudge us the status of friendship. Don't be so snubbing to mere spinsters," said Miss Luke.

"I don't mean we must call Miss Keats a spinster yet; I mean, she has not reached the age of final decision."

"Are you sure that was what you meant?" said Miss Luke, with a roguish eye.

"Can anyone tell me where I am to lay my head?" said Helen.

"On the landing above, in number forty-three," said Miss Luke. "It seems that I have been probing into what is no concern of mine."

"That is very convenient for me. I will go and take advantage of it."

"Well, what is our verdict?" said Miss Luke.

"A most charming girl!" said Mrs. Chattaway. "It is extraordinary to think she has been to Oxford and taken such a high place. She gives no sign of it at all."

"The rest of you find the matter requires consideration?" said Miss Luke, glancing at Miss Rosetti.

"What do you think yourself, Miss Luke?" said Mrs. Chattaway.

"Well," said Miss Luke in a judicial tone, "perhaps a thought self-assured for a young girl and a new-comer, among the middle-aged and established. No, well, that is rather needless. Why should she not be assured? I am sure she has every reason. But definitely and consciously a significant young woman."

"But surely that is not to her disadvantage?" said Mrs. Chattaway.

"Certainly not; to her advantage," said Miss Luke.

"And not to the disadvantage of anyone else?" said Mrs. Chattaway.

"Certainly not," said Miss Luke. "What a line to take, to

be critical of the valuable gift of young confidence, to be blind to the claim of youth!"

"Must we lay the burden of our middle age on the girl?" said Miss Rosetti. "As you said, she did not lay the burden of her youth on us. And I think she was right."

"She was undoubtedly right; and so are you; and I am wrong," said Mis Luke.

Mrs. Chattaway looked at Miss Luke with appreciation.

"I think I will follow her example and go and unpack," said Miss Rosetti.

"I will do the same," said Miss Luke.

Mrs. Chattaway sat with her eyes going after the pair.

"That is a wonderful case of devotion," she said to Miss Munday.

"Yes," said Miss Munday, looking at her empty tea-cup.

Mrs. Chattaway ran to replenish the cup, and came up to her companion.

"It must be a great thing in a life like this, such a friendship."

"Yes," said Miss Munday, stirring the cup and then raising her eyes. "It must."

"Are you interested in different human relationships?" said Mrs. Chattaway, on a more urgent note.

"Yes," said Miss Munday.

"You are more interested in abstract theories, I am sure," said Mrs. Chattaway, with compliment. "But some human relationships, that arise out of certain conditions, are worthy of attention."

"Yes," said Miss Munday.

"Both Miss Luke and Miss Rosetti have great gifts for intimacy."

"Yes, they have," said Miss Munday.

"You have watched them, have known them, ever since they have been here together?"

"Yes," said Miss Munday. "I was here before either of them."

"And they both have great powers of affection?" said

17

Mrs. Chattaway, pausing for result at length to arise from her words.

"Yes, I have found them both very affectionate," said Miss Munday, going to the door.

"I think Miss Rosetti is the less constant," said Mrs. Chattaway, taking some running steps after her.

"I have found them both quite constant," said Miss Munday.

Miss Luke and Miss Rosetti mounted arm in arm to the second floor, and pausing outside their adjoining rooms, confronted each other.

"The new young woman is along the corridor, is she not?" said Miss Luke.

"I hope so, as that was the direction you gave her."

"Is not her room the next but one to mine, next door to yours?"

"I hope so again, as that is what you said," said Miss Rosetti, pushing the other against the wall, and looking into her face.

"Did you approach Mrs. Napier on the matter of the partnership?"

"With no avail."

"She can do without you?"

"That is what she was obliged to explain, at some cost to herself and to me."

"Yes, it must have been at cost to her," said Miss Luke in a low, quick tone.

Miss Rosetti was silent.

"I am at once glad and sorry," said Miss Luke. "Glad to keep you, and sorry not to see you rising above us."

"I am only sorry."

"Ah, you have come to the end of us. But Miss Keats is fresh ground for you to plough, until you can approach your ultimate goal. I believe you have an unconscious affection for our head."

Miss Rosetti turned from Miss Luke, and sauntering past her own door, knocked at the next.

"You are settling in?" she said. "Why not sit down and let me unpack for you?"

"I see no reason against it," said Helen. "At least none that need weigh with me, if it does not with you."

"This is your first post?"

"Yes; or perhaps I should be prepared to be unpacked for by my seniors. It is a custom here? A way of putting new-comers at their ease?"

"Well, I have done it before."

"If it is not invariably done, it does not put me at my ease."

"Is this the latest fashion, and this the one before?" said Miss Rosetti, handling some dresses with open interest.

"It does not put me at my ease to be told that my second gown is out of date. Have you never been taught about poverty not being a thing to be ashamed of?"

"I have always been ashamed of it. I would save anyone in my power from it. I have done so in the one case I could. I can alter the dress so that it bears no hint of it. I am a better dressmaker than I have had any reason to be. You need not be afraid of my old maid's history."

"But why should you trouble about other people's clothes? And I have not convinced myself that poverty is shameful."

"The clothes are not other people's. They are yours. And things like poverty and old age and death are shameful. We cannot help them; but that is the humiliation. To accept conditions that would not be your choice must be a disgrace."

Miss Rosetti went to the door, swinging the dress and whistling to herself.

CHAPTER II

"My father has written to me for my birthday," said Felix Bacon, holding out a letter in his long, pale hand. "He congratulates me on completing my fortieth year. Last year he congratulated me on entering it. It seems inconsistent to congratulate for both, and a little tactless to congratulate for either. He says it is absurd to be doing nothing at that age. He said the same thing when I was twenty and thirty, and everyone knows that different things are absurd at different ages. Do I realise that he has paid for every meal that I have eaten? I had not actually realised it, meal by meal; he must be always thinking about food. That I have been a daily expense to him? Of course, it is a daily expense to pay for a person's meals; but he does not really consider them; it is a false implication. I don't know anyone who thinks less about his child's meals."

Felix crossed the room with a dancing step, and standing before a much older man, who sat by the hearth, waved the letter towards him.

"He says that forty is not too late to turn over a new leaf. Then why make this trouble about it, if it is not too late? I thought the lateness was the point. And he does not say a word about my looking so young for my age."

Felix surveyed in the mirror his small, light frame, his smooth, black hair, his narrow, green eyes, his pale, narrow face, his prominent, narrow features and his subtle, alert expression.

"My figure is remarkably supple and lithe," he said. "But when my father treats me as if I had the gift of perennial youth, I do not believe he is thinking about my figure."

"You have it indeed, my boy, and it is the rarest gift. You have to be old, to realise how rare."

Jonathan Swift rose from his seat, and, putting a hand on Felix's arm, regarded the contrast they made in the glass, his own girth double that of his companion, and the latter's head barely at his shoulder. He was a tall, vigorous man of seventy, with rather formless features, with a likeness to those of his sister, Josephine Napier, the remains of bushy, auburn hair, emotional, roving, gold-brown eyes and an expression at once benevolent and unrestrained. His parents, realising that he bore the surname of a famous man, had given him also the Christian name, by way of doing all in their power towards equality; and possibly reflecting that for his father the precaution had been omitted, and equality had not been the result. They had further put him into the same profession of the Church; and he had himself continued in the line by turning his attention to letters, so that the difference in their practice of these was the only difference between his predecessor and himself. With regard to this difference he had observed that his writings were not in accord with the present taste, and could not be published with advantage during his life. He had helped himself through this period by taking pupils; and the last of these, Felix Bacon, had remained with him for twenty-two years, ever since he had arrived as a youth of eighteen in the escort of his father, a country squire, whose difference from Jonathan's family was illustrated by his ignoring the advantage of the name of Francis for his son.

"My father has not sent me my usual birthday cheque," said Felix, "because I must not get to depend upon it. He must know that habits get set at my age, when he has so often warned me about it. The best way of learning a thing is to teach it to another. He will not pay another tailor's bill this year. I should not want him to; it would look as if my personality depended on externals. But he is really rather womanly in the way he thinks of my food and clothes. Of course he knows that I am motherless."

Felix put the letter in his pocket, indicating by a gesture that it was near his heart.

"My boy, it is the wish of my life that I may cease to be a burden. It is hard on my friends that my work is not for their time."

"The judgement of posterity is known to be the only true one. So there seems no point in getting any other. I wonder so many people do it. You seem to be very wise."

"Ah, they get something besides judgement. But I may get some ordinary work, while I can do it, and do justice with it. God knows, I hope so; God knows, I do."

"He may do something about it, now he knows. I think it must be impressed on him. But perhaps he feels it hardly matters what I wear, as I carry off shabby clothes so well."

"Your father may take his view," said Jonathan, giving his gruff, deep laugh.

"Well, it is natural that they should think about me on the same line, when they bear the same relation to me; especially as the one claims to follow the other."

"I am not going to make a business of accepting what I need from one I love," said Jonathan. "I am simply grateful, as I ought to be."

"I would have a sale of my drawings, if they were good enough to be sold for anything but charity. It is a tribute to human nature that people will only pay for things they don't want, to help good works. What a mean criticism, that they ought to help them for nothing! If I were a woman, I should always serve at bazaars; I never know why men do not serve at them. I should have a regular employment. My father should have had a daughter."

"Does he wish he had had a daughter?"

"Yes. He says he would have found one a consolation. He says too, that I might be a woman, for all the difference he can see. That seems to show that I have tried to be a comfort to him."

"Is he lonely?" said Jonathan.

"You know he is. Pray do not upset me."

"And I am not lonely owing to him."

"Entirely owing to him. He has the first claim. I could not bear to be the object of only one claim."

"We don't often get a chance of a talk like this. Young Fane seems always to be everywhere. I can't think when he does his work."

"I never think about people's work. Work is a thing I do not like to think about. It is odd that my father always connects me with it. He can hardly separate the two ideas."

"Does he suggest anything definite?"

"That I should save him the expense of an agent, and the discredit of having a son who will not live in his house. I don't mean that he actually suggests the whole of that."

"He does not sound addicted to work himself."

"Of course he is not addicted to work. Please do not speak unsuitably about my father."

"You may have inherited his liking for leisure?"

"Children must not be levelling in what they inherit. My father has a great dislike for what is levelling. I should be shocked if he worked. I must always work before him, as I recognise work to be degrading. I am not one of those modern people; I try always to seem a survival from the old world."

"It is generous of your father to continue your allow-ance."

"Yes, that often comes over me, and I resolve to amend my life. Could I teach drawing to the girls in your sister's school? The post is vacant, and I am the soul of delicacy."

"How would that appeal to your father?"

"Well, he says I might be a woman; and he wants me to work, though it is dreadfully unchivalrous of him; it would never do for him to teach in a girls' school. And women who work generally teach girls. Great women have done it, and I had better choose them for my model. I can't help thinking that my drawing is better than theirs."

"Good afternoon," said a strident, self-confident voice, as there entered a spare, vigorous man of thirty-five, with definite movements, openly penetrating eyes, and strongly aquiline features set aslant. "And what are you wagging your tongues about so busily? I hope, as the children say, it was not about me, or I shall perforce interrupt your colloquy."

"I have no respect for people who cannot have their colloquies interrupted," said Felix. "We were not talking about you, but of course we might often do so. I should never suggest anything else to a person who thought he was being talked about. But we generally talk about my father."

"I hope you have arrived at some satisfactory conclusions concerning him," said the new-comer, spacing his words as if they called for note.

"Yes; I have said some generous things."

"Well, it is never too late to mend."

"It is quite early for me to mend. I really think I am one of those people who are as old as they look."

"Well, I don't know what my looks do for me," said Mr. Fane, facing Felix as though without intention. "I may appear a thought jaded at this time of the day. I have earned my cup of tea, whether or no anybody else has."

"Nobody else has. It is extraordinary how many people talk about earning meals. My father is really typical."

William Fane was a local lawyer, who had been introduced to Jonathan as a paying guest, by a former pupil, evincing his sentiments towards his own late educator. It was a need of his nature to feel self-esteem, and as he had no unusual quality but the power of sinking below his class, he esteemed himself for being a man and a potential husband; which human attributes were, to do him justice, less general than many he possessed.

"Well, I have the pleasant weariness that comes after a day of hard and not unremunerative effort. I am a tired but contented man."

"I am glad you do not regard work as an end in itself. But I could never be both tired and contented. I don't think I understand about pleasant weariness. But I am upset when I hear that doing nothing is the most ageing thing in

24

the world. I get into the way of busying myself with little services to others." Felix poured out the tea and brought a cup to Fane.

"You ought to marry, and find scope for your gifts as a family man."

"Please do not look at me with a masculine expression. I may not have the power of making a woman happy."

"A woman asks very little beyond a home and a husband."

"She could not ask for a home from me. My father would have to offer her his; and I do not see how she could be happy with my father."

"I suppose your mother was happy with him."

"Why do you suppose that?" said Felix.

"Well, he has always been very kind and polite to me when we have met."

'He may have made differences between you and my mother."

"Well, I don't see why your mother should have died of a broken heart."

"She died when I was born. It was if she had lived, that I should have broken her heart, my father tells me. It was I, and not he, who had to cause her death."

"You seem quite obsessed by your father."

"So do you," said Felix. "I quite understand it."

"No, no, come, that is not possible."

"It seems to me inevitable, when you have met."

"I repeat that he was very kind and polite."

"Yes, you do repeat it."

"Well, come now, if you ask me, you and he would be doing more for women if you gave a couple of them mates."

"I should not dream of not asking you. You seem to know everything about it; though you have rather soon forgotten my mother. But I have heard that women like men to work."

"Yes, that is a true word," said Jonathan. "Look at my sister, who is to be with me to-night. She likes people to work indeed, dear, good woman that she is! She has been the saving of my boy. She and I are the last of our family, the eldest and the youngest, the first and the last. Yes, that is the right description in another way."

"Oh, a dinner-party to-night, is there?" said Fane.

"No, just my family to see me, if you will bear with it. My sister and her husband, and my son."

"I wonder you do not have your son to live with you, now he is a grown man."

"Surely you do not, when my sister has brought him up from babyhood, and is more than a mother to him."

"Yes, she is more than that," said Felix.

"I think I will go and take a nap, as people are coming to dinner," said Fane. "I don't want to be a damper on the proceedings."

"It will be nice to see him at his best," said Felix. "I suppose he is generally a damper. I wish my father could really observe a person who did regular work."

"My boy, you have had a happy twenty years with me?"

"I have. And you remember my father asked you to make me happy. The one thing he has asked of you, you have done for him."

Felix danced towards Jonathan and took a seat on his knee, the older man moving his arm as if accustomed to the position.

"What would your father say, if he knew all our life together?"

"I don't think he uses words about everything."

"He deserves to be more respected than I am."

"Well, I think he gets what he deserves."

"Do people despise me?"

"Some people admire you for being a writer, but I think more people admire my father for being a squire."

"Well, I believe it is the rarer thing. But I would rather earn my admiration. But I am not of the men who have the facile trick of putting all of themselves on to paper."

"Is it really facile? I daresay they would say it was. We must go and dress. Your family is never late."

Felix ran upstairs and called to the man, who with the aid of his wife, conducted Jonathan's household.

"I will wear my ordinary evening clothes, as they give an impression of greater ease than the new ones. I ought to be a person whose clothes never look new; it shows that no one really conforms to type. But one thing about me is that limpness gives the effect of grace."

CHAPTER III

Jonathan followed Felix downstairs, clad in an old evening suit which he had worn nightly for years, and in which he appeared at once disreputable and dignified.

"Well, I am not dressed for the ladies," observed Fane. "For the lady, to be exact. I am assuming that Mrs. Napier will excuse it."

"That will put your mind at rest," said Felix.

"I am sure she will not mind my little omission."

"It is an advantage to have certainty."

"I make no claim to your elegant appearance. I am content with my own type."

"We most of us are," said Felix. "I am myself. It is the oddest thing in life."

"Now, what exactly do you mean by that?"

"Not at all what you thought I meant. How could you have thought I meant it?"

"I should know Josephine's bell in a thousand," said Jonathan.

"We don't have to distinguish it among so many," said Fane. "Our party is hardly so large."

"I am so looking forward to the evening," said Felix. "My attitude is as fresh and youthful as a boy's."

"Well, it does not do to get too blasé," said Fane, doing his best for his own expectant words.

Josephine led her family into the room, and greeted the men in a quiet manner that was not without a consciousness of her womanhood. Her embrace of her brother seemed to stress the comparative rareness of the salute between the sexes. Her husband followed at a seemingly greater than his actual distance, a tall, slight man of the same age, who gave the impression of being frail and old, with delicate, aquiline features, fluttering grey eyes, and a high, narrow head that filled and broadened at the brow. He shook hands in a gentle, interested manner, turning fully from one to another in his courteous, physically feeble gaze.

A youth of twenty-three brought up the rear, Josephine's nephew and Jonathan's son, whom Josephine had adopted before the dawn of his memory, on her brother's return from a sojourn abroad, a widower with an infant boy. He was a tall, auburn-haired, rather handsome young man, with nervous movements that did not interfere with his impression of ease, and a manner rather elaborate and strained. He began to speak in quick, high, conscious, cultured tones.

"Well, we members of a family meet with all the politeness of strangers! We have never seen the weaker side of each other. I am convinced that my father has no weaker side. It seems to me unnatural for a son to live under his father's roof."

"So it does to me," said Felix.

"My dear Gabriel, my dear boy!" said Jonathan, standing with his hand on his son's shoulder, looking into his face. "I have been living all day in this moment; to-morrow I shall live in the memory of it. I don't think I live less with you, than other fathers with their sons."

"Don't let us talk of other fathers and their sons," said Felix.

"I should say that Gabriel is better off for parents than most people," said Josephine.

"It would come better from me than from you, Josephine," said Gabriel.

"The young man makes free with your Christian name, Mrs. Napier. You allow that?" said Fane.

"I am not asked if I will allow it," said Josephine, slightly raising her shoulders. "There came a moment when it just began, when I suppose it seemed to him that we were a man and woman together. I have no objection if it does not lead to unseemliness; and there has been no sign of that."

The ruling element in Josephine's life had come to be her feeling for Gabriel. She was a woman of emotions rather than affections, and her love for her husband, passionate for years, had failed before the demand of youth.

"He does not call you Simon, sir?" said Fane to Mr. Napier.

"No, he does not give his attention to his address of me," said the latter in his quiet, rather hopeless manner.

"He is making a long stay at home," said Fane.

"Yes, he has left Oxford. He is marking time. Well, time is at his disposal. He will see many things that we shall not."

"Well, we have seen many things that he has not," said Fane, "You have more than I."

"Yes, yes, there is more behind than in front; the past stretches further, the future less far," said Simon, speaking partly to himself. "The road before gets short."

"I admire you for saying that," said Felix.

"We should have admired you more," said Gabriel, "if your saying it three times had not shown how you admired it yourself."

"I admired it more each time," said Felix. "I could hardly believe it the third time."

Simon sank into gentle laughter.

Dinner was announced, and Josephine rose and moved across the room, with simple acquiescence in the convention of her leading the way. Simon followed at a gesture from Jonathan, and Fane stepped at this point into the line, with an air of easy acceptance of the rules of precedent. Jonathan came at the end, with his hands on the arms of Felix and his son.

"I am assuming that you are here as the son of the house, in going in before you," said Fane to Gabriel.

"I try to cultivate that position in as many houses as I can."

"I do not," said Felix.

"To-morrow we are swept away on the full tide of the term," said Josephine.

"I suppose the tide ebbs and flows, Mrs. Napier?" said Fane, surveying the effect of this masculine exactitude.

"No, that is just what this tide does not do," said Josephine, causing Simon to smile. "It flows without any ebb and carries us all away with it."

"The force of nature is nothing to that of my aunt, Fane," said Gabriel.

"You do your part by the tide by watching it," said Fane.

"He is watching it at the moment," said Josephine. "There is a great deal in it that is instructive for him. His own profession is to be education. He can do it for a little longer yet."

"It is hard to be reminded how short the time is, between the preparation for life and the living of it," said Gabriel.

"But better than being reminded how long it is," said Felix. "My father wrote this morning about mine, and its being over twenty years. In my birthday letter."

"Many happy returns of the day," said Josephine, turning to him with a smile.

"Thank you so much; I do hope I shall have them."

"It seems a natural hope," said Simon. "Yes, and it may be a sound one."

"Well, I have already had them," said Jonathan. "But I can do with more, if other people can do with me."

"Well, I come of a very long-lived stock," said Fane, looking round.

"I come of a rather short-lived family," said Josephine in a distinct, open tone. "Both my father and grandfather were fine men while they lasted; but they did not last. They both died in the sixties. It seems strange to me that my brother has already lived longer than either of them."

"You are doing a good work, Father, in getting the

family out of this habit," said Gabriel. "I hope by the time I attain to three score years it will be definitely broken."

"Would any of us like to know how long we shall live?" said Jonathan.

"That is all very well for you, when you are already sure of so much life," said his son.

"Ah, that would make a difference between us," said Simon, shaking his head.

"No one would like a definite end put to himself," said Gabriel.

"Ah, we cannot guess at our appointed time," said Fane.

"Don't say it in that open manner," said Felix. "You should lower your voice when you speak of death."

"Well, I think one does, if one actually speaks of it," said Fane.

"I think that ignorance on such matters is best," said Josephine. "It is natural; and whatever is natural is sound."

"Perhaps with the exception of death," said Gabriel.

"I should be sorry to know that I should live beyond the age of usefulness," said Josephine.

"That seems to me the most embarrassing age," said Felix. "I shall begin to be at ease when I am past it."

"Your duties begin to-morrow, my dear," said Jonathan to his sister. "They won't crowd too thickly on the first day of the term."

"Now that shows what you know about it. The first day is the foundation for the other days. And things do not stop in the holidays; there happens to be the post. You seem to be unaware of that, but I am kept aware of it."

"So am I," said Felix.

"Ladies are never averse from finding an outlet for their energies," said Fane. "They have a great amount of vitality."

Simon lifted his eyes to the speaker's face.

"Surely they vary in that way, and in other ways, as men do," said Josephine; "as all human beings must."

"Oh yes, I was not meaning that they were all on the

dead level. I meant that their vitality was often out of scale with the rest of them. You must have noticed that, in dealing with women wholesale."

"No, I had not noticed it. What I have noticed, since you bring it to my mind, is that in highly developed people the mental force is often out of scale with the physical. I have found that with men as well as with women. I do not think"—Josephine lifted her eyes in reflection—"that it is a sex difference. And I must just say that I do not deal with women wholesale, but as individuals."

"Oh yes, of course," said Fane, his eyes rather wide open on her face.

"Which is it better to be, a man or a woman?" said Gabriel.

"Ah, that would lead us into thorny paths," said Simon.

"I do not at all mind saying I would rather be a man," said Felix.

Fane glanced at Josephine, as his own content became uneasiness.

"Well, a woman would not make a man, nor a man a woman," he said.

"Is that so?" said Simon, "I know it is said to be."

"So you are a feminist, are you, sir?" said Fane.

Simon smiled and made no reply.

"I cannot imagine any useful and self-respecting person of either sex wishing to belong to the other," said Josephine.

"Neither can I, a person of that kind," said Felix.

"I can't imagine him wishing anything at all," said Gabriel.

"I think you are probably useful in ways we do not know," said Josephine to Felix.

"It is to have it known, that I should be useful. But don't you get tired of usefulness even as recognised as yours?"

"Well, I would not say that it does not sometimes get to be much, as the ball rolls and gathers; but I have never yet found myself in a temper of rebellion. Though the question of recognition had not occurred to me."

"Suppose you did find myself so? I can't help imagining it in that case."

"Well, I should just have to conceal it; that would be the only course open to me."

"Did you work the school up yourself, Mrs. Napier?" said Fane.

"From a dozen girls," said Josephine, turning fully to him and speaking in a clear tone. "I could not afford more than a moderate sum to buy the goodwill. A large sum it seemed to me then; a smaller one now, of course. It was all that I could muster at the crucial moment. And a very crucial moment it seemed, a great venture, a great risk. But all's well that ends well; and it has ended as I hoped, and not as I feared."

"You were a brave girl, Josephine," said Jonathan.

"I was not a girl. I was over thirty. It was not long before you returned from abroad, and made me a present of your son."

"Take care, Mrs. Napier," said Fane. "You are furnishing us with data, from which we may deduce your age."

"I need not give you the trouble of deducing it. I am nearly fifty-five."

"I was not going to deduce it," said Felix.

"Well, no one would guess it, Mrs. Napier," said Fane at the same moment.

"Well, there wasn't much fear about you, girl or not," said Jonathan.

"There was a good deal underneath. But if I did not show it, I dealt with it in the way it is best to look back on. I am glad it bothered no one but myself. And I soon had my husband's support." Josephine looked round the table and rose.

"You are not leaving us, Josephine?" said her brother. "Wait until we escort you into the drawing-room."

"No," said Josephine, standing to confront the group.

34

"If a woman comes by herself to a party of men, she must abide by her position and fall in with the custom. I think there can be no two opinions. She is one by herself, and must not mind being by herself. I have no objection to my own company, and I see that, in a certain sense, some of you might have an objection to it; and so the matter ends."

She swept her skirts across the room, seeming to be conscious of this difference from her companions, inclined her head as the door was opened, and passed without looking behind her into the hall.

Felix returned to his seat, his face expressionless. Jonathan looked with proprietary affection after his sister. Fane leaned back, as if freed from some conventional ban on ease. Simon gave a faint sigh.

"I don't believe in sex distinctions," said Felix.

"Ah, a wise woman knows we cannot manage without them," said Fane.

"I always manage without them."

"I saw you open the door for Mrs. Napier."

"But I did not see you. And you and she do believe in sex distinctions. You both keep explaining it. I was adapting myself to others. And I don't call that a sex distinction."

"Living in a stream of women as you do, you must be qualified to judge," said Fane to Simon.

"Living in the stream?" said Simon looking up. "I should rather say that I watch it flowing, and every now and then get touched by the spray."

Fane regarded him in silence.

"You do no other work besides what you do in your school?"

"No, no other. And the school is my wife's."

"What a way to talk!" said Gabriel to Fane. "What work do you do, besides what you do in your office?"

"You are interested in your work?" said Fane, not taking his eyes from Simon.

"Yes, I am interested. I could wish that my pupils were

35

sometimes more so," said Simon, between a smile and a genuine sigh.

"If I ever work, I shall try to have just that touch," said Felix. "I don't think my father talks more about work than other people."

"Let us talk about something else, for heaven's sake," said Jonathan.

"And for my sake," said Gabriel. "I am conscious of my present position."

"That is the worst of a temporary arrangement," said Felix. "One is never at ease. It is better to make it permanent."

"Could I let my aunt support me?"

"Yes, if you don't believe in sex distinctions. Men often support people. Nearly always, my father tells me."

"You have to be able to accept, my boy," said Jonathan, looking with affection at Gabriel. "It is one of the things we have to learn. Unwillingness implies a lack of generosity, a reluctance to grant anyone else the superior place."

"My father has never appreciated me," said Felix.

"I suppose that is why a gift is so often called a loan," said Gabriel.

"Ah, a good deal is done under the guise of borrowing," said Fane. "I have never borrowed; I can say that for myself."

"I have never borrowed. But I have accepted," said Jonathan.

"Two noble things instead of one," said Gabriel.

"Well, good things enough," said Jonathan. "Let us go into the other room. We are forgetting that your aunt is alone."

"We are, for the advantage we have taken of her absence," said Gabriel. "She left us to be men together, we have decided vaguely against borrowing."

"Well, this is a subject it is safe to broach with you, Mrs. Napier," said Fane, entering the sitting-room. "You have never borrowed. I am sure of that."

36

"Yes, I have borrowed," said Josephine, laying down her book. "I borrowed a small sum from a friend in the early stages of my school, the very early stages." She paused with almost a grim smile. "I paid it back within three months."

"So you had to be thankful without any permanent benefit," said Gabriel.

"I was very thankful. And I began to earn as fast as ever I could."

"Do you know many people who earn?" said Felix.

"Yes, a great many. And a goodly proportion of them I have put in the way of earning myself."

"Could you put me in the way of it? I have heard that you want a drawing-master; and my drawing is very good; and my father says that I might be a woman."

"Now I think that is a foolish joke. I do not regard teaching of any kind as a matter for jesting. You will forgive my taking my own profession seriously?"

"Of course, when it is my own profession."

"Now," said Josephine, leaning back and betraying in her voice a hope that it might be as she said: "am I to take you as being in earnest or not?"

"It shows what harm I have done to my reputation. I am like a man out of prison. If no one will employ me, how can I redeem my character?"

"You would not object to having a man teaching in your school, Mrs. Napier?" said Fane.

"No," said Josephine. "I do not see any reason for objecting to it. With certain things granted, of course."

"They are all granted with me," said Felix. "I do not even like to have such things talked about."

"Do you feel you have a gift for teaching?" said Josephine, looking straight into his face.

"I feel I have a gift for drawing. And that has always been a reason for teaching it."

"Yes, and there might be worse reasons," said Josephine, sitting back and speaking as if to herself.

"Thank you so much for engaging me. I will try to do my duty. And I will write to my father to-night."

Simon fell into rather doubtful mirth.

"The whole business is settled, then?" said Fane, looking about.

"Are you thinking about my stipend?" said Felix. "I am not at all ashamed of talking about it."

"You ought to be, if you talk about it like that," said Gabriel.

"Why should you be?" said Josephine. "The labourer is worthy of his hire."

"Yes, that is it, I know," said Felix. "But I have conquered myself."

"Now I hope," said Josephine, "that you have no feeling of its being beneath you to teach, or to teach girls?"

"I see now why workers have unions against employers."

"Well, shall we proceed to the practical side the next time we are alone?"

"The practical side! That is what I should have said. Are we ever alone?"

"Do you know what my last drawing mistress, teacher had?" said Josephine, in a voice that seemed to be lower, in spite of herself.

"It was a mistress," said Felix. "I have found out what she had."

"Then what about half as much again?" said Josephine, bringing her tones to an open level.

"You are not in favour of equal pay for equal work! Fancy being as experienced as that!"

"No," said Josephine, leaning back. "Men have more material responsibilities than women. I do not pretend to think that the same standards can apply."

"I am glad you do not take my father's view of me."

"Did your last teacher live in the school, Mrs. Napier?" said Fane.

"My drawing master or mistress is never resident."

Simon frowned slightly, his eyes down.

"Would not a woman serve your purpose as well?" said Fane.

"Yes," said Josephine. "Fully as well. But no woman of suitable attainments has presented herself."

"Pray do not conspire against my livelihood, Fane," said Felix.

"You are not allowed a say—do not have a say in the matter, sir?" said Fane to Simon.

"He is very kind in giving me his advice," said Josephine. "The school owes him a great deal."

"Well, you will have a companion in distress," Fane said to Felix, unable to adapt himself beyond a point.

"How many companions shall I have, Mrs. Napier?"

"I do not remember at the moment the exact number."

Fane looked at Josephine.

"All ladies but the two gentlemen here?"

"No, not all."

"Oh, you have other men in your school?"

"Yes."

"And what do they teach?"

"Each his own subject," said Josephine, speaking the truth of her visiting masters.

"Oh, it would be regarded—it is a high class of school?" said Fane.

"I should soon give it up, if it did not merit some description of that kind. The keepers of schools cannot but be the makers of the future. I would not face the responsibility of not doing the work faithfully."

"Of course everyone goes to school," said Felix. "It does exalt my profession."

"Will you put your nephew into the school, Mrs. Napier?" said Fane, feeling that matters might go so far.

"No," said Josephine in a full, rounded tone. "He and I have lived so much on equal terms, that I feel he might not fancy me as a task-mistress. He looks to me for other things. And we must not put all our eggs into one basket. My school might fail like anyone else's."

"Then I should be out of work," said Felix.

"No," said Josephine quietly. "No one would be out of work. My testimonial would secure that. The school has its past. And now we have talked of school out of school long enough."

"Thank you all for taking an interest in my future," said Felix.

"It would be shocking to be a woman, and have less pay for the same work," said Gabriel. "For more work in many cases."

"Yes, on the whole, women are harder workers than men," said Josephine, her voice making no comment on this difference.

"There doesn't on the face of it seem any reason for it," said Jonathan.

"No," said his sister.

"You find that you get more out of your women than your men, Mrs. Napier?" said Fane.

"No, I do not find that," said Josephine, bending her head as if to suppress a smile. "But I have to inculcate more lessons on the sparing of themselves."

"They have fewer interests for their leisure," said Fane. "Public matters mean less to them."

"I think that if you were to hear my debating society, you would modify your opinion there."

"Perhaps the women you employ are hardly average women."

"Well, you would hardly apply the term 'average', to a Cambridge wrangler, and two first classes at Oxford, women or not," said Josephine, looking at the window.

Simon slowly raised himself in his chair.

"I wonder they don't want to try their wings further afield," said Fane.

"Further afield?" queried Josephine.

"I mean in a more significant sphere."

"What sphere is more significant than education?"

Fane did not suggest one.

"Pray do not belittle my calling, Fane," said Felix.

"Does an element of self-sacrifice add to a life or take from it?" Simon asked himself in a low tone. "Some great men have seen no beauty in it. Well, so it is."

"There is very little self-sacrifice in the life of my mistresses," said his wife. "I see to that. And very ashamed I should be of myself if I did not."

"I am very fortunate," said Felix.

"Now, make no mistake," said Josephine. "I expect your best, your whole best, and nothing but your best. Then you shall find yourself as fortunate as I can make you."

"I need not suppress any charm that is natural to me, need I?"

"You need not indeed. I am the last person to want my pupils to be blind to charm, or to belittle it myself in my staff. I am fortunate in having got together a good deal of it."

"Do you think I shall have the most charm on your staff?"

"Well, I can hardly say," said Josephine in a serious voice. "There are some very charming women on it. I am sometimes struck by it, when I come on them unawares. I must be on my guard against taking a rare thing for granted."

"Yes, you must," said Felix.

"I will indeed," said Josephine. "And now it is time for me to get my cloak. Men of mine, be ready to escort me home."

"What purpose are you serving by this scheme?" said Gabriel to Felix.

"I want to see some life, and to wear out and not rust out, and to retaliate on my father."

"You won't see much life in a girls' school."

"That is where you are so superficial. I shall see an unusual sort of life."

"Yes, a school is a miniature world," said Jonathan, giving a yawn.

"That is just what it is not," said Felix; "or I should not take any interest in it. My father is a man of the world. It is little, unnatural corners of the world that appeal to me. I am very over-civilised."

"That is nothing to be proud of," said Fane.

"Oh, I don't agree with you," said Felix.

"No, it is hard to agree to that," said Simon, shaking his head.

"I will go and get a telephone call to my father," said Felix; "and tell him that his birthday letter has fulfilled its purpose, and led me to work; and that as he compares me to a woman, I thought it would be best to teach drawing in a girls' school."

"You will do nothing for our friendship by this," said Gabriel, following him into the hall.

"I don't want to do anything for it," said Felix, dancing towards the telephone. "It is not a thing I take any interest in. We are on the telephone at my father's expense. He does not approve of modern inventions, but he knows that I cannot be homesick when I can always hear his voice."

Josephine appeared on the stairs and bent smilingly from her height.

"You are going to telephone?" she said in a pleasant manner.

"Yes, to my father," said Felix.

"Will you please remember me to him," said Josephine in the same manner.

"My boy," said Jonathan to Gabriel, "the evening has meant much to me. You will spare me another? I make no claim; I have no claim. I depend on your generosity."

"I think you depend a little on my generosity, too," said Josephine, adjusting her wrap with her husband's aid.

"I know it; I am grateful. I have a great deal to be thankful for; I hope I am thankful. Good-bye, my dear sister. Good-bye, my son."

Jonathan embraced both his sister and his son, according to his custom, while Felix stood with his eyes averted, as if by

42

chance, from the family scene, and Fane with his attention held by it.

"Well, I have a great deal in my life," said Jonathan. "They give me a generous affection that I have done little to deserve. Is that the telephone? Any message for me?"

"No, it is for me," said Felix. "A word from my father on the coming change in my life. I will be back in a few minutes."

"It must be quite that," said Fane at length. "Ah, we thought your time would be up, Bacon."

"I refused a second allowance of minutes. It was astonishing how much we said in the first. I began to realise how it would be, if we did not waste a moment of our lives."

"Well, what does your father say to your plan?"

"That it was what he would have expected. That is quite untrue. He would never have expected me to teach in a girls' school. That if I choose to behave in an undignified manner for a pittance, it is my own affair. That is the best definition of work I have heard. When do my so-called duties start? I said the day after to-morrow. Shall I wear petticoats to fulfil them in? I said I should wear my two everyday suits alternately, that I had no petticoats. As he pays the bill for all my clothes, he ought to know that."

"I admit it seems odd work for a gentleman," said Fane. "I don't make any secret of it."

"My father didn't think it was a secret either. To me any work seems odd for a gentleman; but I think that is rather a secret."

"There is plenty of work suitable for a man of any position. We have conquered the old prejudice against the learned professions."

"Teaching ought to be a learned profession. Have we conquered the prejudice?"

"Wouldn't it be better to teach boys, if you must teach?"

"My father said that, too. It is impossible to think of anything he did not say. And then they asked if I would

43

have some more time! How clever it was to hit on the amount that just gets everything in!"

"Well, I will go to bed," said Fane. "I have a day's work before me."

"I wonder if I shall say that as often as other people."

"Ah, it is easy to begin to work. It is when the novelty wears off that the crux comes."

"I shall be glad when the novelty wears off."

"He is an inquisitive fellow," said Jonathan, as the door closed.

"Well, it is natural to be curious about my teaching drawing to girls. I am sorry to think my own affairs interesting, but I do not think they are at the moment."

"Ah, Felix your mind will be on Gabriel, and I shall be forgotten."

"I shall come home to you a tired bread-winner. I suppose I am a bread-winner, even if all the bread I win is for myself. Bread-winners' own bread hardly seems to count. But there has been so much talk about who pays for my meals."

"Felix, I ask you earnestly not to do for Gabriel what I have done for you."

"People are so open about wanting others to learn by their mistakes, instead of feeling that the less said about them the better. They almost seem to have made them for others to learn by. I have heard that there is self-indulgence in all sacrifice."

"Ah, I will conquer myself: I know I am thinking of myself: I do not think of a boy. I am a miserable old man, useless at the work I love, a burden on the friend I love, jealous of my own son. But I will be happy in what I have had, happy to give it up, now that the time has come. I am not one of those who have had nothing."

"I think I am going to be one of them," said Felix, taking his usual seat on Jonathan's knees. "I think I should have had something by now, if I were not."

CHAPTER IV

"Why, Adela," said Josephine, shaking her latchkey at a maid who was waiting in her hall, "what is the good of my burdening myself with the insignia of a householder, if you are to stay up and make it useless? I undertake to be equal to the work of the morrow, late hours or not, but I have not the handicap of youth. A lady to see me, who insisted on waiting? Well, I have known people come at stranger times. Parent, pupil, former pupil, future parent? Which of them needs my help to the point of snatching my sleep?"

She entered the house, to be met by a clear, carrying voice, as a tall, dark woman broke out of a room to meet her, pushing back her veil to reveal the full, black eyes, the crinkling black hair, and the keenly cut nose and chin of a friend of her youth.

"Home, sweet home at last! Yes, it shall be sweet, though I have lost so much since I left it, and come back to it so old and poor and sad. I will have the spirit to make it so. You, who remember me of old, will not doubt the spirit. Both of you have had the early hopes fulfilled? I am too glad, for my heart to grow sick with my own still deferred. You will tell of the happiness to an ear so ready to listen."

"Elizabeth! Elizabeth Giffard!" said Josephine. "After all these years of silence! The voice struck my ears like an echo from the past."

"This meeting has been in my mind many times," said Simon, advancing with gentle eagerness. "The many imaginings have made it true."

"I had almost given up hope of it," said his wife. "And now it has come to pass, I think the heroine of the occasion should be sitting in this easy chair, and having a glass of this wine, and some of these sandwiches, that are not put

45

here to be looked at. Now I think that is a great deal better."

"Such a lot of thought and kindness, that I am sure the old affection is underneath! It lies too deep in my own heart not to have its place in yours. So many storms have passed over it, and left it unscathed! Now, tell me of your life together, and the adopted son, and the success. Yes, I heard of the so brave ventures. I had no fear when I heard of them, when the little bird with the tidings flitted between you and me. Yes, little birds have known where they would find a welcome. I have not sent them back with only sad words to say. But now I will feel the happiness, though it is not mine. It shall be mine indeed."

"This is Gabriel Swift, our adopted son, my brother's boy," said Josephine. "I took him off Jonathan's hands, when he was a few months old, soon after I set up the school, and a short time before I married."

"Yes, yes, I know it all: I have not a short memory where my friends are concerned. And I heard you were to have a husband to help in the brave undertakings. My daughter was born at the time of your marriage, a few months after her father died, the father she never saw. So my child lost a father, and yours gained one. Well, that was how it was to be."

"It sounds a reproach to me," said Gabriel. "Is there anything I can do to atone?"

"Ah, I daresay there will be something. My girl will be glad to have a comrade. But at the moment my mind must be given to these old comrades of my own. I heard of the wedding when I could not write, when my baby was a few days old. I could only think of both of you. My heart was too full for anything else, too full of joy and sorrow. Both were there; yes, I will be just. And my heart found room for friends again; it was closed for such a little while. It was on your honeymoon that you heard that I had a daughter?"

"It was then that we heard of your husband's death,"

said Simon. "We heard the good and the sad tidings at the same time."

"I sent the other word to Josephine, when I was first alone; when I felt so weak, and remembered her as so strong. But it was not the moment for it; poor Josephine, it was not! I was so sorry afterwards to have sent such a sad, sad word. Yes, when I knew, I understood; I am not a person who misunderstands; I only feared I had done harm. But Josephine was herself, and went on her own brave way. And now I see her in the midst of all that came of it."

"We neither of us heard before our marriage," said Simon. "We had the letter that came on our honeymoon. I remember we sent the answer at once."

"Such a sweet answer! It gave me courage to go forward. I did not know how hard the world was to the widow and the fatherless. Well, I did not keep silence, to bring the sadness after all. So let me hear some of the dear, good news."

"I am sure we heard of your husband's death on our honeymoon," said Simon.

"I remember making it clear to you then, anyhow," said Josephine. "It would have been too much to be sure of accomplishing before. If Elizabeth meant to write a letter, or we meant to read one, when we were all immersed in the deeps of our experience, we shall none of us misunderstand."

"Well, a letter in the past is not to be compared with friendship in the present. I will take the one in exchange for the other with all my heart."

"Now, do you want this callow youth as witness of your reunion?" said Josephine. "I will spare you the constraint of his presence, and myself the discredit of missing our evening hour together, or any other lapse along that line. It is for my peace to keep in his good graces, but it makes less difference to yours. Don't think that I don't remember the old bond between you two. It is a pity for a tie of that kind

47

to be broken. It seems to me such a sad thing, when the deep relations of life blot out the lighter memories that are the heritage from youth. So I will leave you to clasp your hands over the gulf of your experience. Don't think we want to be witnesses of that dramatic scene."

Elizabeth turned her smiling face from the closing door.

"So you heard that I was a widow, after you were married yourself, Simon?" she said, her voice making the sound of the name sweet.

"Yes, that is how I remember it," said Simon, his lips just framing the words.

"Well, and how did that come about? Well, it came about in one way or another. It was best for you to go to the chosen life, chosen, I am sure, so wisely for you, undistraught by anything that might lead you aside; or it was thought best. We are in the hands of—what shall we call it? Fate? Let us call it Fate. That is the best word, or shall we say the wisest?"

Simon did not speak.

"We must be good and wise. And it is never good and wise to think of what might have been, never good and wise to judge. I think that Josephine seems greater and wiser than ever now, Simon. Her face has gained with the years, if I may say a pretty thing to you about your wife. There is something there, that sits better on it than youth. But I did not realise that youth was so far behind: perhaps life is not always in such a hurry with its later gifts?"

"You have not let me hear from you for over twenty years," said Simon.

"Ah, you did not let me hear from you, when the months were as long as all the years afterwards."

"What are your plans for the future? I may ask that, even if I have no claim on the past."

"Ah, plans are for the more fortunate. They are not for lonely widows, lacking in the world's goods, not for the people who need them. I am lodging here, to live for a while in my memories, and give my girl a glimpse of the scene of my youth. Through her childhood I have done whatever would keep her with me, always trying, trying to keep above it all. Trying with who knows how much success? I don't know what the verdict will be."

"Well, I do," said Josephine, returning to the room; "and one flattering enough even for you; and I remember how exacting you were in the matter of a compliment. Not that I think that any kind of work needs so much keeping above, you know. That is my own prosaic opinion. But what are you running away for? Can't you be comfortable here a little longer? I don't see anything in this room to frighten you."

"There is so much for me to see and appreciate and—no, I won't say envy—put from me as above my own claims, that I think I will run away, as you use that word. But I will run back again; a glimpse won't hurt me; it will only confirm that my friends still have the best. I have so prized our dear meeting after all these years. So now fare you well. Not that I need to say that to you. Does Simon have to leave the fire to speed poor me on my path?"

"Now, you stay where you are," said Josephine to her husband. "You and your chill have not yet parted company. Do you think I didn't notice your appetite at dinner, or your lack of it? I am used to doing the honours in this house. Such a great barrack of a place it seemed at first, for me to do the honours in!" She followed her guest to the door, continuing her speech. "Well, it is my lot, what I have undertaken. I meet it day by day, as it comes."

"Well, you have your husband to help you," said Elizabeth, walking in front. "He and I were great friends once, you know. You do know; you left us for a minute to remember it. We found the minute enough; we remembered many things; our old times together, his feelings when I was engaged, dear Simon, his surprise when he heard too late of my husband's death. You thought it best he should have the surprise. Ah, poor, foolish girl that I was!"

49

"You were a woman when your husband died."

"Yes, poor, foolish woman that I was! It was more foolish in a woman. I should have known the risk; I had known you." Elizabeth quickened her pace, almost as if she were fleeing from Josephine. "But yet I had not known you; perhaps I could not; perhaps the difference between us was too great. I have to blame my own innocence. Yes, it was strange in a woman of my age. You must find it strange. At the same age you had not that innocence."

"You know that Simon is always your friend," said Josephine, as the door of the hall brought them to a pause. "We did not suspect that you had this other feeling. Believe me, we did not; perhaps we had our own innocence. Your secret will be safe, even safe from Simon, and it is from him that you will want it to be safe."

"Yes, I think the secret is safe from Simon; that many things are safe from him."

"My dear, it was when you were the widow of another man, that you wrote to me, or thought you wrote. If Simon and I were blind to anything outside each other—perhaps we should admit we were for a time; well, we will both admit it—and a letter got passed over or put aside, it could have meant very little. It was when your future was dawning, that you wrote the letter to be answered, that could be answered by people in our state of mind. And we answered it at once; I remember reminding Simon, that it was his words rather than mine, that would bring you comfort. I was glad to hear you say that they brought it to you. He has to be kept to those little duties, as you who know him so well, must know; though that was a deep and pressing duty to both of us; you know that too. But the things you have said, would give even me a wrong impression, if I let them. But I will not let them; do not fear; do not let your hard experience warp your judgement. Tell me your troubles, and lean on me. I am so used to being leant on."

"My troubles," said Elizabeth, weeping into her hands, "are poverty and loneliness and anxiety for my child. I must earn my bread and hers, and I have nothing that people need. I have suffered to the last in eating bread they thought I did not earn, those people who seemed so much below me. It has been bitter bread; and no one in my life has helped me."

"Now can I help you?" said Josephine, in an open considering tone, as if the foregoing talk had left little impression on her mind. "You would at least be with friends, if you took a place in my house. I have to replace my housekeeper, who is leaving me to be married. If her work would be easy for you, it is time you found things easy. And nobody would taunt you with eating bread you did not earn, even though it were a little more than bread. And in a school your daughter would find a place. I don't know how that sounds to you?"

"Such a blessing, such a breaking of light. I would accept it so gratefully, if I felt I was deserving. But I have said things out of the bitterness of my heart, when in yours there was kindness."

"Well, be thankful you said them to someone who knew you could not mean them. And tell me when you will come and bring your daughter, for both of us to care for together. I shall be grateful for your help as soon as you will give it, as I have put your predecessor's convenience before my own."

"Then I will come at once, to get used to my duties. Such sacred duties they will be to me, so faithfully discharged! So much I shall have to learn from you, and will learn so readily, or I should not be the woman I am. I think you remember my old self, though I have shown it through such a darkness. I am that old self still at bottom: I don't know if I look at all the same at the top?"

"You have altered much less than I have. People would hardly guess we were the same age. It is strange how differently the years deal with us, what divers things they give and take."

"So you have forgiven my yielding to bitterness at the

contrast of our lots? It is seldom that I sink so low. But enough pressure forces us to anything, and I had had enough. My measure was full to overflowing, and it overflowed. I had drunk too deeply of the bitter cup; but it will be mingled with sweetness now." Elizabeth went with her light, quick steps towards the door. "Our old friendship is the basis of a new life together, with you at the top and me at the bottom, and such a lot of love in all the space between. The spirit that broke its bonds just now, has escaped. Your success shall be sweet to me. And so for such a short time, good-bye." She held out her hand, but Josephine drew her forward and kissed her on the cheek, and then, as if asking nothing in return, released her at once from her house and her embrace.

Simon hardly looked up when his wife returned.

"Well, still out of bed?" she said in a rather excited voice.

"You did not tell me, Josephine, when Elizabeth's husband died."

"Yes, I told you, and urged you to write her a letter, and had almost to sit over you while you did it, if my memory serves."

"That was on our honeymoon, when he had been dead for some months, if your memory serves there too. She said she wrote to you when he died."

"Well, now she says she did not write. And what an ugly, bitter, little voice! Poor Elizabeth! We need not load up on her every word she said, in a moment of emotion and what not. It is a good thing she chose to utter her retracting words to me. I could see her making her choice, and had mercy on her. You see, I knew her so well."

"Her voice did not sound as if she were uttering such words."

"Oh, we had the bout of emotion we were bound to have, as two weak women alone. You would not have expected her to have it with you. I had seen it gathering. Poor Elizabeth is often not mistress of herself."

"Did she retract her statement that she wrote to you at the time of her husband's death?"

"No," said Josephine, slightly drawing herself up. "I knew she was prepared to retract it, and so I did not require her to. I did not wish her to take more on herself than had to be: I saw that she was not in a fit state. I don't want to push my advantage to the uttermost. I never have any use for that line."

"Are we to see her again soon? I hope we shall often meet."

"Well, I am glad to hear that," said his wife, with a faint note of triumph, "as she is settling here at once as housekeeper. We shall meet her every day, whether we want to or not. And we ought to want to; she is an old friend of us both." She ended with her voice dying away, and her eyes on the bookcase, and walking forward, took a book.

"Did you arrange that just now?"

"Well, it was obvious that we did not arrange it when she was in here," said Josephine, turning a page.

"Was it her wish?"

"My dear Simon, it was she who was worked up, because we did not see the desire in her mind, not I. Because I did not see it. She acquits you, I am sure; Elizabeth would always acquit a man. It is a woman whose instinct is supposed not to fail, as mine failed, I admit."

"She is coming here as housekeeper?"

"That is what she wanted. That is what I perceived her to want. That is what I ought to have perceived before. That is what I offered her, when I perceived she wanted it. That is what she forgave me for not offering, when she accepted it. Well, is that all you want to know?"

"I am very glad," said Simon.

"So am I," said Josephine, in an open manner. "I am fond of Elizabeth, and shall enjoy having her working under me; working with me, for there is no question of top and bottom in my conception of work. She went about the business in a baffling spirit, but characteristic, poor, strung-up creature that she is!"

"I hope it will be a suitable post for her."

"Well, you are a nice kind of customer! Of course it is suitable, when she needs it, and has no other, and can have her daughter with her, when another might involve a parting."

"Her daughter will live here, will she?"

"My good Simon, how can we separate a mother and her child, when the mother is a widow, and the child of the dependent sex? You are not a fiend, and neither am I; so it is no good our pretending, convenient though it might be. And don't keep looking at me as if I were one. You have been adopting that expression for some time, and it is the reverse of becoming. You must see that what either of us wants, has no bearing on the matter."

"I do, indeed, see it, Josephine. I have been let into a sorry muddle."

"Well, don't keep harping on it. A muddle is not any better because it is sorry. The sorrier, the worse, in my humble imagination. I don't wonder that you became muddle-headed in meeting the romance of your youth. Don't think that I don't know about that. I heard enough of it at the time when her affections were in process of being transferred, and she was keeping you as a sort of second string to her bow, as far as I could gather. I even had a word of that time to-day, when she was referring, and frankly, too, to the changes that time had wrought in you and me. Ah, Elizabeth had her ways. A leopard does not change its spots, or change his feeling that spots are rather a credit. Well, women of her kind have a right to put their gifts to their natural use. We must not find fault with what is natural. And in spite of your concern for her, it did not occur to you to escort her home. It is a good thing that you were out of her mind."

Elizabeth went from Josephine's door with rapid feet and upright head, her face betraying her inward rehearsal of a humorous scene. When she reached her lodging, she leaned over the steps and tapped with a sprightly hand on the window.

"Such nice, prompt attendance! Thank you, pretty parlourmaid," she said, as her daughter came to the door. "It is late at night to bring the wretch from below. Such funny things I have witnessed, late though it is! A little refreshment will help me to evoke them. So surprised would Josephine be by my needing it, when so much has been offered me. I could not feel tempted, when it all seemed so valuable and so valued. Now I can't waste my gifts on a lackadaisical audience: let your mother keep what is her heritage, what has stood between us and so many things. The truth defies even my talent for pictures in words. Josephine, looking like a statesman in a woman's dress! Such a sinking of the heart I had, when I remembered we were young together! The funny sight, but sad too, poor Simon! And the end the funniest part of all, that I am to be housekeeper in the school where she is head mistress! Such a contradiction of all memories!" Elizabeth wiped her eyes, as if her tears of mirth had changed their kind. "I wonder if Josephine will think of it. Well, what do you say to your news?"

"I have hardly had my own news yet," said her daughter, in her husky, languid tones, turning to her mother her dark, unusual face, with its absent, indifferent eyes and curved and protruding lips. "What part am I to play in this comedy, tragedy, tragi-comedy? It is the first of the three, I gather, with the hearts of clowns as sad as they are said to be."

"As if that were not the point, that I am to keep you with me! As if I should have yielded to pressure, if they had not pressed that! Ah, they saw your mother and remembered her. And it need not be such a place as some of them have been. I know you have been brought to a dark outlook. Yes, a sad burden to bear, and shoulders tried by bearing it! But young shoulders are supple, and the least harm comes to the bravest. We have spirit to recover, and I think that the time has come for recovery. Keep up your heart, or your mother's heart will fail. There will be enough to make it in this new life based upon the old. But poor Josephine and Simon! I feel so much sorrier for them, than they for me, if only they knew."

"We can hardly expect them to guess it. Is the problem of my clothes to be left to solve itself? I suppose I shall need the outfit of everyone, with everything made a little stronger, to stand an extra strain. The bright side of not being trained to any one thing is that you are qualified for all things."

"No, it is not to be left to solve itself; it is to be left to your mother to solve. I have brains and hands, and the skill and will to use them, and an extra spur this time to urge my gifts to their best. There will be other eyes than mine to be rejoiced by the sight of my daughter. I am not making a mistake in taking you to Josephine's house. It is not for nothing that I have an eye to character. I am not of the meek who inherit the earth. Enough of the earth will do, to make a share for you. Ah, Cinderella in her ashes was a princess. And it is not meet that some should be so light, and others so heavy laden."

CHAPTER V

JOSEPHINE ENTERED THE room known as the library, which was the scene of her family life, and coming up to the table, paused with her hand upon it.

"Well, I have welcomed the junior staff. They have gone to their quarters, taking with them a word from me. I have done for them what I did for their seniors yesterday. I cannot bear the thought of these women, coming from some distant place, it may be, not meeting with any respect and understanding in their work and their lives."

"You do not assume that we find the thought bearable?" said Gabriel.

"Can I be of any help to you, Josephine?" said Simon, in a manner of saying what should be said, whether or no with hope of result.

"No. Everything is on its foundation now. The class-rooms are arranged and assigned; the one thing was as much of a business as the other. The new basis of the accounts is settled. That took some delving into the deeps of one's mind; but, as it hardly seemed advisable to add a chartered accountant to our staff, I delved until the result commended itself. The time-tables are organised, in so far as it is possible for human capacity to bring them to such a stage. The preliminary steps are behind; it is only the term that is ahead."

The intensity of Josephine's tone caused Simon to lift his eyes, and she continued in a different manner.

"The worst of it is, that another little piece of energy is behind too. Well, we can only go on until our store runs out."

"I am glad you have come in while you have some left," said Gabriel. "We should not expect to make a move towards our own refreshment. And pouring out tea would stress my position as companion."

"As companion you need do no more," said Josephine. "And I am very used to making any moves that are necessary."

"The best companionship is known to rest upon difference," said Simon, with an indulgent smile. "The impulse that has had its result in the school, as yet hardly repeats itself."

"Impulse!" said his wife. "It takes something more than impulse, to set on foot a large, organic concern; to give it its life, to breathe its vitality into it every day, to keep from somewhere at its source, a hand on the pulsing current that looks to you for its force. Not much in that line would be done, if we trusted to mere impulse."

"It would be safer to trust to every human quality we possessed," said Gabriel.

"Yes, that is just about what we have to do. And the more we possess, the better."

"It was not a considered word, Josephine," said her husband.

"Now don't get absorbed in discussion just as the kettle is boiling. I am housewife as well as head mistress, and laxity falls as hard on me in one sphere as in the other."

"And I am master in logic and history," said Simon.

"And be thankful that you have the work to do. What would any of us be, without our work?"

"I should be a leisured man," said Simon.

"I should be what I am," said Gabriel.

"You are a boy, just through your boy's training. But your uncle talks as if he carried the weight of the house, when his work would not keep the wolf from the door."

Simon's face relaxed into a resigned, but settled hopelessness.

"The wolf is always represented as at such close quarters," said Gabriel. "Why may he not lurk at the outer gate?"

"He is not at any distance at all, thanks to the school that you both regard with such bare tolerance."

"I admit he would be too much for me single-handed," said Simon. "But I am grateful for myself for my privilege of a day's work."

"It is a foolish theory that a man should not give his life to teaching girls," said Josephine. "A woman would not be ashamed of teaching boys; and the two things are just the same."

"They may be said to be the opposite of each other," said Simon. "But I am of your mind, my dear; I am not above teaching anyone."

"We should be strange people, indeed, to be above that."

"We should, in two ways," said Simon.

"I am above teaching girls in the despicable way," said Gabriel.

"You are a very young man," said Josephine. "It would not be suitable for you or for them. But your opportunities would have been very different, if I had been above teaching them, or below it. The one, as your uncle says, was as likely as the other."

"Don't say it was all done to prepare for my future, the future that does not come to pass."

"Are you at home, madam?" said the maid at the door.

"Well, I think we may say we are, Adela," said Josephine. "I cannot see any reason why we are not."

"Adela means, are we ready for guests?" said Simon, with his faint frown.

"Well, I think we are. Here is a good fire, and a good tea, and everything governed by law and order. It seems to me rather an opportune moment for guests. The more, the merrier, I say for my part."

Simon for his part said nothing, and Felix Bacon entered the room.

"Well, how are you?" said Josephine. "Have you come to see us professionally, or as a friend? I need not say how welcome you are in either character."

"I have come professionally. Perhaps I am not any longer your friend. I am here because I heard you were seeing your staff to-day. I am the last person to presume on the past."

"Will you have some tea with us, and then come with me to my study? Your colleagues have tea in their room upstairs, but you are rather late to join them. You have the run of the common room, when you are in the house. Some people separate the men and women in a school; I believe it is the usual thing; but I have never seen any reason for doing so myself."

"It would be dreadful if you saw reasons, especially in a school for girls. I am surprised that the men and women have to be separated, and that it is the usual thing. I will do nothing out of my sphere; so I will come with you to your study. Am I the only newcomer this term?"

"There is Miss Keats, the new, young, classical mistress," said Josephine, walking at his side to the door; "a very gifted and accomplished girl. You will be interested to meet her."

"I have always wanted to meet someone really accomplished, to compare myself with. Do you sit alone in this study? I think I am glad I belong to a common room. It seems to be you, who really have to be separated."

"Yes. It works out like that," said Josephine, looking for something in her desk. "Yes, here is your time-table. Your hours and classes are marked. I hope you will enjoy your work here, the more that I knew you as a friend before we came together as colleagues. That has not often happened to me."

"I hope it does not give me an unfair advantage?"

"Now, you will know better than to talk about advantage, when you have known me as a head mistress a little longer."

"I already know better. I am very uncomfortable at fancying that I might be singled out. How many of us are there, equal in the common room?"

"In the senior room, where you belong, Miss Munday, Miss Rosetti, Miss Luke, Mrs. Chattaway and Miss Keats; besides the visiting masters, who are there at times. You know them by sight, except Miss Keats. She is young to belong to that room, but is there by virtue of her work. Mrs. Chattaway is there by virtue of her age; her work is in the junior school. It might be uncongenial for her to be always with younger women."

"Am I there by virtue of my age or my work? It would not be uncongenial to me to be with younger women."

"Now I daresay it would not," said Josephine, pointing at him with her pencil. "But I would have you know that there are other things here to command your attention."

"But it would be more congenial to be with the older ones, though you may not believe it."

"Yes, I believe it; I think I should have guessed it. You are in that room by virtue of your work. When that is the case, the question of age does not arise."

"That is a good thing, as I do not confess to my age. I suppose Mrs. Chattaway does to hers. It shows how untrue it is, that women are less ready to admit their age than men."

"I do not know her exact age. I have found her very kind and charming as a friend, as I have all the members of my staff."

"I did not mean to talk about Mrs. Chattaway's exact age. I hope they none of them presume upon their friendship?"

"I trust that they deal with me fully as a friend. I hardly understand that phrase, 'presume upon friendship'."

"I quite understand it. Shall we have a gossip about your staff?"

"No!" said Josephine. "When you have known me a little longer, you will know that my mistresses, in their presence and in their absence, are safe with me. I hope I could say that of all my friends."

"I hoped you could not. But it is interesting that they

would not be safe, if we had the gossip. They must have treated you fully as a friend. I almost feel we have had it."

"You will find that not much gossip is done here," said Josephine, smiling as if in spite of herself.

"I suppose it hardly could be in a common room."

"Either there or elsewhere."

"And in the community of women! I am glad I am seeing life for myself, as all the theories about it are untrue. Now I see that you are dismissing me with a look. Of course you are one of those people whose glance is obeyed."

Josephine gave him a bow from her desk, and when he had gone, returned to the library.

"Well, there is another person sent on his path with a word! I could hardly be blamed if my stock of apposite words gave out, with the demand upon it. Happily it seems to increase with need. Nothing would do for Felix, but that he should be initiated with due and official ceremony."

"Do you think you will get on with him in his new character?" said Gabriel.

"Well, if I do not, he will be the first person I have not got on with."

"You have never dealt with anyone who has been a friend first."

"Friend first, fellow-worker afterwards; fellow-worker first, friend afterwards! What is the difference?"

"The others may feel there is one."

"Indeed they will not. I can set your mind at rest there."

"Will the mistresses like him about in their common room? He will be there oftener than the other men."

"Well, I should think they will. I find him very charming; and I do not see why they should not do the same. I make it a rule in making arrangements for people, to judge them by myself. It is the best, the simplest, and the friendliest thing."

"Suppose you have to give him notice?" said Gabriel.
Simon laughed.

"Well, I have had, of course, to break my relation, professionally, with certain people. That is simply as it has had to be. But I have never terminated it in any other sense; they have always remained my friends. In one case a woman came back to me and was married from my house: I found she regarded it as her home. It was a good thing I did not realise that before, or I should have felt some scruples in parting with her. But now, with my trained judgement, I should not be mistaken."

"It will be difficult to steer between our old and new relations," said Gabriel.

"You will only have the old relation. And for your uncle and me, Felix will do his work in one capacity, and depend upon our friendship in the other. He is a gentleman." Josephine moved her hand. "There should be no difficulty."

"I seem to be a person not versed in the ways of gentlemen."

"What you are, is a jealous boy. You want me to have no other friend but you. But I am very used to having streams of people pass before my eyes. Felix is only one of a group to me. I had to prepare him for that: I did not find him exactly in a state of preparation."

Felix was presenting himself to his future companions.

"I have come to introduce myself. I daresay you all know me by sight. I think my face is one that you would remember."

"Do you know us by sight?" said Helen. "Or are our faces less memorable?"

"Perhaps it is a sex difference," said Miss Luke.

"It is men who generally look at women's faces," said Miss Munday.

There was a pause.

"I am a little taken aback," said Felix. "I did not expect that your touch would be so much like my own. And I don't think you are trying to put me at my ease. Did you know that I was a person who could not feel awkward?"

"Yes, I think we sensed it," said Miss Luke.

"I am not surprised by your saying that. Mrs. Napier told me about your high level of charm."

"That was surely a rash thing to say," said Mrs. Chattaway.

"Perhaps it would not have occurred to Mr. Bacon, if he had not been warned," said Miss Luke, joining in the amusement at this possibility.

"I rely simply on being my natural self," said Miss Munday.

"Have you ever seen a more distinguished plainness than mine?" said Felix.

"No, certainly not," said Mrs. Chattaway. "I do not mean that there is any plainness in question."

"It is known to be a thing that is often forgotten," said Felix.

"I have seldom heard about plainness, without hearing too that it was forgotten," said Helen. "There hardly seems any point in mentioning it."

"Is ⸴ the first time you have done regular work, Mr. Bacon? ⸴aid Miss Luke.

"Do you not like to talk about my looks?"

"Yes, very much," said Miss Luke, yielding to the situation.

"I thought you would. We cannot often agree that a person is plain, to his face."

"Or that something makes us forget the plainness," said Mrs. Chattaway, with a touch of archness.

"Oh, do you really think I am plain?"

"They were your own words, Mr. Bacon."

"I had no idea that they would be anyone else's. They never have been before."

"You may not have started the idea before."

"I never will again, for fear the same advantage is taken of it."

"You will find it a change to be occupied every day, Mr. Bacon," said Miss Luke, with a touch of firmness.

"I have heard that women are cruel. I cannot expect them to let bygones be bygones."

"Surely there is nothing to be ashamed of in having the opportunity of a leisured life," said Mrs. Chattaway.

"No, I really agree that it is a thing to be proud of."

"So do I," said Miss Rosetti. "But you betray what you think of our position."

"I have always felt very chivalrously about it. But now we are all in it, we will not tolerate pity. I did not know before that pity really could not be tolerated."

"What drove you—what led you to take up the position?" said Mrs. Chattaway.

"Thank you for remembering in time about pity. My father makes me too small an allowance, but only small enough to lead and not drive me. And he could afford to make me a large one."

"I am sure he could," said Mrs. Chattaway.

"Do you expect us to think more of you for that, Mr. Bacon?" said Miss Luke.

"Yes, but not as much more as you fear. I am very sensitive to atmospheres."

"Is this atmosphere different from others?" said Helen.

"No, very nearly the same. No one admires riches as much as he feels it natural to admire them."

"He has always found out that they are not the one thing in the world," said Helen. "What is that bell?"

"Oh, how many years is it since we said that?" said Miss Luke.

"What is the bell?" said Felix. "Not a knell, is it?"

"It is the knell of someone's innocence of a working life," said Miss Luke.

"No wonder you hesitated to talk openly about it."

"It is the dressing-bell for the mistresses' first supper," said Miss Luke, with an atoning manner of full information.

"Then I have stayed to the last moment. I am not embarrassed by doing that. I do not recognise the politeness of leaving early. We ought always to seem as if we could not tear ourselves away. I really hardly can to-day, I have so enjoyed my first hour of work. And I am so sorry that I shall not see you all dressed."

"A most charming man!" said Mrs. Chattaway, as the footsteps died away. "He really seemed as if the society in this room were the one thing he would choose; and that is the essence of good manners."

"It must have been polite fiction?" said Miss Luke.

"Well, he seemed too good to be true," said Helen.

"It is a pity he did not see us dressed," said Miss Munday.

"I believe in some schools the mistresses do not dress at night," said Mrs. Chattaway.

"I know they do not," said Miss Rosetti. "I have lived and not dressed in them."

"It seems odd," said Miss Luke, with a slightly puzzled frown.

"It is only a superficial difference," said Mrs. Chattaway.

"Now is it?" said Miss Luke.

"I will put on my satin one evening early enough for Mr. Bacon to see me in it," said Miss Munday, meeting without flinching the mirth caused by a happy view of her appearance at its best.

As Felix reached the Hall, Gabriel crossed it and went towards Josephine's study.

"I bid you good-night with the respect I owe to a member of my employer's family," said Felix.

"I respond with the respect carefully paid by that member."

"It is not true that people have real esteem for workers. I thought my view of work as degrading was original, but it is almost universal. People who think it not degrading are too proud of thinking it, for it to be their natural opinion."

"How did you get on with the learned ladies upstairs?"

"I found I had a great deal in common with them; and

66

that rather put me out. I thought I should be so different. I think perhaps I must have found my vocation."

"It is the same as mine, then," said Gabriel. "My elders don't seem to know of another. It is time I departed to pursue it. And I find it is easy to get exhausted without doing any work."

"I am only beginning to know about work. I am glad it is not that, that causes exhaustion. But will you not find it a refreshment to see me flitting through the house about my duties?"

"Oh, don't apply any more emotional pressure. I shall faint beneath the heat and burden of the day." Gabriel broke off as Josephine came from her room.

"Well, you have met your colleagues?" she said, giving a word in passing to Felix.

"Yes. I nearly outstayed my welcome. I left them barely time to dress."

"Well, I daresay they like time for that," said Josephine, and turned to her nephew, as though the attention at her disposal for Felix were spent.

"Well, lazybones, standing dreaming instead of bringing me those books! I haven't the time to waste that you have. Where would you be without your man of the family?"

"I might be a man myself," said Gabriel, using a voice not often heard from his lips.

"Why, what is this? What is it?" said Josephine, with instant grasp of the position, while Felix vanished, as if of previous intention, from the house. "What is this line you take? What have you had from me but kindness?"

"It is time I did something besides take kindness: it becomes a reproach and a burden. People are so conscious of what is taken, and so unconscious of what they take. I can't be anything but a fund of easy companionship. Apart from anything else the life is too exhausting."

"Oh, is it? Exhausting is hardly the word I should apply. You had better find some life that is less exhausting. That is the cure for that sort of mood."

"I had better have found it months ago. I recognise the mistake."

"Ah, your real self was not hidden for long," said Josephine, in a tender, almost shaken tone. "And I saw it through the cloud. You may trust me not to take you at a disadvantage. You have a right to ask that from your best friend."

"I must claim the right to my different moods, as other people have it. I can't be simply an automaton of flattery. It is not a reasonable thing to ask, nor a possible thing to do."

"An automaton of flattery! Well, I don't recognise much sign of your being that in the last few minutes. Have your moods; I will not quarrel with them, as long as they are yours. It is your own self that I want."

Josephine passed into the study, and Gabriel wandered about the hall, wearing a hunted look.

CHAPTER VI

On the next evening sounds of arrival were heard of a more insistent nature than the many of the previous days, and Josephine came from her study, and hastened to the outer door.

"Welcome!" she said, in a deep, vibrating voice, drawing Elizabeth into the hall, and keeping a hand over her daughter's shoulder in avoidance of premature signs of intimacy. "Welcome home! Come and say a word to the masculine side of my household. The two complete families greet each other at last."

"So we exchange a word of friendship before we go to our own place? We take a breath of affection, and carry away the fragrance, fresh and sweet? So your boy and my girl meet for the first time, Simon, as you and I met so many years ago! There were meetings between the boys and girls in the old days too. The old days pass, and the new days come, and we do our best with all of them. We will, indeed, do it with those that are to come. But we are to linger for a first dear moment?"

"You are to linger for more than a moment, sorry as I am to dispute your first words in this house," said Josephine. "Our family dinner awaits your pleasure. You have come to friends and not to strangers, and at the risk of imposing directions at too early a stage, I would have you remember it."

"Such a happy remembrance! Such a sweet reminder! My Ruth is as glad as I am of the respite before the usefulness. She has been so blithe and busy in helping us to flit; but the spirit of weariness will creep apace in spite of the brave resolves. And the privilege when it is so sweetly offered, is doubly sweet. We will not be so churlish as not to welcome it."

"You will be doing us a kindness in keeping Josephine's attention to her own fireside," said Gabriel. "Her family is never enough by itself. She has been gadding off to-day to some part of the building unknown to us."

"Now, I have been doing nothing of the sort," said Josephine, in a distinct, conscious tone. "I had to have a word with my younger mistresses; and found myself committed to further communion before I knew where I was. They only wanted to make some confidences after the separation of the holidays; there is not so much in that. So away with your gadding and the rest! I had no anticipation of being detained, when I entered their presence."

"Well, you will be able to prophesy the result of further visits," said Elizabeth, in a bright tone.

"Yes, I think I shall," said Josephine frankly. "I had happened to introduce myself to their quarters before; and when you take an unprecedented course there is no certainty about the result. I could not be sure if my effort through the years to observe a simple equality toned up rather than deteriorated by the spice of control, had met with success. In its nature it must be a precarious effort. But the least element of failure would have been revealed to me to-day. Why, Simon, have I shaken your chess-board and baulked your genius? Well, a game is not of the things that mould the future, and Gabriel is saved from another signal defeat."

"Gabriel plays for the game and not for victory. These things do not repeat themselves," murmured Simon, pressing his fingers to his brow.

"Well, the game is not like Humpty-Dumpty, impossible to put together again," said Elizabeth. "The king's horses and the king's men can do their work this time."

"Josephine, you distinguish too much between your own employments and other people's," said Gabriel. "We see why your being asked to remain upstairs was not so certain."

"Well, we see that it was certain. And my poor young

mistresses! I wonder what they would say, if they knew how my lingering in their quarters would be taken hold of in mine. They would not have had the courage to press me in their pleasant, spontaneous way. Their eagerness could not have seemed at all such a simple, natural thing."

"It is strange to think that we have people fulfilling their destinies within our doors, whose lives are all but a sealed book to us," said Simon, his eyes on his moving fingers.

"That could never be the case with me. It would go too much against the grain." Josephine smiled at Elizabeth, as if her words foreshadowed her own relation. "It would simply be a contradiction in terms. I know what is to be known about each individual who comes under my survey. And often what is not to be known as well. Ah, what they tell me in their eyes and in their very silences, these women who have poured past me, working out their history! Ah, if we knew everyone's story! Well, if we are supposed not to know, we do not know; that is how it has to be."

"I was beginning to hope it had not," said Gabriel. "How do they have so much in their lives, when the outer world is so uneventful? Do you suppose Felix will be as fortunate?"

"Mrs. Napier," said Ruth, "you will let me say how I appreciate your not treating Mother just as one of the women who work here? I am the last person to speak; but it makes such a difference. Her being obliged to work does not mean that there are not ways and ways of letting her do it."

"My child, your mother and I are old friends. With others I have not been so fortunate. I have had to build up the background, that in this case is ready to my memory. But I never treat anyone 'just as one of the women who work here'." Josephine bent to Ruth with a smile. "You need not fear, stranger though you are in yourself to me, that you would meet such dealings at my hands. It is not only as your mother's daughter, that I shall deal with you to the best that is in me." She ended on a lighter note. "I find so many of my matter-of-course actions taken as benevolence, that I get into the way of making provision accordingly."

"It would not do to make differences for us, dear, that the others would resent," said Elizabeth.

"I should hardly have the opportunity. We work too much in our different spheres. The room set aside for your activities belongs only to you; 'the housekeeper's room' is the legend on the door, if there is anything in an inscription. Then there are the common rooms for the senior and junior staff: Ruth has the run of the latter in her own right. And I have my room across the hall, and possess it in solitude, as you do yours. I do not move amongst you all, dispensing benefits. I sit and work alone, realising that I am receiving them. That is a far more accurate picture of me."

"Well, we will make the most of the evening of simple friendship."

"Pray let us do so," said Gabriel. "We seem to be using it entirely for professional purposes. Is there anything we ever talk about, apart from the school?"

"I do not want to discuss the school at this end of the day," said Josephine. "Too many problems have arisen by that stage, to be dealt with in a drawing-room spirit. So, if our guests have absorbed enough of its atmosphere to possess their souls in peace, let us choose any subject that is congenial."

"Let us ask them to supply it," said Gabriel, "and give us a glimpse of the outer world."

"It is the inner world they must be thinking of at the moment. Their rooms are waiting for them, and they will dress and eat before they are at your disposal, though their experience of the outer world may well be larger than yours."

"It must be, as mine is non-existent."

"Well, it may not sound such an enviable place, when you hear it described with all the vigour and realism of which Mrs. Giffard is mistress. Perhaps she would not have chosen this world, if the other had made such a great appeal."

"Still, I think I can let you have your glimpse," said Elizabeth, rising and taking her wraps. "I have been in the outer world a good deal, as I daresay you can gather from signs that I betray unconsciously. I must not expect not to bear the marks of the fray; they are honourable signs of war. My experience shall be at your service. We will not hide it under a bushel, if it is to be our talent, or the material for our talent. It is an ill wind that blows nobody any good. Do we go straight up the staircase, dear Josephine?"

"Straight up and straight along. I am not giving you an escort. The sooner you know your way about your home, the better."

"Shall we come down when we are clothed and in our right mind?" said Ruth, a drooping figure in the door.

"Come down as soon as you will spare yourselves. I won't suggest how soon that will be. I do not know your ways; if you like to be unpacked for, or to unpack for yourselves, or to superintend the unpacking. The third and middle course commends itself to me, but I do not claim the same knowledge of you. I find that I must not burden my mind with such details about my charges. Not that they would be a burden, if my mind had room for them. As it has not, I appoint a deputy, and I recommend the experienced corridor maid in the part."

"Well, shall we unpack for ourselves or not?" said Ruth, as she followed her mother upstairs. "Can it be that we are people to be waited upon? I fancy I detected signs that was not really the case."

"I think we will superintend the unpacking, the third and middle course," said Elizabeth, holding her hand to her lips in silent laughter. "That is the method I shall adopt with a hundred boxes every term; so it is as well to get into the way of it. It might have been recommended with confidence. Well, how do you like my family of friends?"

"The proof of the pudding is in the eating. I have taken

73

such a very small bite as yet; though I believe it was regarded as a large and succulent portion."

"I am sure that one of them is inclined to like you."

"Oh, people might like me, if I ever happened to pass before their eyes. They cannot form opinions of a young woman who does not come within their range of vision."

Josephine came to Elizabeth's room before the family dinner-hour.

"Now, I hope you will excuse my prowling about your passage? I prefer people to keep to their own quarters myself. Not that there is any particular point in it; it is just a feeling I happen to have. But I thought, as mine are open to you, that yours would be to me on this occasion. I want to introduce you to my mistresses myself. They are eager to welcome an old friend of mine, and there is no reason to defer the pleasure. Have you any feeling about the manner of your introduction?"

"I will leave it to you, my dear, the head of all matters in this house."

"Then I will do it in the way that seems to me natural." Josephine knocked at the door of the common room. "Here is Mrs. Giffard, my old friend! As I had a natural wish to present her to you myself, you will pardon my breaking in upon your privacy? If you have had too many glimpses of me to-day, you have not of her. And I warn you that she is not accustomed to being a sight to be wearied of."

"Such a lot of clever faces! Such a lot of lore and learning confronting poor me, who am so eager to lap it all in comfort! It gives importance to my so unimportant work. Will you grant it a little importance, and me as well, because I do it? Importance is so much the fashion that I must have my little share."

"Your work is the most fundamental of all," said Miss Luke.

"Now I regard my work as equally fundamental, though I say it as shouldn't," said Josephine playfully. "Because all work is equally so; for that reason and no other."

"I wonder some of this accomplishment does not break out into the world," said Elizabeth. "We must indeed take care of it, or it will escape."

"Oh, we are content with our narrow sphere," said Miss Luke, laughing.

"And it is not as narrow as you would think," said Mrs. Chattaway.

"Experience is not a matter of doors and walls," said Josephine, glancing round. "Though other things may be a matter of them sometimes."

"The deepest experience always takes place within them," said Miss Rosetti.

"Yes, yes, indeed," said Josephine. "That is profound."

"I have a great deal of knowledge of life," said Miss Munday.

"If I may say so, I have noticed it," said Josephine. "And again if I may say so, I have noticed it increasing."

"You may say so again," said Miss Munday.

"Well, we all have this in common," said Elizabeth, "that we must put our gifts to the purpose of honest self-support."

"Have we?" said Josephine easily. "I happen to have passed that stage."

"So have I, in the last years," said Miss Rosetti.

"I am provided for," said Miss Munday.

"I am partly," said Miss Luke, laughing at the turn of subject. "I am engaged in building upon the rather frail foundation."

"I am dependent upon myself, being just the person who ought not to be," said Mrs. Chattaway.

"I am too. I feel it is rather a heroic position," said Helen.

"Yes, yes, it has a dignity in a way, that no other position has," said Josephine. "I remember feeling that I was losing something, as I left it. Well, I must return to my family. Thank you very much for your welcome of my old friend."

"Why do they lead this life, if they need not, Josephine?" said Elizabeth, as they went to the stairs.

"Why, we all choose some life, don't we? There would be no explorers or scientists or poets or politicians, according to that view."

"Miss Keats is very much younger than the rest. She has an unusual type of face. Do you find her a magnet for Gabriel's eyes?"

"No, I do not; I can give you a simple answer there," said Josephine, with a little sound of mirth. "The mistresses in that group do not contrive to be that. He is a very one-idea'd young man. It is not the result of any training of mine. Sometimes I get quite borne down by the unvarying direction of his emotions. But they will settle into a steadier current in the end."

"He is very young as yet."

"I think it is not a question of youth. Twenty-three is the romantic age. But some people must deal with romance in their own way, have it in their own form. But the idea of his turning to my staff for his satisfaction in that line"— Josephine's voice broke again—"gives me to smile, I admit."

"My dear, you are more than wonderful in your touch with all of them. I shall get to be in awe of you, if you go on being so wise and great and good. You have left the past so much further behind than I have. We were not so good in the good old days, or the naughty old days, whichever they were. Well, this is the library, the dear home room? Well, Simon and son, I have returned from my venture into the lions' den. Such a feeble, feminine creature I have been brought to feel, such a light, bright, opinionless person, with such a woman's mind! Josephine came to my rescue and coaxed them back into their cage. And I am ready to tell Gabriel the story of my life in the wide, wide world. Such a different thing I see it has been from being in the cage! When he is ready for the feast of words, I will lay it out for him."

"I think the feast we are ready for, is of a more tangible kind," said Josephine, moving to the dinner table. "Quite such an unsubstantial repast is hardly adapted to our immediate needs. Plain living and high thinking are very well; but as our living does not look so very plain, and as the thinking did not sound as if it were to be so very high, we won't concern ourselves just now with the combination. Mrs. Giffard may be too tired to amuse you to-night, Gabriel; and as your path and hers will not often cross, you may have to learn that her energies are not to be dissipated in masculine service."

"No, no; we have dedicated ourselves to feminine service. That is in the inside world, and we must be content to fulfil it there. And content to be there, too." Elizabeth gave a bright glance at Josephine. "We have so much cause for content."

"Is not Miss Giffard to join us this evening?" said Gabriel.

"My poor, weary girl!" cried Elizabeth. "She is wandering companionless in these perplexing corridors!"

"Leave this to me with confidence, Mrs. Giffard," said Gabriel.

"Well, I should hope so," said Josephine, looking up. "I was wondering how far Mrs. Giffard would get, with a young man sitting looking gracefully on. Go and find her daughter and escort her here. This is a difficult house for a stranger, the great rambling, complicated place! I often wonder at myself for having got it added to so often, unawares. You go too far in recognising only one woman in the world. I am ceasing to be flattered by it."

"I am ceasing to flatter you by doing it. I am occupied with the picture of our guest. I know that passage which is the undoing of strangers."

"And when you guessed all about it, too!" said Josephine, with a sigh.

Gabriel came upon Ruth at the expected place.

"I have been blamed for not guessing your predicament, and more blamed for guessing it."

"I am the person to be blamed," said Ruth, hardly hastening her steps. "This is a pretty way to be useful, isn't it?"

"You are not going to be useful to-night. If you knew the atmosphere of this house, you would understand the arrogance of that speech."

"Yes, I will believe it is arrogant. I am learning about the dignity of toil. I would modestly relinquish the distinction."

"I would relinquish my distinction of being the only person in the house without yours."

"We ought to be shaken up together," said Ruth, lifting her large eyes to his face. "Instead of which I suppose we shall live at opposite poles."

"We are reaching the pole at which my life is spent. Poles are known to be chilly places. We will venture sometimes into the warmer climes between. Josephine, I have found the lost sheep, but in a state of exhaustion."

"Well, that is natural, when she forgets her dinner. Come in, my child, and make up for lost time. I hope you will forgive our beginning? We would have waited of course, except for involving your mother. Yes, Simon, you may help yourself; Ruth is safely supplied. Will you allow my husband to use your Christian name in private life? He will not in professional relations."

"I feel so guilty that anyone has waited, Mrs. Napier."

"My dear, we do not serve men before women," said Josephine.

CHAPTER VII

"MAY I COME IN?" said Josephine, hesitating after her knock at the door of the common room, as though uncertain that the formal command to enter extended to herself. "Or am I intruding?"

"You are intruding, of course," said Miss Luke. "You should hesitate to enter a room in your own house."

"I certainly should," said Josephine, advancing with a still tentative step. "This room is not in my province: it is good of you to make me welcome in it. And I don't know why I should have the easiest chair, unless it is because I am the guest. I should certainly give it to any one of you in my rooms. Well, they did not play me false in the matter of the springs; that is one thing. Miss Munday, I believe I am turning you out of it?"

"Yes," said Miss Munday. "I was sitting in it."

"I am indeed sorry to be displacing you; but there is a matter that I wish to discuss with you all. I hope you will give me your advice?"

"Yes, we will," said Miss Munday.

Josephine joined with some vagueness of thought in the mirth that ensued.

"We will advise you to take any step you have decided on," said Miss Luke. "It must be advisable to take a step. There is more point in a step when it is taken."

"Now it is very nice to see tea coming in," said Josephine, not passing over this item in her companions' lot. "I don't know if you are going to allow me to share it with you?"

"We will not enlighten you," said Miss Luke.

"Are we going to send for another cup?" said Josephine to Miss Munday, somehow attaining a decision, but hesitating to take upon herself the office of hostess in the room.

"Will you bring another cup and saucer, please?" said Miss Munday to the maid.

"Thank you," said Josephine to Miss Munday.

"We have hot scones on the day when our head comes to tea," said Miss Luke.

"You always have hot things brought to you, I hope?"

"I do not know; I do not care for them," said Mrs. Chattaway, looking faintly startled.

"I meant, we did not always have this rare kind," said Miss Luke.

"I hope you send for any kind you prefer," said Josephine, in the tone of what went without saying. "Or more than one kind, if you care for it."

"Oh, surely no one could do that," said Mrs. Chattaway, with a suggestion of shuddering, which she checked with a glance at her friends.

"Oh, thank you; am I to come first?" said Josephine.

"Yes, before me," said Miss Munday.

"Well, I should think so!" said Mrs. Chattaway, replying to Josephine, and running forward with the sugar and tongs, and for the last steps without the tongs.

"Thank you," said Josephine, taking some sugar with her fingers, as if unconscious of another method.

"I am very clumsy," said Mrs. Chattaway. "I never had clever hands."

"Neither had I," said Josephine, with a faint note of surprise. "But as we both live rather by our heads, it is not of any great consequence. Not that I am not an admirer of a delicate hand."

"Our eyes turn to Miss Rosetti's," said Miss Luke.

"Yes," said Josephine. "If I may be very personal, I have seen no one else with hands of that type, unless it is my nephew, Gabriel. I say to him that his ought to be the woman's and mine the man's, a speech which does not appeal to his sense of fitness."

"You wear such beautiful rings, Mrs. Napier," said Mrs. Chattaway, her tone suggesting full compensation for Josephine.

Josephine gave a perfunctory glance at her hands.

"They were presents," she said in a careless tone. "One naturally puts presents to the use for which they were intended."

"Are you going to begin with a scone, Mrs. Napier?" said Miss Rosetti, sauntering forward with her hands under the dish.

"Yes, I am, please. I think tea should go through all its proper stages. I hope it does that with all of you?"

"Yes," said Miss Munday.

"It is not for lack of temptation if it does not," said Mrs. Chattaway, who had run back for the tongs, and forward again to Josephine, as if the latter also might remedy her omission.

"Yes, I will have a little more sugar. Thank you," said Josephine.

"It is a pity we only have four meals a day," said Miss Munday.

"I should be sorry to have any more," said Mrs. Chattaway. "I can hardly manage those there are."

"Why not miss some of them?" said Miss Rosetti.

"It would be unsocial," said Mrs. Chattaway, just inclining her head.

"It would indeed," said Josephine. "And what is more, it would be very bad for you. I hardly like to hear of it even in jest."

"I like to hear of more than four meals a day even in jest," said Miss Munday.

"Well, I am on the side of Miss Munday, in the sense she means," said Josephine. "Why not have as much as we can of a pleasant and beneficial thing? That is, if the diet merits that description where we happen to be. In some households I should not want to hear of more than four meals a day, even in jest. Jest would be the last word to apply to it."

"It would be wrong to joke about it," said Helen.

"Now I am glad that you concede significance to the material life," said Josephine. "When the health and comfort of many people were about to depend on me, I asked myself: 'Am I prepared to adapt my own instincts to the extent that may be demanded?' And having answered the question, and lived the answer for over twenty years, I feel myself a larger rather than a lesser woman."

"What led you to take up educational work?" said Mrs. Chattaway, sensitively cloaking any harshness in the truth.

"I might put that question to you."

"Oh, well, I had no choice: I was left very badly off," said Mrs. Chattaway, in a parenthetic manner.

"Then our initial reasons were not so different. I was myself too poor"—Josephine gave the last word a full utterance—"to do all that I wished. But the reasons that lay deeper were my love for teaching; my belief that seeds were sown in youth that would bear fruit in the later days; my passionate desire——" She held her expression carefully still—"to sow with my own hand some of those seeds. Do you not think that the resemblance between us goes further than the beginning?"

"Yes, oh, yes," said Mrs. Chattaway, her voice hardly in keeping with the extent of her claim. "But in your case the stage will soon be reached when you can leave all such necessity behind."

"Have I not made it clear that I shall never reach that stage?"

"Oh, that is just what you say," said Mrs. Chattaway, again making rather light of Josephine's meaning.

"How I hate myself for saying a dull, dutiful thing!" said Miss Luke. "But some of us have to be at classes at five."

"Now that brings me to the point of my dilemma. I think you are too much tied to classes, especially to those that make no claim on you as individuals. I have been thinking that an extra junior mistress is indicated. Well, the truth is, that my friend Mrs. Giffard, was so anxious to have her daughter with her, that I found myself doing what is really against my principles, and creating a post. But do you not think, quite apart from any whim of mine, that you would be better for a little less routine?"

"Yes," said Miss Munday.

"Most human beings could say that," said Miss Rosetti.

"I am so glad that you agree with me," said Josephine, her voice losing a little in fullness.

"Now, I don't know; I have not said that I agree," said Miss Luke, standing with a considering, honest air. "I don't take to the idea of admitting to too much work. It is one of those little, unsatisfactory things that one somehow does not do."

"You have certainly not done it," said Josephine, her manner sacrificing her own point of view.

"Mrs. Napier may not require a unanimous vote," said Miss Rosetti.

"No, no, that is quite fair," said Miss Luke, sitting down. "I am taking advantage of the rest of you. I can only admit it, and say no more."

"I cannot say that I have too much work, Mrs. Napier," said Mrs. Chattaway.

"Can you not?" said Josephine kindly. "I am very glad to hear it. But we are considering a question of general policy. How the matter works out, is for all of you to settle between you. It is nothing to do with me."

"You are so kind in your manner of doing things, Mrs. Napier. We all ought to be most grateful."

"No," said Josephine, "it is I who should be that, if what you generously say has any truth. It is what we meet with, that brings out what we have in us for help or hindrance."

"You are doing Mrs. Giffard a great kindness," said Miss Rosetti.

"No kindness comes into it. She was my girlhood's friend; and I am not happy in seeing her life go too much awry. I am considering myself, as I believe we all do really."

"I believe we do," said Miss Luke. "I believe that is so; that characters make history."

"It is extraordinary what reversals of position life brings with it," said Mrs. Chattaway.

"Why, what reversal is there here?" said Josephine. "Mrs. Giffard and I were old friends then. We are older friends now. Surely life may be allowed to bring those changes?"

"You are too kind to admit my meaning, Mrs. Napier."

"Yes, I think I am. I shall see no difference in the value of our work, as we do it side by side. You will all do me the service of observing that spirit towards her daughter?"

"We can do nothing else, with your example before us," said Mrs. Chattaway, making no personal claim.

"Well, in a way I resent the young woman," said Miss Luke. "She will be taking on herself what I have a right to feel depends on me."

"Now you are to fall in with my scheme, and realise that I think it best for you," said Josephine. "I cannot have objections raised to a decision for your welfare."

"It must be sad for the girl to give up her youth to routine," said Mrs. Chattaway, attending without delay to Josephine's request.

"It is different for mature and settled spinsters!" said Miss Luke.

"Now, I can tell you that there is no conflict between the two spheres of work and marriage," said Josephine. "If there were, marriage could not be what it is, a different usefulness."

"Indeed there is none, when abilities are up to both," said Mrs. Chattaway.

"I would not claim that abilities have much to do with marriage," said Josephine, bending her head as though to cover a smile, and then raising it frankly. "The forces that unite two personalities, defy definition, though the business is attempted without any beating about the bush in some modern books I could mention. But there would be no meaning in these things, if each case did not work itself out for itself and by itself. Do you not say that that is so of every human experience?" She turned about her to relinquish any claim to an isolated position.

"Now," said Miss Luke, drawing quickly into herself; "let us admit it. When we meet a married woman, do we not feel a certain respect for her?"

"Well, I hope so," said Josephine. "Poor woman, why should you not? I hope you feel a certain respect for me, as I sit here."

"Now, now, Mrs. Napier, again you are too kind to admit our meaning."

"Well, then, let us be plain," said Josephine. "We feel a certain respect for the woman who attracts and possesses a man? Is that it? My words are what yours would be? Well, and why should we not? We should feel a certain respect for any human ability."

"Ah, but they are the elemental things, the love between man and woman, marriage, motherhood," said Miss Luke in a deep, quick tone, placing herself fully outside her initial heading. "The things untouched by civilisation, primitive, immune from what is called progress."

"Yes," said Josephine gently.

"I was forgetting that Gabriel was not your own son," said Miss Luke, very low.

"In this case it must be exactly the same," said Mrs. Chattaway.

"No," said Josephine; "it is quite different. In early days it could not but have an element of sameness. It fades with every day now."

"You are always conscious of the difference?" said Miss Rosetti.

"He is always conscious of it. He does not let me forget it. He is my masculine companion, my protector. And that reminds me that you yourselves have a new masculine companion. What is your verdict on Mr. Bacon's presence in your common room?"

"By no means an open verdict," said Miss Luke.

"I am sure it is not," said Josephine, with a smile of fellow-feeling. "But, seriously, do you not think him a very brilliant and polished man?"

"We could not think it more seriously than we do," said Helen.

"I am glad it is to be such a high quality of companionship," said Josephine, with a touch of earnestness. "He will spend some time here between his hours of work. I should not care for you to be thrown with every man of my acquaintance. By the way"—she spoke with sudden concern—"you do not object to his presence here, do you?"

"No," said Miss Munday.

"It seems a strange profession for him," said Mrs. Chattaway. "I mean, the mere fact of working, when he has been used to a life so different, may put a strain that he does not anticipate."

"I daresay he does not," said Josephine, with a touch of grimness. "I did not myself. We have to make the effort. I made it; and I venture to think that it will not hurt him to do the same."

"I cannot bear to think of it," said Helen. "I feel like the savage women, who do the work while the men sit idle. Perhaps the extra mistress will be a help to him. I feel inclined to let him have my share of her."

"Well, I hope she will be a help to all of you," said Josephine, rising. "That is the purpose of her, after, of course, the fulfilment of her own life. I hope she will give just that little extra easing, which makes so much difference in any arduous lot. And I am not going to sympathise with you over its being arduous: I should envy you that side of it, if I did not share it. Now it remains for me to thank you for your hospitality, and to betake myself to the masculine side of my world. I wonder which side is more dependent on me? Or to which I owe the greater debt? That is the truer question."

"Is there much difference between the sides?" said Helen.

"Well," said Josephine, "there is a difference, and there is not. I see it so plainly, and I see it does not exist, if you know what I mean." Nobody gave any sign of not knowing. "Well, it is my lot, what I have undertaken. I must not complain; I do not. I would not change it, even when I find it much. And I don't know what my men would say, if I made the suggestion."

"Your nephew is making a long stay at home," said Miss Rosetti.

"Well, he has spent his college days apart from me," said Josephine, in a condoning manner. "I must not be surprised if he wants a little of the other thing now. I am not surprised; though I admit I was not prepared for the violence of the reaction. And I find that we must not joke about apron-strings. I have to be very respectful to young manhood, very heedful of a young sensitiveness. It is not a charge in which I would fail, not the least of my duties."

"You will find it a change when he marries," said Miss Rosetti.

"I must recognise that I have no prospect of such a change. His attitude towards me must keep me a prisoner: I don't know what any young woman would say to it. Well, I must remember that the tie of blood between us is not of the deepest kind. Anyhow, it is put aside by my young gentleman, in determining the basis of our intercourse. I am not his aunt any more than any other woman."

Josephine moved to the door, and Mrs. Chattaway was a moment behindhand in running forward to open it. Josephine paused, as her exit was impeded rather than eased, and acknowledged with a bend of her head a courtesy due to a guest.

CHAPTER VIII

"WHAT SHALL I wear for the school entertainment?" said Gabriel.

"Anything tidy that you have," said Josephine. "You must be properly dressed to show the people to their places."

"What will Miss Munday wear?" said Gabriel. "I should like to be equal to Miss Munday."

"Well, you can't be," said Josephine. "Miss Munday is the senior mistress, and you are a foolish boy. There is no question of equality. You can put on anything fit to wait upon her in."

"Felix will wait on Miss Munday," said Gabriel. "The junior mistresses have fallen to my portion."

"Well, I hope you will attend to them properly. Felix is so very dependable in that way. I feel that his compeers have definitely been better looked after since he has been with us."

"What about the question of all questions, my dealings with the parents?" said Simon.

"Why is it more of a question than the others?" said his wife.

"Ah, we know why," said Simon. "Yes, I fear we know why."

"But I feel that Josephine is right in repudiating the truth," said Gabriel.

Josephine laid her hand on her nephew's head, and hastened from the room. In the hall she came upon Ruth, and paused to speak to her.

"You have done the programmes, my dear? I am afraid you had not much time."

"I had not, Mrs. Napier, and so there are not many programmes. More time would have resulted in a larger number."

"Well, I hope you will enjoy the afternoon after all the preparations."

"Oh, does one ever enjoy a thing when one has been involved in the preliminaries? And it is the people who have not been involved in them, whose enjoyment matters."

"Dear, dear, I should have thought that that was the best foundation for enjoyment," said Josephine, laughing and passing on. "I am quite prepared to find it so myself."

The mistresses came into the concert hall, with their demeanour modified as much as their dress, indeed modified by it. Mrs. Chattaway cast furtive glances from the others to herself; Miss Munday's expression suggested humorous awareness of her own festive aspect; Miss Luke, by moving rapidly amongst her companions, laying her hand on their shoulders and indulging in lively talk, proved that she was without any such awareness.

"I feel a little conscious of my appearance," said Felix, coming up to the group. "Perhaps it is being one of the few people who can wear formal clothes."

His speech was met by incredulous mirth, his hearers keeping their eyes on his face, in case of further entertainment.

"Well, I hope that no one will be conscious of mine," said Josephine. "It is not my habit to be aware of it; but when I am oblivious, it may be hitting other people in the eye. I got into the garment in time, but I admit it does not add to the occasion."

"People always seem to think admission alters things," said Helen, "when it really rather helps to establish them."

"You are right; I have been remiss," said Josephine, catching the words and giving her a smile as she went to her place; while her mistresses regarded her in silent appreciation of the difference that had raised her above themselves.

Josephine listened to the concert with a demeanour that

proved her unprepared for its items as they came. When a girl performed especially well, she leant across her neighbour and inquired the name of both pupil and teacher, and gravely nodding her head, sat back in her place. Jonathan heard the performance with his face covered with his hand, and his body swaying to the music. At its conclusion he emerged into the open room, but perceiving his sister mounting the platform, resumed his seat and his expression.

"Now I feel that I am not doing well by my speech in choosing to make it directly after the concert. That had the excuse of honest preparation, one which as a school-mistress I feel should command indulgence. And this has no excuse at all; hardly even that of being felt a duty; for I should have taken leave to doubt the need of it, if I had been permitted." Josephine smiled at her mistresses, and pausing in what might have passed for a recourse to her memory, if it had not been for her confession, continued with an air of confidence gathering, as she found that words came. "What I am conscious of, as I stand here, is that I am the last and the least of the people present; the least as the head mistress, as the simple means to an end; and that anything about me that is not in some way revealed by my pupils, can have no meaning. So I will ask you to take the simplest word, born of the moment, as fulfilling the moment's need. I find that I would only, that I should only, that I can only say one thing; and that is that I am grateful; to my pupils, to their parents, to my staff; to all who give me of their best in return for mine." Josephine paused, and perceiving that this limit to her words had caused a miscalculation, waited with her eyes down, as if under the influence of her feelings, until a little girl, carrying a bouquet, approached the platform.

"Now, here are two charming things!" she said, standing with the bouquet in one hand and the other on the child's head. "I do not know which gives me more pleasure, but I do know which is the more important; and I think I cannot end better than by saying that there can be no one present, to whom it is more important than it is to me."

There was applause, whether for Josephine's self or her devotion of it to others, was not apparent, and Mrs. Chattaway turned to her friends.

"An extraordinary speech for the spur of the moment! Just the sort that one would think would need the most preparation. One can hardly believe it."

"No," said Miss Munday on a rather high note.

There was a tendency to titter, and Miss Luke set her teeth through her own participation in it.

"Come, come. What we could not do ourselves may be possible for others, for one other, anyhow."

"And we have Mrs. Napier's word," said Mrs. Chattaway.

"I admire the speech more, if it was prepared," said Felix. "Fancy planning to make that kind of speech and not an elaborate one! I had a glimpse into my own soul."

"What is the jest?" said Josephine, as she passed.

There was a pause, and then Miss Luke stepped forward to do all concerned the justice of truth.

"It was suggested that you had prepared your speech, Mrs. Napier. The idea of your not being above human weakness struck us as ludicrous, you see."

"Oh!" said Josephine. "I had not that temptation. I speak much worse, when I do not speak extempore. I am afraid that your impression that I was doing myself more than justice, had a certain truth."

Jonathan for the second time emerged from his seat.

"Well, that was a pretty sight, a satisfying feast for the ears. A very high standard, Josephine, my dear, both in you and your pupils; my congratulations. Well, Miss Munday, we are both interested in education: I have given much of my life to it. Miss Rosetti, I have promised myself a talk with an old friend. Yes, is there anything more to come?"

"The exhibition of drawings," said Felix. "You need not be afraid of their quality: I entrust the mounting to no one but myself. I should be ashamed to let a pupil take home a drawing that had no merit. The old-world atmosphere is so important, and I pay it strict attention."

Josephine glanced at Miss Munday and Miss Luke, and raised her brows in mock despair.

The father of a pupil came up to Felix.

"So you are the drawing-master of the school?"

"Yes," said Felix in a cordial tone.

"And you are quite settled in the post?"

"Yes. I do not lose my positions."

"Have you had many?"

"No; that would mean that I did lose them."

"You find the work interesting?"

"Yes. I was saying what interesting work I did."

"Why did you choose to teach girls rather than boys?"

"Everyone asks me that. I wonder how girls get educated. I knew people didn't always believe in women's higher education; but I find that they don't believe in any education at all. I wonder why they send their daughters to school. I suppose you have your own reasons?"

The guest smiled and moved on to Josephine.

"He has his own touch, that drawing master of yours. He seems to take his work in a serious spirit."

"I should hardly have thought that that was the phrase to describe his talk with you," said Josephine, with a smile.

"I was speaking of his real attitude, apart from his talk."

"I hope that goes without saying of anyone who teaches here. And in his case the attitude cannot arise from his background. It is his own."

"Where does he come from? Was he not intended for the life?"

"He is the son of Sir Robert Bacon, whose place is about thirty miles to the west," said Josephine, her easy voice easier as she ended: "The only son."

"Oh yes, of course," said the guest.

"Is there any 'of course' about it? Men whose roots are in the country, generally give their hearts to hunting and such like, don't they, rather than to the furthering of art?"

"Oh yes. No doubt you are fortunate to have him."

"Yes; I think it shows a genuine inclination," said Josephine in an even tone.

"It seems an odd life for him, teaching drawing to girls."

"If I thought teaching girls an odd life, I should not have chosen it. You cannot expect me to agree with you there."

"No, no; but I meant for a man."

"Well, you cannot expect me to agree with you there either, or I should not have men on my staff."

"Well, I must say that I agree," said Fane, pausing with the simple purpose of sharing the talk. "I thank heaven that there were other choices open to me."

"Then I think we all thank heaven for it," said Josephine, smiling.

"Yes, yes, indeed," said the guest. "Do you find that men teach better than women, Mrs. Napier?"

"No, but I find they teach as well; so that there is no reason for debarring them from the work."

"No, no, of course not," said the guest, inwardly confronting the question of human eagerness.

Jonathan left Miss Rosetti and came up to his sister; and the guest gave a glance at this further masculine element as he went his way.

"Well, Gabriel is still domesticated, my dear. Is enough getting to be as good as a feast?"

"I don't think anything is as good as a feast, at tea time after an amateur concert. And Gabriel will certainly not cease being domesticated just now. He will bring refreshment to these kind ladies, who have borne the concert with such fortitude, knowing how unwillingly I inflicted it on them. So allow Miss Rosetti to drink her tea in peace."

"Miss Rosetti and I are old friends. It was I who introduced you to her."

"Well, having done one great thing for the school, come and do another, and talk to some parents. That seems to me a great thing at this moment, distorted though I admit my sense of values to be. We will leave the qualified ones to make merry at the expense of the concert. I'll warrant that will be the better of the two entertainments to-day. Why, what a crash! Has somebody come to grief?"

It was seen that a pupil, who had been carrying tea to the guests, had stumbled with the tray to the ground.

"Dear, dear, what is this, what is this?" said an old gentleman. "All the best cups and saucers! Well, I hope nobody is hurt. The china is hurt quite enough."

"Here is somebody in trouble!" said Fane, as Gabriel and Felix approached in haste. "Now there is no need for a fuss. Accidents are bound to happen."

"Are you shaken, my dear?" said Josephine to the girl. "No, don't trouble to pick up the pieces; my nephew is here. Yes, you must want a chair; thank you, Mr. Bacon. Now they will fetch you some tea for yourself. You have had quite a shock; the state of the china shows that."

"Your pupils expect gallantry while they are at school, Mrs. Napier?" said Fane.

"Surely school should be a preparation for life."

"I hope they will get what they have been taught to expect."

"I hope so," said Josephine, with a touch of gravity.

"You treat school-girls as if they were grown-up women?"

"Always, when it is possible. But perhaps there speaks the educationist." Josephine smiled at Fane, and turned to the mother of a pupil.

"Who was the girl who played the violin, Mrs. Napier?"

"I am afraid I do not remember her name. I know her well by sight."

"Of course you cannot give personal attention to all the girls."

"I can see that they all have personal attention. That is what I do with my time."

"Do you know who teaches her the violin?"

"Yes, I have just asked. I too, was struck by her playing. And I ought to know the good gentleman: I find I have a talk with him every term."

"Would you recommend my girl to learn the violin?"

Josephine placed her hand on the speaker's shoulder.

"I should not, at the moment. I must find what her talents are, what her health is, in a word, who she is, before I offer an opinion. There are people who will tell me all these things."

"The girls of to-day are fortunate," said the mother, realising the distance between her child and the person in charge of her. "Will you ask someone to write to me?"

"I hope to write to you myself," said Josephine, emphasising her second word, and leaving her companion in favour of the state it indicated, as compared with certainty.

"May I have tea with you?" said Felix, joining the mistresses, who were still a group by themselves. "I want to seem a person apart from the other masters."

"Well, that is the way to do it," said Miss Luke. "Their bearing seems to indicate that we are the subordinate half of mankind."

"So many things indicate it, and yet is never really settled," said Felix. "I hardly think you can be, or it would have been proved by now."

"Do many things show that man is the ruling half?" said Miss Rosetti.

"Yes, a great many," said Helen. "And yet that is never settled either. It may mean that we cannot judge by appearances."

"I believe you are a feminist, Mr. Bacon," said Miss Luke, her tone hardly bearing out her own opinions.

"He is indeed," said Helen. "He said that it was not settled that women were subordinate to men, and he could not be more of a feminist than that."

"Here is an impressive-looking person!" said Mrs. Chattaway. "Whose father is he?"

"Oh, he is mine," said Felix. "And he said he could not come. He must think it his duty to take me by surprise. I hope I have not caused him inconvenience. I must behave to him very carefully. People's manners to their family are such a test."

An upright old man about seventy-eight, of the same height, but of heavier build than Felix, with the latter's features in a more solid and regular form, was advancing across the room, impeded by his fellow guests, one of whom addressed him, as they were compelled to a pause.

"This is a pretty sight. All the young faces."

"Ah, yes, indeed," said Sir Robert, turning his glasses about him.

"You have a daughter, you have a grand-daughter; you have come to visit one of the girls?"

"I have come to visit my son."

"Your son?" said the other.

"Yes," said Sir Robert, with grave simplicity. "He is the drawing master here."

"Oh yes; I have heard people speak of him. I hear that he puts his heart into his work."

"I trust he does, as he has undertaken it."

"My father is the first person to take the right view of my profession," said Felix. "I am glad to see you looking so well, Father. Will you come and see the exhibition of drawings?"

"No, I will take them for granted, thank you," said Sir Robert, shaking hands with his son, with his eyes on his face.

"Then will you come and be introduced to my colleagues?"

"No, I will also take them——ah, I shall be most pleased," said Sir Robert, observing the sex of these persons, and accompanying Felix towards them.

"May I introduce my father?" said Felix, pronouncing the names of the women in turn, and causing each to give a conscious little bow, and Sir Robert a series of salutes that had not merely a numerical advantage.

"Are your son's surroundings what you expected, Sir Robert?" said Miss Luke.

"Ah, yes; a pretty sight," said Sir Robert, giving a general glance about him after his words.

"Confess you would like him to give up his post to-morrow."

"I should be sorry to see him change his mind so soon."

"He says that in your view he might be a woman," said Miss Munday in a plaintive tone.

"A father is disposed to take a hopeful view of his son," said Sir Robert, bowing as he turned away.

"Do you not want to have a talk with your father?" said Mrs. Chattaway to Felix, with an improved opinion of this opportunity.

"No. I look rather undistinguished beside him. And he might try to make me look foolish; and it would not be fair to Mrs. Napier for me to look both. One cannot only consider one's own family."

Sir Robert was approaching Simon.

"You have great doings here to-day."

"Yes, it is our great occasion."

"A pretty sight, the young faces," observed Sir Robert, after a silence.

"Yes, here to-day and gone to-morrow!" said Simon, in a rather drawn-out, dreamy tone. "A world of fleeting generations."

Sir Robert agreed, and moved off to offer a formal hand-shake to Jonathan. Jonathan returned it in a cringing manner, stooping and looking shorter than he was, and vanished into the crowd.

"It is a pity that I have not inherited my father's appearance," said Felix. "I am really almost a trivial figure in comparison. Here is Mrs. Napier, bringing another father to see us! I see how much mine is above the average. I am not at all self-conscious about being the only man."

"Not as self-conscious as Mrs. Napier is about being the only woman with the father," said Helen to Miss Rosetti.

"Now, here are the senior mistresses grouped for your introduction to them!" said Josephine, keeping her eyes averted from Felix, to give full weight to the convention of precedence to woman. "They will be interested to know that you hope to place your daughter with us next term."

"Will you pay extra for drawing?" said Felix, as he was presented.

"Why, I don't know. Is that the thing to do?"

"Yes, quite the thing," said Felix.

"Mr. Bacon is the drawing-master, and anxious for the success of his subject," said Josephine.

"Well, it shows that he takes his subject seriously."

"I am shocked by people's attitude to their daughters," said Felix. "They all express open surprise that their education should be taken seriously. It is a good thing that they entrust it to other people: they are evidently not without parental instincts. But they don't seem to give any real thought to their being the mothers of the race."

"Well, but too much education may not result in their being the mothers of the race," said the father, lifting his eyes lightly from the mistresses, as if they had not had this direction, and then hastening his words. "Well, we spend nearly as much on the girls' education as on their brothers' nowadays."

"It is so savage of us to be proud of that. We aim at real equality; and every extra is a step towards it. So as drawing is an extra, I am sure that your daughter will take it."

"But I am not sure she has any talent."

"But I am sure she has. You see the difference between the parent and the teacher. Will you come and see the kind of talent she will have?"

"I would rather see some average drawings, and know what is done by the ordinary girl."

"You shall see any kind you like, though I cannot bear your daughter to be called ordinary. I will show you some drawings that are not yet mounted, and then you will know that she will do much better. You won't come and see how much better she will do?"

"No, I will be content with the average. Though I shouldn't be surprised if my girl is a thought above it."

"I knew it," said Felix. "You see how well I already understand her. You will wait for me while I fetch the drawings?"

"I will send for them," said Josephine, turning to Elizabeth, who was standing near. "Mrs. Giffard, you will do me a kindness, and fetch a portfolio from the left-hand bookcase in my library? You will not mind an odd job to-day? We are all occupied with them."

"An odd job?" said Elizabeth. "If I minded odd jobs, dear Josephine, I don't know what would have happened in this house to-day, or failed to happen. But this odd job doesn't sound as if it called for my peculiar talents."

"It does not, and that is why it is an odd job," said Josephine, coming to her side and lowering her voice. "I think, you know, that I would call me Mrs. Napier, if I were you, on these formal occasions. And I will make a point of calling you Mrs. Giffard. You must trust me to take on myself an equal share of a bargain."

"Now that you break one that has lasted for forty years! But I am yours to command, as we are both aware."

"I am always sorry to be compelled to any such awareness. But if I must recognise that I am, I will request you to do as I asked."

"There are several maids about with nothing on their hands."

"Well, if you are happy as the housekeeper," said Josephine, using an audible tone, "in allowing the maids *carte blanche* on my shelves, I will follow my rule and leave your own work to your own judgement."

"Simon, are you coming to help me to accomplish my duties?" said Elizabeth in ringing tones. "They are branching out in so many directions. Shall we follow the example of our boy and girl, and address ourselves together to usefulness?"

Josephine glanced at Ruth and Gabriel, who were dispensing refreshments together, and summoned an indulgent expression to her face.

"Simon is occupied with his guests," she said, turning back to Elizabeth. "If there were any need for assistance, I should have provided you with it. There is only one portfolio."

"Well, he and I have so often done one thing between us in the past, that we can safely essay another in the present. If practice makes perfect, you will soon have your prize."

"I am sorry to have caused any trouble," said the guest. "We could have seen the drawings another time."

"That would be a pity," said Felix. "It would postpone your recognition of the inferiority of other people's children. The parents of daughters are not so unnatural in that matter as in others."

"You seem to know a good deal about parents. I suppose you have been here a long while?"

"Anyone would suppose that," said Felix.

"I daresay your staff has not much to complain of, Mrs. Napier."

"Hear, hear!" said Miss Luke, stepping impulsively forward from her place.

"Hear, hear!" said her companions, moving forward a shorter distance, and dropping their eyes as they voiced their exclamation, Mrs. Chattaway with emphasis, Miss Rosetti with acquiescence, and Miss Munday in a falsetto tone, which provoked a twitch on her own face. Miss Luke joined in on a lower note, proper to support of her own initiative, and the guest made a movement to tap his stick, as if hardly accepting his own isolation.

"Well, what am I to say?" said Josephine. "I think I will say that I have been told to 'hear', and that I have heard, and that if it is enough for you, it is indeed enough for me."

The guest fulfilled his impulse and desisted, finding himself without real faith in the method.

"Well, I will go and pursue those drawings," said Josephine. "They seem to be shy about not being passed for exhibition."

She went down the room and crossed the hall to the library, from the open door of which voices came to her, with their meaning blurred by her own emotional mood.

"Yes, I sat here alone, Simon, waiting for you to come in to me with Josephine. I sat and called up the past, until your family came and brought the present. Such a strange present it was for a moment, while it pressed back the memories and took possession! Yes, it has possession now."

"You are a great help to us in it, and it is in the present that we live. Shall we let the dead past bury its dead, and deal with it in the better way?"

Simon steadied himself on the ladder where he stood and turned towards Elizabeth. A step was heard at the door, Josephine's step; and Elizabeth sprang away from the ladder, unconscious that she held it, unconsciously tightening her hold. Its balance was shaken, and it fell to the hearth, carrying Simon with it, and casting his head against the marble curb.

Josephine entered and started forward to her husband, who lay as he had fallen. The two women bent over him together, stood up together, and faced each other, as the truth was flung upon them; and Elizabeth found herself hastening for help at Josephine's word.

Jonathan and Gabriel came to Josephine, and she turned to them almost with a smile.

"Gabriel, I have to call on you to do your first action as a man."

Simon was lifted and carried to his room. The doctor gave the diagnosis of instantaneous death. The temple had been struck on the fatal spot. The routine of the house went on, and it was known that there was emptiness in Simon's place, and how near to the heart of things that place had been. In spite of the violent incident of his death, he seemed to have died with the evenness with which he had lived. It seemed that nothing sudden had taken place. There was less a blank than a difference.

At first Josephine was calm, alert, alive to every need. Then she drew apart, gave some rapid, final directions in a failing tone, and hastened from her husband's room. She went in search of Gabriel, and found him alone, and drew him into a solemn but sustaining embrace.

Jonathan stayed for the evening, and sat at dinner in Simon's seat, in obedience to his sister's quiet word. The hour was to be marked by no particular observance. Josephine was gravely cheerful, and refused to be relieved of the duties of her place. She talked to Gabriel with reassuring ease, and made no demand on him for grief, assuming simply that the loss was light to his youth.

She went herself with her brother to the door. "My dear sister, my heart is full for you. You are beyond praise. Just take each moment as it comes."

"There is no fear that I shall do more than that; and no fear that anything will go amiss with anyone else, as long as I do it. That at the present must be enough for me. Yes, I must find it enough."

CHAPTER IX

THE NEXT MORNING Josephine came downstairs at the usual time. She assured herself that Gabriel had slept, and making no response to the similar question to herself, moved to the breakfast-table.

"You did not sleep, then, Josephine?" said Gabriel.

"Well, no, I did not, naturally, my dear. But I am glad you did; that was just as natural. Now let me see you do the natural thing by your breakfast, and do it justice."

She supplied his needs as usual, moving her hands with energy, and adjusting the things on the table, as though she hardly took into account that they served any purpose for herself.

"Are you going to have absolutely nothing, Josephine?"

"Yes, I am this morning. I shall eat as soon as ever I can, I promise you. I am not a person to take a pride in not being able to eat and sleep. I am proud of things that do more for other people. As soon as Nature can control my foolishly responsive organism, I shall let her and be thankful."

She raised her eyes with courteous interest as Ruth Giffard appeared at the door.

"Dear Mrs. Napier, Mother has arranged for the dressmaker to come to the house. Do you think you could bring yourself to see her? She is in the housekeeper's room. You know certain things have to be done."

"Dear child, how thoughtful of your mother! Of course certain things have to be done. I cannot be seen at all as I am now; and as I have no intention of immuring myself for the rest of my natural life, I will go and submit to the necessary steps to prevent it." Josephine rose with a movement that revealed her unused plate, and, throwing her napkin over it, went to the door. "And will you stay and say a word to this poor Gabriel of mine? I cannot bear that mine should be the only woman's face he sees to-day."

"So brave and good this is, my dear," said Elizabeth, as Josephine opened her door. "You need hardly be conscious of what is happening, if you will put yourself in our hands."

"I must do so indeed. I plead guilty to being a very dull and unresponsive subject, and must simply hope to be borne with. I confess that I had not thought of this necessity, which was parasitic and dependent, and really exacting of me. I will be frank, and ask you to do your best for me, without expecting return; which is frank indeed."

"Which gown shall we take first?" said the dressmaker.

"Good morning, Mrs. Faulkner," said Josephine, roused to observation for the first time. "I hope you will excuse my not seeing you before."

"I thought this for the day," said Elizabeth, showing a material. "That very deep mourning is not worn now."

"Simply the deepest mourning that is made for a widow," said Josephine, in an almost light tone. "That is all I have to say."

"But you will get tired of such heavy black, as the months go by."

"Will you not sit down, Mrs. Faulkner? No, I shall not get tired of it, dear Elizabeth. I shall not give it a thought. That is where I have to ask you to be patient with me. And the same with the other things." Josephine turned to the woman, and hurried her words, as if anxious to get the matter behind. "Simply the deepest widow's mourning that is made. And of good quality and no definite date. I shall wear such things for a long time."

"Well, you must have your own way," said Elizabeth.

"It is not my way. It is my character, and has nothing to do with me. I have no way in the matter. It is settled for me from within, as it were behind my back"

"Will Mrs. Napier be going to the funeral?" the dressmaker asked Elizabeth, possibly hardly going to meet

Josephine's methods of decision. "Because, if so, we must hurry some of her things."

"No, I shall not be going," said Josephine, turning on the speaker quiet, serious eyes. "I have no opinion on the question of women's going to funerals. I simply know what I can do and what I cannot."

"That will make things much easier. What I mean is, we shall not be so pressed."

"I am glad of that," said Josephine.

"I am sure you are wise, dear," said Elizabeth.

"Well, there again it is settled for me. Now, if I have done my part, I will leave you both to do yours. Thank you for coming to the house, Mrs. Faulkner. And, Elizabeth, you will let me give you your dress for the service on Friday, and arrange for Mrs. Faulkner to make it? You will not deny me a small privilege just now?"

"No, dear, no; I shall not be going to the funeral. I will stay behind with you."

"Simon would have liked you to go," said Josephine, bending and looking into her eyes.

"No, I don't think so. I find funerals upsetting. And I shall not need black clothes. I shall have no right to wear them, no use for them afterwards."

"Black is always useful," said Josephine gently. "I often wear it myself; often did, I mean. But perhaps you are right, that there is no need for us both, for anyone but me to be involved in the sombreness. You will have something else for a gift, some remembrance of Simon. He would have wished you to have one." She turned to the dressmaker and took a kindly leave.

At the funeral luncheon she presided herself, calm, considerate, self-controlled; talked in a normal, if rather absent, manner on matters of the day, and met with kindness rather than solemnity the mourners' farewell.

"Keep your thoughts on one thing," she said to Gabriel, her low, clear tone not approaching a whisper, "that your home and your life are safe. You are too young to be held by sorrow. I will see that the future is fair to you."

On his return she gave him a cheerful welcome, drew him out on the funeral for his own relief, and left him while she went herself on a pilgrimage through her awakening house.

On the mistresses' landing she came upon Mrs. Chattaway, who turned and ran back as she saw her, and then turned again and ran forward, as though reconsidering the question of an encounter.

"Well, how have you been in these last days?" said Josephine, with an open smile for this vacillation. "You have found me but an indifferent head, but I can assure you only in one sense. Has everything gone well with all of you?"

"Yes, indeed, Mrs. Napier; as far as it could, considering the trouble of the house. It is a small matter how things have gone with us; the question is, how they have gone with you. Of course, there is no question; we have been so grieved for you."

"Now, that does not alter the fact that the question exists with you. Believe me, you have been much in my mind. If I had thought that you could doubt it, I would have made the effort, made a point of coming to see you."

"No, of course not, Mrs. Napier. How could we think of such a thing? I cannot express what we should have felt. We should have sunk through the floor with shame and compunction."

"Well, I hope you will let me do so almost at once, and that you will not sink through the floor, but will all sit comfortably in your chairs. It will be a satisfaction to me to see you. Will you give your companions that message?"

Mrs. Chattaway remained still for a moment, and then openly abandoned her errand and ran back to the common room.

A little while later Josephine knocked at the door.

"May I come in?" she said, entering with hardly a

question in her tone, in simple acceptance of the concessions to her situation.

"Indeed you may," said Miss Luke in a low, deep voice.

Josephine sat down, and placing her elbows on her knees, leant forward over folded hands.

"I have not seen any of you for several days. Have you all been well?"

"The point is, how you have been, Mrs. Napier?"

"I have been well," said Josephine, in an incidental cordial tone, that at once assigned her health to its place and readily bore witness to it.

"You have been constantly in our thoughts," said Miss Luke.

"I have felt it. I assure you it has been a support to me."

"Oh no, Mrs. Napier; if we had known——" Mrs. Chattaway broke off.

"I know," said Josephine, leaning forward to touch her hand. "It was clear to me; I am grateful."

Mrs. Chattaway withdrew her hand and replaced it, withdrew it again, and again set it at Josephine's disposal; and Josephine turned as if unconsciously to Miss Munday.

"I have to thank you for taking prayers for me. I must not impose my duties on you any longer."

"You should not return to them yet, Mrs. Napier," said Miss Rosetti in a friendly tone. "You must spare yourself."

"No," said Josephine, her voice rising; "that is just what I have been doing, and what I must not do. I do not see any of you doing it, and that should make me pause and take myself to task. It has made me do so."

"You must not pretend that it is not quite different," said Miss Luke.

"Yes, it is a little different; well, quite different, as you are so kind as to see it. But I must not yield to the difference. I have faced it; you need not in your kindness fear for me."

"It does not seem to me right," said Mrs. Chattaway.

"Well, you know it does seem right in a way," said Miss

Luke, wisely making the move to normal ground. "What did not seem right, was that Miss Munday should take prayers."

"Prayers do seem rather too right a thing for Miss Munday," said Helen.

Josephine gave a ready laugh.

"No, and it is not right," she said. "She has her own duties to complete, without mine."

"You will not take prayers in the morning?" said Miss Rosetti. "I hope you will not be down as early as that."

"Now," said Josephine, looking straight at her, "why do you hope it? You will all of you be down, and I should take my place with you."

"Well, it will relieve me of the strain of being in time," said Miss Munday.

"Yes," said Josephine, with an uncritical smile, "I thought of that; of your waiving your personal inclinations in deference to mine. I have not thought little of it."

"Are you eating and sleeping, Mrs. Napier?" said Miss Luke.

"Now," said Josephine, "what an awkward question! Suppose I asked any of you, if you had taken your proper recreation during these last days! What answer should you make?"

"You are thinner, Mrs. Napier!" accused Mrs. Chattaway.

"Am I?" said Josephine, absently lifting her bodice a distance from her figure. "I daresay I may be."

"Your dress is quite loose," said Mrs. Chattaway.

"Well, we could not expect the dressmaker to foresee the changes of the immediate future. Exacting as we are with dressmakers, we do not expect from them the gift of prophecy."

"No one could have foreseen that anyone could be so affected in so short a time," said Mrs. Chattaway, half under her breath. "It shows how much more sensitive some people are than others."

"Well, in that case, I think they should hide their sensitiveness," said Josephine. "It is a quality that should work both ways."

"How is your nephew, Mrs. Napier?" said Miss Rosetti.

"Keeping up his spirits, thank you. It is a great relief, that he is not letting them get out of hand. Happily youth is resilient."

"It is a great loss for him," said Miss Rosetti.

"Yes," said Josephine; "so great, that I shudder at the thought of a greater. There are some things—well, the heart stands still before the imagination."

"Your courage must have done everything for him," said Miss Luke; "or rather, done the one thing, and held out hope for the future."

"What I have tried to do," said Josephine, "is so to appear to him, that he should not have to counterfeit a maturer than the natural grief. That is often the saddest side of sorrow for the young. That is the principle underlying the course I have been seen to be taking."

"We have thought you so brave," said Mrs. Chattaway, disclaiming misconception of Josephine's demeanour.

There was a knock at the door, and Josephine turned on Miss Munday a look of question.

"Come in," said Miss Munday.

Felix came in, and perceiving Josephine, made as if to withdraw.

"Now, I don't know what is the matter with me," said Josephine, in another tone. "First Mrs. Chattaway runs away from me in the passage, and now Mr. Bacon gives a glance in my direction, and prepares to flee! I had better take myself off, and leave you free of the sight of my sable form. You will become inured to it by degrees."

"I am glad that I am not capable of real grief," said Felix, as he closed the door behind her.

"Most people would not like to feel that. They are so blind to their own advantage," said Helen.

"I am afraid I should not show the dignity of it."

"You can plan your own death after everyone else's, without a misgiving," said Helen.

"You have a right to, as regards most of us here," said Miss Luke.

"Oh, I shall really have a great deal of real grief," said Felix.

"I have not been marked out for sorrow," said Miss Munday.

"What I cannot understand," said Felix, "is how all of you, who knew Simon Napier, are not in real grief and showing its dignity."

"I thought I was showing it," said Helen. "I am."

"We did not see much of him," said Mrs. Chattaway.

"Well, that is some excuse."

"But not enough," said Helen.

"Did you—you were very much attracted—you liked him very much, Miss Keats?" said Mrs. Chattaway.

"Yes, very much," said Helen.

"So did I," said Felix.

"I had great respect for him, of course; but I cannot say he was my ideal for a man," said Mrs. Chattaway.

"No—no—perhaps not," said Miss Luke.

"He was mine," said Helen and Felix at once.

"You two seem to think very much alike," said Mrs. Chattaway.

"Exactly alike in this matter," said Helen.

"When people feel that there cannot be two opinions, they have to share one," said Felix. "I am glad I am not alone in feeling an admiration for a fellow creature. I might be thought to be easily pleased, when really my standard is very high."

Josephine had gone downstairs and entered the library, unreminded once again of the scene it had witnessed.

"We have reached the stage when realisation sweeps over us, Josephine," said Gabriel.

"Don't realise more than is necessary, or more than is natural," said Josephine, taking the hand he held out to her. "That kind of realisation tends to become imagination, as the days go by, if we do not put on the curb in time. I am thinking of myself more than of you, as my danger is greater. I shall put myself under a tight rein. Think what it would have been, if we had lost each other."

"You talk of putting curb and rein on imagination, and then allow it to become utterly unbridled."

"Yes, it was going too far, imagining too much. I should not have said it; I do not say it. We shall be nearer than ever to each other. You have a right to demand it. I am under the duty to meet the demand."

"Will you keep on the school?" said Gabriel, after a silence. "Of course you have hardly had time to decide."

"There is nothing to decide. The parents and pupils will wish it; the staff and servants will wish it; and I consider all and each of them before myself. And there is someone, for whom I am putting by money with every year that I keep it, and for his sake I shall hold to it as long as I am able."

"You must not save money for me," said Gabriel, in a new, sharp tone. "You have done enough for me, and must do no more. I shall be going forth to work for myself as soon as I can leave you."

"Well, that won't be soon," said Josephine. "I have done a woman's part by you, and you must do a man's part by me. To leave a lonely widow by herself would hardly be doing it."

"I could not take Uncle Simon's place in the school."

"No, you could not," Josephine gently agreed. "It is not a thing I should care for, that you should make your career in a girls' school. Your uncle had the difference within himself; it was involved in his being as an individual, and for him it was possible. I mean nothing but appreciation of either of you, when I agree that for you it is not possible."

Jonathan and his friends were to come to dinner, to help his family over the funeral night.

Josephine gave them her usual welcome, and showed particular concern for their comfort.

"My dear, you must think of yourself, and not of us," said Jonathan.

"No, that is what I must not do. That is where my danger lies. And it is best to avoid danger. Surely discretion is the better part of valour."

"It is good of you to tolerate the company of a comparative stranger, Mrs. Napier," said Fane.

"I must have ceased to regard you in that light, or I should not have expected you to tolerate my company, even the glimpse of it that I shall give you." Josephine put a cushion behind her brother. "Now, are you all as you like to be?"

"Are you not going to stay, Josephine?" said Gabriel.

"No, not to-night, my dear."

"Then are you not going to have any dinner?"

"Yes," said Josephine, in a light tone. "I am. I am rather faint, rather hungry. It will be brought to my room."

"Why do you not stay and have it with us?"

"Why, you do not want to know my reasons, do you? They are not of a surprising kind."

"You will get into low spirits, if you do not take care."

Josephine gave a low laugh at this account of her situation.

"Of course you are already in low spirits. But there is no point in letting them get lower."

"I am going to let them get a little lower than you have seen them," said Josephine, almost brightly. "That is my object in going away by myself, since you insist on a precise explanation. There is just a little point in it for me, you know; I am not an abnormal woman."

"Ah, your aunt is a courageous creature, Gabriel," said Jonathan, when his sister had left them.

"I am less proud of her at the moment than I have been."

"Ah, the spirit is willing, but the flesh is weak," said his father.

"You will have to fill your uncle's place, Gabriel," said Fane.

"I am far from such an ambition. I shall have all I can do to fill my own place, when I find one to fill."

"Is not your aunt very dependent on you?"

"She is dependent on herself, as you can see. It is I who ought to be dependent on myself. I hope to get a post in my old school, and cast off my reproach."

"I shall not miss you," said Felix. "You have killed my feeling for you. And I find that I like women better than men."

Jonathan looked from Felix to Gabriel, as if rejoicing in his possession of each.

"I suppose all men do in a way," said Fane.

"I did not mean in a way," said Felix.

As Jonathan and Gabriel laughed, Josephine came into the room, and giving them a smile of sympathy for their mood of mirth, crossed to the bookcase, and taking a packet of letters, left them without a word.

CHAPTER X

"Well, I am grateful," said Josephine, looking over her desk at Miss Luke and Miss Rosetti, who sat before her. "It is a load lifted, to feel that my husband's work will be done, until I can fill his place, in the ways in which it must be filled." She ended in a manner of forced cheerfulness. "We must be thankful that we can deal in such a healthy way with the gaps in life."

"It is a privilege to do what we can, Mrs. Napier."

"Well, that is another demand of your kindness, that I am afraid I do rather feel it a privilege," said Josephine, with a touch of amusement at herself. "Even if I cannot be blamed for that, you miss your proportionate gratitude. And I fear you will miss it. I am not going to express suitable appreciation even now. You will be lenient towards my inevitable attitude?"

"The largest share of the work is falling on you, Mrs. Napier."

"Well, I should hope so. I should not have much right to expect your help, if that did not go without saying. I am not so muddle-headed about the rights and wrongs of a case."

"We shall have the practical advantage. We are not doing the work for love, not on an intangible basis, in a word, not for nothing," said Miss Luke, amused by the final length to which she went.

"My husband's labour is surely worthy of its hire. Or do you not think, now that you come to experience it, that it is?"

"It seems, in other hands than his," said Miss Rosetti, "hardly worthy of so much hire."

"Well, that is perhaps another point on which I am

adapting matters to my own feelings. I hope that you will allow me the indulgence? Believe me, I do not intend any overreaching of my place. If it is a convenience to you, I am glad; though I have not thought of it more than you have. And now you do not want the burden of my society at this particular juncture of my experience. I am under no delusions about it, though I may say that I have appreciated yours, and taken its lesson. As this nephew of mine appears to desire it, we will allow him to take the step over which he properly hesitates, and supplant you. I will not offer more thanks. I told you that you would not get your share. And now, young man, the next time you make your appearance with a lady, you will allow her to precede you, I hope."

The women left the room as Gabriel entered it, leading Ruth by the hand.

"Well, amusing each other, like the good children of old friends? It is kind of Ruth, my boy, to adapt her leisure to yours."

"We wanted to see you about something important, Mrs. Napier, or I should not have left my work."

"I meant simply what I said, my dear, I do not communicate by implication. I am grateful for any happiness that you will give Gabriel just now, when the companion of his life is so little to be recommended."

"In that case, you will be grateful to Ruth, Josephine," said Gabriel, coming nearer with a stumble, to avoid lifting his head. "She is giving me a happiness greater than I had conceived."

"Then it must be on a generous scale indeed, indulged boy," said Josephine, her tone out of accordance with the change in her eyes. "Let us hear about it before I resume my labours. Come to the point, and enunciate some demand of youth."

"It is the demand that I was bound to make one day. It is naturally often a demand of youth. This breaking up of our life seemed the best time to make it. The lesser change must count less at the time of the greater. I make the demand with confidence, having been taught, as you will say, to make demands. I have said enough for you to understand me?"

"No," said Josephine, in a quiet, conversational tone; "I don't think so. You have not said anything definite, have you?"

"Mrs. Napier, Gabriel and I find that we belong to each other," said Ruth, standing with clasped hands. "We are waiting to tell the world, until we have your sanction."

"No, come, I don't think so," said Josephine, seeming to suppress a smile. "Quite apart from telling the world, which would never be necessary, what you imply would involve issues of which you have no understanding. I don't want to snub youthful earnestness—you know I am not a person to do that; my life is based upon the significance of youth—but you will forgive me for not taking you very seriously? Silly little people!" She ended on a tender, final note, her hands trembling beneath her desk. "You would be nicely up a tree, if I did."

Gabriel looked as if he had met what he feared, but Ruth shrank back and lifted her eyes to his.

"You must surely understand the feeling between a man and a woman, Josephine?"

"Well, let the feeling help you to do more for each other than it is doing, or it will not be at all the feeling between a man and a woman, that I understand. No, I have had understanding of a very different kind. Even in this break of my last and lasting experience of it, I can look back on the earlier ones"—Josephine raised her eyes and seemed to be counting on her fingers—"and see them unsullied by any simple grasping for self."

"Early love may be the only love, Mrs. Napier."

"No, my dear, it may not."

"We are living our youth, of course, as we are young," said Gabriel. "There must be something in the first love, that anyhow is its own."

"Come, don't be highfalutin. You will be sorry for extravagant speeches soon. You will look back and squirm over them. I remember my own youth."

"Perhaps it would be as well if your own youth had borne more fruit," said Gabriel. "I don't remember any feeling between you and your husband, that can be taken as an example."

"Don't you, my dear, don't you?" said Josephine with almost fervent hopelessness. "You think that that was not much, that daily feeling that you saw; that humdrum, tried affection that was before your eyes! You think that most married lives hold more; that this that you were trying to imagine, would hold more? Do you, poor boy, poor boy?"

"I am speaking as a man, Josephine."

"Oh, no, you are not. When you refer to the person, whom from your childhood you have known as 'Uncle Simon', as my husband, you are speaking as the silly boy you are. It is natural: as you said, you are living your youth, and youth has its own ways of dealing with its setbacks, its innocence, its spleen." Josephine spaced the last words, uttering them with quiet philosophy. "Ah, a man would know that there are many claims to be fulfilled, before a boy can take his place. No, be a boy a little longer; and you, my child, be satisfied with your youth; and presently find a parner more advanced to man's estate, than this beardless boy of mine."

"Of course I admit the appearance of ruthless egotism," said Gabriel.

"No. Why should you admit that? There has not been much appearance of it, has there?"

"I mean the leaving you by yourself in your new loneliness."

"Oh, I thought you said 'appearance'. You meant reality, did you? The less said about that, the better. We certainly will not turn our eyes on the figure you cut in any real sense."

"We are pledged to each other," said Ruth. "We are not people who could break our faith."

"Now, now, you know we none of us can take that stand. I, for one, should be ashamed of taking it, of resolving never to change. If we can never change, we can never learn. And that admission means more for me, than it would for you. Why, you have broken your promise to me, that you would throw yourself heart and soul into your work. You must have had a wandering mind of late, while I have been—well, also breaking my promises, and yielding to the claims of my own life. So I am not going to take you up hardly for it. We have to go back on promises too lightly or confidently made. We know there is a real promise to be made by both of you, by and by, and that this preliminary is better quickly put aside, if it is not to cast its shadow forward over the real thing that is to come. That is a tragedy we do not want for you."

"Would you not like to see Gabriel's children, Mrs. Napier?" said Ruth, in a pleading tone.

"Gabriel's children?" said Josephine, with a little frown. "How do you mean, my dear? Do you—can you mean your children and his? Because it is not for me to refuse to follow you wherever you care to lead."

"Josephine, that is absurd," said Gabriel. "It was a perfectly reasonable speech."

"Yes, it was very reasonable," said Josephine lightly. "As reasonable and tangible and practical as it could very well be. It was I who was not tangible enough, I quite agree."

"You do not try to understand, Mrs. Napier."

"My dear, I understand without trying," said Josephine, almost tenderly. "It is a difficult moment for you, a moment that does call for courage. It must be, when we make a mistake in the deeper things, as we do in youth. We need the courage to admit the mistake to ourselves, and to see that what we thought we had attained, is still beyond. But you have it; you are your mother's child. The spirit you show in holding to your purpose proves it. It is only the adjustment that is needed. Gabriel has not been unworthy of himself in his first stumble"—she gave Gabriel an almost radiant look—"of the many that are to come before the final steadying."

"To refuse to accept a simple truth is neither moral nor reasonable," said Gabriel.

"Well, may I ask what you will live on, since I am to be so reasonable? I admit that I was rather trying to be the other thing, by way of covering what needed covering, and saving the faces that required to be saved."

"I shall get a post at my old school. They give a preference to old boys, and my degree is good. We shall be able to manage."

"Well, well, manage then. I am glad you have the grit to face it all together; to meet the grinding daily round of contriving in pence, and cutting off amenities that have come to seem the decencies. For it does need character. I for one have never done it, or thought I could do it. I admit that for me life is dependent on a certain seemliness. If you can do more than I, be it so. Though it has never been so, has it, in our years together? And now you know that my work cannot wait, and that it is necessity and not indifference, that drives me to dismiss you. You can tell me the details presently, of all you have arranged. It must have been a complicated piece of planning; I feel how much you have had on you."

Ruth and Gabriel found themselves in the hall, and breaking at once into talk, forgot where they stood, and before many minutes Josephine emerged and came towards them.

"Now," she said, brushing past them with some letters in her hand, "let me pass, chattering pair. What are you doing blocking up the hall for people who need it? I suppose you think no one has more to do than you have. If that is your influence over each other, you must see that you do not exert it for too long."

Her manner put them behind her in thought as well as in deed, but in a moment she turned her head and came to a pause. Then waving her letters to them, she went her way.

CHAPTER XI

THAT EVENING, WHEN Josephine and Gabriel had dinner as usual alone, Josephine made no mention of what had passed, and appeared in a more than usually genial mood. When the meal was over, she set the places at the hearth, so that the grouping seemed complete.

"Josephine, may I ask Ruth to join us?" said Gabriel, springing to his feet.

"What, my dear? Yes, fetch anyone you please," said Josephine, stooping and making a noise with the fire-irons. "We ought to make our party brighter in the evenings, and remember that you are young, and that neither of us is old. What about bringing Mrs. Giffard as well, asking her if she will kindly join us? I must not forget, in the egotism of trouble, that she is my old friend, and that it is because of her that her daughter is in my house."

Gabriel carried the message, and presently Elizabeth came by herself.

"Why, what is this that happens, or threatens to happen, Josephine? Have the boy and girl confided in you, and not in me, when one of them is all my own? Such a jealous real mother I shall be, if the adopted mother is given the first place! Well, she is used to it, and must not be grudged her dues. But what do our little people say, that shows that they are little and ours no longer?"

"There has been some talk about their being engaged, or being unengaged or something," said Josephine. "I never know what they mean, these dilly-dallyings between the very young. They mean that they need to be thrown together, I think, so that any spurious ebullition of feeling may wear itself out. It almost seems that they are of that mind, and disposed to apply the curative method to themselves."

"But they want to be married, the naughty ones to want to leave us?"

"They are going to be married, if I heard aright before dinner," said Josephine, with a little laugh. "They may not be going to by now, for all I know. Gabriel's wanting to fetch Ruth in this public, family way, rather looks as if there was a settlement of things."

Gabriel and Ruth returned to the room together.

"This is well thought of on your part, Josephine. As I am to be Mrs. Giffard's son-in-law, it is meet that she should know the group that I regard as my family."

"It is only you and I now, dear; hardly a group," said Josephine, in a low voice.

"So sweethearting has been going on, when we none of us suspected it!" said Elizabeth, throwing a bright glance at Gabriel. "It is all settled, is it? Such a lot of being unsettled I had, when I was at this stage! Such a lot of shiftings and shilly-shallyings, naughty one that I was! But my daughter has hidden her lights under a bushel; and this is the first time—well, nearly the first time; I must not tell tales, must I?—that she has let them shine before men; as represented, shall we say, by a certain young man?"

"This is a thing to be told in Gath, and published in the streets of Athens," said Gabriel. "People had better prepare themselves for it."

"They won't want preparation, dear, for such an everyday occurrence," said Josephine, reaching for her knitting. "They are accustomed to its happening amongst their younger friends."

Ruth looked at Josephine, as if the latter might be changing her ground.

"It is everything to us, Mrs. Napier."

"Yes, yes, my child. We were talking of the other people who exist in the world beside you."

"I don't see why we should trouble about the other

people in the world," said Gabriel, in his less familiar tone. "It is not the custom in our position."

"Well, you are not troubling about them, are you?" said Josephine, rapidly changing her needles. "You are behaving in completely the customary way in your position. You need not fear that you are affording us a glimpse of anything out of the common. We can set your mind at rest there."

Elizabeth gave a swift glance from face to face.

"People always give up their old life when they marry," said Gabriel.

"All living creatures mate while they are young, if their life is natural," said Ruth.

"Well, I suppose that is the level of the beasts," said Josephine, laughing as if in genuine amusement. "And they mate afresh every year, don't they? I confess I had not thought about them, at any rate in connection with our own life. And if I wanted to live at their level, I don't know that I should put it as plainly as you did, you frank, modern child."

"You seem to be knitting for dear life, Josephine," said Gabriel.

"It rests me, my boy," said Josephine, leaning back and then resuming. "It won't do for me to give up any means of rest, if I am to need them more than ever. I may be knitting for dear life soon; you seem to be planning that I may."

"I wish you would give Ruth a chance to know you, Josephine."

"She has had every chance to know me," said Josephine gravely. "I have been her principal, her adviser—her benefactor; if we are to get down to rock bottom, as she does. In all those capacities she does know me. If she is to know me now as a human woman, with human claims, it will not do her harm. I am giving her the chance to know me, that she has not had."

"My marrying her will make no difference to my feeling for you."

"I wondered when that was coming," said Josephine, with a note of contempt. "It would have made no difference to my feeling for you, would it, if I had abandoned you in your orphanhood?"

"Josephine, I simply don't understand you."

"No," said Josephine gently; "I expect you don't. I have given you no opportunity. You have only had to conceive of the side of me that gives. I see you have actually had no glimpse of any other."

"There must always be give and take in any human relation."

"There must. That is my point. I have done my share of giving. Now is the time—yes, I will say it—for me to take."

"I don't think you understand the nature of giving."

"Well, show me that you understand the nature of giving back. That is all you have to be concerned with. No one is asking you to take any initiative in the matter."

"You would share our happiness, Mrs. Napier," said Ruth.

"My child, happiness must come out of our own lives, not out of other people's. I think you must know that. Indeed, the course you have been taking shows that you know it. I might say that you would share my happiness, if Gabriel remained in his old place. But be assured that I shall not say it." Josephine bent towards Ruth with her old smile. "I have not so little knowledge of human nature, or so little sympathy with it."

"But we must think of our happiness, as you think of yours."

"The time for it is all to come," said Josephine, moving her hand. "When you have earned it, is the time. It will perhaps not be just yet."

"I think I had better take Ruth away," said Gabriel.

"Yes, you take her away," said Josephine, pointing at him with her needle; "and make your peace with her for dragging her into this morass. She wants a man ten years older than you. She has not forgotten, if you have, that a woman is ten years older than a man. It can never be out of the poor child's mind. You overrate your claims quite pitifully, or shall we say youthfully? I hope Ruth will let us say it."

"Well, so it is all to be held up, Josephine?" said Elizabeth, as she and Josephine were left alone. "It is not the romance that must come in the end to my orphan girl?"

"My dear, I hope not much experience of that kind has fallen her way yet?" said Josephine, bending towards her friend with a concern so kindly as to preclude any doubt of her soundness.

"The real experience must come in the end. We shall have to find it in us to give it a welcome."

"We shall find it in us," said Josephine. "Do not fear I have no fear for you. We shall yield when the moment comes, yield to keep more truly. But this time it has not come; and we must not take the easier path, must not disport ourselves in the broad and flowery way. We must face a little bitterness of spirit; at least I must. And I can face it for Gabriel's sake, and a little for my own as well. I wasn't quite insincere in saying all that I said; it had its elements of truth. I am not a person to rate my own claims at nothing, or to think it well for other people to do the same. I have too much respect for my fellow creatures and myself, especially when one of the fellow creatures happens to be my adopted son."

"I wonder if the news is all over the school?"

"Yes, I should think so," said Josephine, in a careless tone. "A girl, you know, any ordinary girl, would be eager to record any score along that line. It is understandable. I think we must understand it."

"Of course, there is no real objection to the marriage."

"Now, I do hope," said Josephine, "that you do not feel I have not watched over her, that she has made a false step, and one which I am afraid is a pity. But I have been torn aside by personal sorrow, and it may be that I have been less alive to other people's needs. If it has been so, then so it must be said."

"We could have expected nothing else from you. She had her mother to watch over her, and there is no harm done."

"Yes," said Josephine seriously, "I think you could have expected something else from me. I hope you will always expect it. And the harm done is of the kind that I forgive myself the least, needless suffering for youth."

"They should have enough to manage on, if Gabriel takes a schoolmaster's post. There is no real obstacle in their way."

"No obstacle is real to young people, who find their purpose criticised, and criticised justly." Josephine smiled into Elizabeth's face. "You have learned your lesson well. I recognise the arguments of this afternoon."

"They held good this evening."

"Yes," said Josephine, with sympathy in her tone.

"Shall we send for them, and talk it over again?"

"No," said Josephine, more sharply. "I have had enough of that, all that I can bear of it, if you will pardon me."

"Of course you must be considered."

"Yes, I begin to see that I must."

"Love never takes heed of other people," said Elizabeth, looking at Josephine.

"No, that is as I said. But when it is as young as this, it soon passes. Yes, that is the sorry side of love between a boy and girl, often in itself a beautiful thing, that it does tend to pass."

"Are you talking about me and my early marriage?"

"There! You see that in every case some truth comes home. No, I was not talking about you; and I am sure you know I was not, and should not, in that veiled way. It is simply that the cap fits you or me or anyone; and so it probably fits your child and mine."

"Did your first love come to an end?"

"Yes," said Josephine, with a look of reminiscence; "and my second and third, since you ask me piercing questions. I see I have perhaps laid myself open to them. I think and hope that they also came to an end on the other side; that I have no harm to look back on. But you see the cap fits me as well."

Elizabeth took a step towards Josephine.

"You will take my daughter's lover, as you took mine?"

Josephine moved a pace apart, her eyelids falling and her head back, seeming to force a contempt through her silence.

"I think it is time for me to go, Josephine," said Elizabeth, beginning to weep. "In my present mood I am a stranger to myself. And in yours you cannot bear with a stranger."

"If I had regarded an old friend as a stranger, I should certainly not have been able to bear with you. And as things are, if I betrayed myself, I have; so I will not flatter myself that I can contradict what I have not hidden. To be something and then deny it, is not a combination that holds water, is it?"

CHAPTER XII

JOSEPHINE MADE NO mention of Gabriel's marriage during the next weeks. She went through her days in outward calm, holding at bay the danger that seemed too great. The only change to be seen was a general increase of kindliness, an instinctive laying of the foundations of a different life. Gabriel spent his time with Ruth between her hours of work, and in his intercourse with Josephine, showed himself affectionate and filial, as though forbearing to feelings he could not explain. One day he and Ruth came to her study together.

"Josephine, we have another demand to make. Ruth has lost her zeal for professional life, and requests you to release her at the end of the term."

"Well, she can request me then, can't she?" said Josephine, looking up from her work, and resting her eyes on their locked hands. "I am not an ogress."

"Well, you are rather. That is why I feel it my duty to come between the two of you."

"And what are you doing, I should like to know, coming between me and a member of my staff? That is a duty rather off any known line. Now let Ruth—Miss Giffard you ought to call her in this capacity—speak for herself."

"I don't feel it is honest to go on, Mrs. Napier. My heart is not in my work. I find that I can only live in my future with Gabriel."

"Now, that is a nice confession for a mistress of mine to make! How long have you been feeling like that, I should like to ask, you travesty of a professional woman! And will I release you? Indeed, and with all my heart. And glad I am, that I have not had to ask you to release yourself, you awkward daughter of my old friend! And at once, if you please, and no mention of the rest of the term, if you love me, from someone who openly confesses that her heart is not in her work!"

"It is better to be open about what is inevitable, Josephine."

"I should rather prefer a decent veil to be drawn over it, myself."

"You do understand, Mrs. Napier? You don't think that things are going on, except as they are? Mother would be so distressed, if we gave you a wrong impression."

"What, my dear?" said Josephine, in an absent manner, bringing her hands alternately down on her desk.

"You don't think that either of us is deceiving you?"

"No, I do not," said Josephine, turning roundly on her. "Think you are deceiving me, when you boldly state that your mind has not been on your duties! I do not think you are deceiving me at all. I half wish you had deceived me. You give me a sense of compunction for my school, the feeling of all others, that I desire to avoid."

"I wish that so much of yourself had not been given to the school," said Gabriel; "and that there was something over for other purposes."

"Oh, do you?" said Josephine, with suddenly flashing eyes. "Then you wish that I had not sent you to Oxford, do you, and that I would put you now to some grinding toil and moil, instead of leaving you to meander and philander through your days, while I give so much of myself, as you put it, to the school? It is a nice, unselfish wish, but it is rather late."

"I shall soon be working now," said Gabriel.

"And how long would you have been working, if I could go back and take you at your first word? *Soon* be working? Soon! It is an amusing phrase. Still in the future, is it? Well, well, well!"

Josephine made no comment on this scene, and maintained her silence until the morning when there lay on the breakfast table Elizabeth's invitations to her daughter's wedding. Elizabeth had taken rooms for the occasion in the town, and despatched the invitations without a word to Josephine, taking advantage of her position as mother of the bride.

Josephine sorted the letters for the household herself, and added thereby to her knowledge of it; though she would have scorned to open the letters, and depended upon as accurate as possible a deduction of their contents. Gabriel saw her recoil before the significant envelopes, and brought himself to words.

"You have the invitations to the wedding, have you? They bring home the fact that I have no wedding garment."

"Invitations? No, I have no invitations, dear. A letter from my cousin, whom you have never seen; a line from my lawyer, that you would not understand, and the usual missives, reasoning and otherwise, from parents, with which I will not bore you. That is the sum total of my favours this morning."

"I mean the invitations for the other people in the house. Mrs. Giffard would hardly send one to you. It is assumed, of course, that you will be there."

"The invitations for your wedding and Ruth's?" said Josephine, saying the words clearly and fully. "For her friends in the house, I suppose? The envelopes with the oblong shape? I took them for a set of appeals for charity. Though I should not have escaped one myself, in that case, I suppose. I should be the first person to be approached. I believe I am approached, on some such grounds, in some of the others." She laid her hand on some envelopes.

"They are in a sense a set of appeals for your charity."

"Why did they come through the post? What a needless complication, to send letters to the post from their eventual goal!"

"But by no means a crime."

"Oh, no, dear. Nothing worse than the outcome of a lack of training."

"It was to let you know of the wedding."

"Well, then it had a reason. But why could you not tell me of it?"

"You know very well why, Josephine."

"Well, it seems that you too had your reason. But, my dear, when you have not courage to speak of a thing, examine into your own heart. What is the reason why it should not be spoken of? What is there against that thing?"

"Nothing in this case," said Gabriel.

"Then you have nothing to worry about," said Josephine. "By the way, what arrangement are you making about Miss Giffard for the future?"

"She refuses to allow me to support her. I can only hope that she will do so in time."

"You did not insist upon it?" said Josephine, just raising her brows.

"I had not enough to offer, to warrant that. Josephine, you will come to my wedding, won't you?"

"I suppose I naturally shall. Nothing else would be practicable, would it?"

"I meant that you had not much time in these pressed days."

"Why, it won't take long, will it? You can tell me when it is time to start, for the matter of that."

"You will get to care so much for my wife, Josephine. You will come to think of me the unworthy member of the partnership."

"My dear, I have many people to care for. Miss Giffard came to me as a member of my school, the school that you have such a dislike to hear mentioned, and that happened to be the solution of her life. For, for home life as you know, or will know, she is not fitted. It was in that capacity that I saw to it, that I indeed cared for her. I did not undertake a relation with her in any other, or put any other at her disposal."

"Well, you will do your best?" said Gabriel.

"I will, indeed," said Josephine in a cordial tone, that

did not hold any confidence of result. "What is that other letter you keep staring at?"

"A letter it is natural to stare at. It is from Fane, in his capacity of lawyer, and states that a client, who must remain anonymous, will pay me two hundred a year through Fane's office, on the condition that I make no attempt to discover the donor! A client! The donor! No clue of any kind! Neither he nor she! I suppose it is Father; unless it is you, Josephine? Of course that question is breaking the condition of acceptance; and I confess my inclination to accept."

"No, my dear, it is not my way to do things anonymously. I should frankly say it, if I were to offer you an allowance. And that reminds me that I was about to offer you one; of lesser munificence; a hundred and fifty a year; openly tendered from myself. Would it be of any good to you? It would have even more point, combined with the other. Yes, no doubt that is from your father, and given anonymously, lest you should fear that he could not spare it. But he must know his own affairs. I think you would be right simply to accept both offers."

"My breath is leaving me at the rosiness of my future. I was wondering how I should manage on a salary not meant for a married man. And now my way is not only smooth but paved with gold. It is very generous of both of you."

"I was wondering how you would manage, too. But why is it generous of me? Of your father it is much more generous. Money and the material things of life are not what I have had traffic in. My truck has been in different commodities."

"It is I who am having to do with material things," said Gabriel, hastening his words, as Josephine rose and came towards him.

"My son, is it too much to ask, that for your own sake and mine you should give this first fancy a chance to prove itself? That you should spare a few years out of your many, to help the few that are mine?"

"Josephine, you know you ought not to ask it."

"Well, may I ask if you definitely accept my allowance?" said Josephine, moving away. "That is the sort of thing I ought to ask, is it? Would the hundred and fifty a year be of any use?"

"You know it would: I don't know what to say."

"Well, you don't say it is not the sort of thing to talk about, anyhow. You don't give vent to that particularly unhappy little saying. It is all right to make mention of it, I gather. Or ought it to have been anonymous like the other? Oh, never mind, my dear. I have taught you to be as you are. It is more blessed to give than to receive, is it? That is your motto in disposing of me?"

"You make things more than difficult for me, Josephine."

"Make things difficult! 'Make them easy' is the phrase I should use. A hundred and fifty a year is a lubricating kind of obstacle, in my opinion."

"I see how magnanimous it is of you, in the face of this unforeseen help, and of your disapproval of the marriage."

"I can't see that those things make any difference," said Josephine, with a faint irritation, as if at obtuseness. "The unforseen help makes it more worth while for me to add my quota; and it is your comfort that we are considering, not the means by which you have endangered it. It won't look after itself, because it has a less experienced person to look after it. It is because of my disapproval of the marriage, that I am trying to arrange that things should not be worse than they must be. I don't want hardship for you; I should not have looked after you as I have, for all these years, if I had wanted that. I believe you think me capable of a sort of revenge. I hope you are not like that, yourself, my dear? They say that we judge other people by ourselves. I certainly am not, because I wanted a little support in the days of my loneliness." Her voice shook and then rose on an easy note. "Now take these piles of letters, and put them including the invitations, on the post table. And then leave me in peace to deal with my own. When I have breakfast without you, I shall have disposed of them by this time."

"I am humiliated to think of your finding letters a substitute for my companionship."

"No, you are not, my dear. It is what you are deliberately planning. It is the thing you ask of life, as far as I can gather. It is I who am humiliated by it. I don't make any secret of that. I have not made a secret of it on purpose. It is well that people should know what they are doing, that they should not go blindfolded through their lives."

CHAPTER XIII

FROM THIS MOMENT Josephine showed herself in another light. She referred to the marriage as to a normal event of the near future, and addressed herself to the preparations in an open, kindly spirit, arranging for her staff to attend the ceremony, and organising a celebration for the school.

"We must celebrate the marriage of the son of the house. I want to feel that you are all rejoicing with us."

When someone observed that it was not entirely an occasion for her to rejoice, she replied with an air of amused admission.

"Well, my nephew and I may stand a little aloof in our hearts. The force of advancing life has been too much for us, and deprived us of our bearings; and we find ourselves clinging to each other as the only rock left. But do not breathe a whisper, and you shall see that we shall not betray ourselves."

On the day of the wedding, at breakfast with Gabriel for the last time, she studied some papers during the meal, looked up to speak as if for the sake of convention, rose prematurely from the table, and returning as though recollecting herself, laid a hand on his shoulder.

"Why, what an absent-minded woman, adopted mother, lifelong friend! Too many capacities to be absent-minded in, at our last breakfast! I ought to suffer a lifetime's remorse."

"Don't think that you will dispose of me at that light cost," said Gabriel. "You will often have my wife and me seated at your board. Your house is the old home to us both."

"Yes. What a way to celebrate our last experience of our real home life! What an unsentimental pair we are!"

Josephine conducted the early luncheon with liveliness and ease, appeared to eat herself with interest and appetite, admonished Gabriel of his duties as host, and talked on topics unconnected with the occasion. She had made no difference in her usual dress, and wore simply her better outfit of widow's weeds. Her bonnet, with its crape and veil, lay ready at the side, indicating that her toilet was complete.

"Try to manage a little more, Mrs. Chattaway. I think we have plenty of time, and anyhow they would hardly begin without so many of us."

"No, thank you, I could not, Mrs. Napier. I have had too much, and we must not delay the hero of the ceremony."

"It is our safeguard, that we have him with us," said Josephine, smiling at Gabriel. "There have been so many preparations unconnected with him, that we forget he has quite a prominent part to play."

"We are hardly in danger of feeling that we are the protagonists," said Miss Luke.

"I am not putting myself in Miss Giffard's place," said Miss Munday. "I do not mind if you cannot believe me."

When the other women went to dress, Josephine moved to the side table, pushed aside the bonnet, and began to turn over her accounts.

"You are surely going to appear in something more festive than that?" said Gabriel.

"No, why should I, my dear? This is what I wear at this time of my life. What else should I wear? What else could I? I can put on my simpler things, if you would prefer them though I think they are a little soiled. This is my dress for occasions; and I thought you would wish me to appear in it. I can change it, if you would like." Josephine took some steps towards the door, moving with deliberation, as if time were of no account.

"I did not know that people went to weddings, dressed so completely as widows."

"I suppose widows dress as widows, just as bridegrooms dress as bridegrooms."

"It is quite a long time, nearly six months, since Uncle Simon died."

"Five months, twenty-three days and nineteen hours," said Josephine, with her voice dying away and her eyes on space.

"Haven't you anything less funereal? Surely you got something new for the occasion?"

"My dear, it was for you that I got things, not for myself. You are the instigating character of this festival, not I. And I had not personally thought of it as a festival, if you remember."

"I took it for granted that you would dress in a suitable manner. You might be going to a burial in those garments."

"Well, I might have gone to a burial in them. That was their purpose. I should have gone to one in them, if I had been equal to it, if you remember that, too. That is why they are suitable for me at this stage of my life. Not that I want to remind you of it, at this stage of yours. So if you have done advising a middle-aged widow on her apparel, suppose you go and brush your own! It is not too late for that improvement, and it is a distinctly more appropriate one. It is you who are to appear as the bridegroom, not I."

"Well, I should soon be starting," said Gabriel in an aloof tone. "I have to do some confabulation with Felix. And the other carriages will soon be here. You were to arrange with Mrs. Giffard about going up the aisle."

"Yes, I believe something of the sort was planned," said Josephine, moving to the table for her bonnet, and assuming it with simple regard to neatness, and with no attempt to suppress the veil. "You are a practical person to remind your aunt. It is encouraging to see that my training bears fruit, on the day when you are dispensing with it."

Gabriel made a movement to embrace her before he left, but she raised her eyes from arranging her skirts, and parted from him simply with a nod and a smile.

She drove to the church in a carriage by herself, and

walked to her place in a manner that somehow drew attention to her widow's garb. She was calm as the ceremony proceeded; followed the words of the service; watched with interest as Elizabeth gave her daughter away; and at the significant moment turned her face to the kneeling figures in natural emotion, and openly wiping her eyes, returned to her book.

At the subsequent gathering she was a benevolent, dignified figure. She looked maternally at Gabriel's wife, made a point of talking to her staff, and on passing Elizabeth in her place as hostess, went up to her with a friendly word.

"It is all so very, very nice. You will let me pay you a compliment? I don't know why we should congratulate other people to-day, and not you."

"Now it is you whom I am going to congratulate, Mrs. Napier," said Fane. "Keeping a stiff upper lip, as you have! Well done!"

As he raised his hand to pat Josephine's back, he found it turned towards him, and for some reason drew back and failed to avail himself of the convenience.

"Ah, we must feel that Gabriel's happiness makes up to us for our loss," said Jonathan.

"When people are happy in leaving me, I do not admit that they are a loss," said Felix.

"And all this business connected with them takes a good afternoon out of a good working day," said Josephine in a hushed and rueful manner.

"Have you filled Ruth's place?" said Jonathan. "It is strange to me that I have a daughter."

"There is no place to fill," said Josephine, in the same conspiratorial tone. "I have tried to make one, tried to keep it, tried to regard it as deserted; but I confess that on all those scores I have ignominiously failed."

"Mrs. Giffard will miss the girl," said Jonathan. "I almost feel that she and I are related. We must make a point of seeing each other."

"Yes, she will miss her for a time," said Josephine;

137

"until the pendulum swings and the girl's lifelong feelings reassert themselves. Gabriel will miss her then, if the same thing has not happened to him."

"My son," said Jonathan, approaching Gabriel, "my token to you has been in my mind. This is a great occasion for a father."

"Then you are not guilty of the Titanic gift?"

"You are no nearer to the truth about that?"

"It is a condition of acceptance that we are never to be nearer to it."

"Well, let us consider the sentimental token. In a way that is the significant thing."

"Ah, you are the guilty one!" said Gabriel.

"Now we will leave impersonal things, if you please, to their proper fate. Anonymous people have a claim; there is a duty we owe to them."

"I suppose I must not utter gratitude?"

"How can you utter gratitude to a person or persons unknown? If you as much as harbour suspicions, you are guilty of a breach of faith. And ought you not to be standing by your bride, instead of trying to shock your father? I don't grudge you to your wife to-day, my son."

"Don't you think that the bride's appearance does us credit?" said Josephine, pausing by her mistresses.

"Indeed, yes; she could not look more charming," said Mrs. Chattaway.

"Ah, youth and happiness and looking forward! the permeating things!" said Miss Luke. "We must not underrate them."

"Are we inclined to underrate them?" said Miss Rosetti.

"I admit that it was clothes I was thinking of," said Josephine, dropping her eyes in mock guilt. "I must be in a very unspiritual mood."

"Ah, but the wedding-day is a great moment," said Miss Luke, adhering to her stand against the natural opposition. "It must be the climax, the coping stone, the peak of youthful experience."

"Oh, don't use the word 'climax'," said Josephine. "It has such a suggestion of anti-climax. And we hope that things are not over for them yet."

The bridal pair were leaving by an early train, and the intimate group assembled to speed their departure. Josephine quietly stepped into a prominent place, and when Ruth's farewells were accomplished, moved forward to Gabriel, in a manner of approaching the culminating moment of the day. She relinquished him with her eyes held from his face, and waved a perfunctory, cordial hand as the carriage drove away.

An hour later she stood at the door of the common room.

"Have I given you time to change the charming dresses, that have been such an asset to the occasion? Being outside the necessity myself has perhaps made me unimaginative."

"The time has sufficed for those who cared to avail themselves of it," said Miss Luke, looking down at herself with a little laugh.

"You are very wise," said Josephine.

"You are fortunate, Mrs. Napier, in being exempt from these exactions," said Mrs. Chattaway in a rather artificial manner, keeping her eyes from her own dress.

"Fortunate?" said Josephine, looking up amusedly from under her brows. "I am not sure that that is quite the word."

"I was not speaking in jest," said Mrs. Chattaway vaguely.

"It is I who was doing that," said Josephine. "Though the question of dress has been little enough of a jest for me to-day. If I had known the fuss there was going to be, I should have done something else than follow my instincts. I see it was a selfish line to take, but I honestly had not meant it so. It was more that I had not thought of my appearance at all, than that I was self-indulgent over it."

"Your brother was anxious for you to do him credit?" said Miss Rosetti.

"My brother! It was my nephew! It was he who fussed

and fumed, and almost forgot to go to his own wedding, because his adopted mother and best friend—they are his words; I am not originating them; occasions of emotion loosen the tongues of the reticent—had omitted to drape her mature form in a manner he approved. I might have been the bride instead of her imminent aunt-in-law. Well, I am cured of taking the line of least resistance as regards my apparel. And here is Mr. Bacon, come to complete the lesson with an illustration."

"I am proud of being able to enter this room without knocking," said Felix. "I have only just brought myself to do it."

"It must be a pleasant privilege," said Josephine. "I happen to be the only person here without it."

"I hope you are not hinting for it."

"I am not indeed; I have no claim."

"We have been talking about the clothes we wore for the wedding, Mr. Bacon," said Miss Luke. "I already speak of them in the past tense."

"I am glad you did not wear those you have on," said Felix. "We should not have liked to say anything about them. I think you carry off changing them. I should feel a little uncomfortable if I had done it."

"Oh, pray let us drop this subject of clothes," said Josephine.

"You will miss your companion, Mrs. Napier," said Mrs. Chattaway.

"Oh, we do not lose the people whose lives take a different turn from ours," said Miss Luke, quickly and slightly averting her eyes.

"Well, I have not lost Gabriel," said Josephine in an almost comfortable tone. "I must take myself to task, and remind myself how much I have in the concentration of his feeling; and not fret about his having had to tear himself away in the flesh. But poor boy! His face at parting does come back to me; it will. I am not one to make a fuss about nothing; but this is not quite nothing."

"A wedding upsets me," said Miss Munday. "I am very sentimental."

"So it does me," said Felix.

"Well, do you know, so it does me," said Josephine. "I cannot explain it, but there it is."

"I can explain it," said Felix; "but I do not think I will."

"I explained it," said Miss Munday.

"We feel that the bride and bridegroom care more for each other, than anyone cares for us," said Helen.

"I do not feel that," said Josephine. "You must find some other explanation for me."

"I suppose that Gabriel and Ruth are very devoted?" said Mrs. Chattaway.

"Devoted?" said Josephine raising her brows. "Ask me another. I am not in a position to give you an account of their feelings. They draw the modern veil over them too successfully."

"Gabriel does not confide in you?" said Miss Rosetti.

"Oh, I have had it all," said Josephine, almost airily. "How hard it is to throw oneself into a new life, when the old is tugging from the past—that was the word, tugging; not elegant, is it?—and how long it will seem before the upheaval is over, and the old peace returns. Oh yes, I have had it."

"It does not sound the deepest devotion," said Mrs. Chattaway.

"Well, I think hardly any modern young people's relation sounds like that," said Josephine leniently. "But I have seen cases that suggest that things may be more often than we think, the same at bottom. We must hope this is one of them; I indeed have reason to hope it."

"Do you find Ruth a confiding daughter-in-law?" said Miss Rosetti.

"No, I do not. She has honoured me so far only with plain, laconic statements about her material future. But I daresay she found me a great rock to come up against; a formidable bulwark, built out of lifelong feelings; offered to her as an allurement, poor child, when she could only see it as a menace. I was obliged to put the question of ways and means too; and that was not a popular measure, until I added an item of my own to one side of the account; when they liked my exposition better; both of them; not only Ruth; and I admit with reason."

"You are a very unselfish aunt, Mrs. Napier," said Mrs. Chattaway.

"Yes, I have been unselfish," said Josephine, without emphasis. "There is not much temptation to be anything else, when you are considered harsh for doing what you may not leave undone. If you can do something to balance things, you find yourself simply doing it. And I have little use for material things. In other words, I have not been unselfish."

"Many people would have a use for them."

"Then they would be unselfish."

"Will you convert your nephew's room into an extra class-room?" said Miss Rosetti.

"No, I shall not. There would be a fine to-do, if I did. I am not courting such a shindy. It is to be left as it is, with the adventure books by the window, and the photograph of myself by the bed. I repudiate that version of myself; I would gladly throw it on the fire; but I am taking no liberties with my instructions. When young master comes home he is to find things as he left them."

"I did not know he was masterful," said Miss Rosetti.

"Oh, well, this is a matter of his private and precious feelings. He is not in a general way. I am the only person who has been shown his masterful side. I am sure he will make a most amenable husband."

Josephine took her leave with a somehow fallen face, as if baffled by something she had looked for. As Felix's step sounded behind her, she turned to meet him.

"I could not stay with the women who have no sorrow to hide, and not enough to hide of anything else. I am ill at ease with people whose lives are an open book. There is so

142

much in me, that must at all costs be hidden. Jonathan and I were coming to dinner; so may I stay and not go home to dress? My wedding clothes are nearly as becoming as my evening ones."

"Stay by all means. Your clothes do not matter at all."

"I noticed that you thought that about clothes; and I see that your clothes did not matter; but I don't think mine can be dismissed like that."

"I am sure your clothes are admirable. I cannot imagine you without them—without your own kind of them, I mean."

"I don't think it matters which you meant, as you cannot imagine it."

"I admit I was ashamed of my clothes to-day," said Josephine. "I see I should have thought of Gabriel."

"I am coming into the library to gossip about Gabriel. Do you think that Ruth is worthy of him?"

"We may be pardoned for thinking she is not."

"I don't think we ought to be pardoned. My feelings, when I think it, are quite unpardonable."

"We may surely hold unbiased opinions on occasions."

"I don't think ever on occasions."

"Ruth looked very pretty to-day. You will say that there is an example of the importance of clothes."

"No. I certainly shall not. I cannot consent to be dragged down too far."

"Did you not think that she looked particularly well?"

"Yes, but I did not know it was clothes. I was afraid it was happiness."

"Well, you need not accuse me of dragging you down," said Josephine.

"We are always hard on our faults in others; we know how inexcusable they are. I have never met any of those faults that are almost lovable. I have been more unlovable on Gabriel's wedding day than ever before."

"I have not been at my best," said Jonathan, coming into the room. "I feel the loss of my son more than I have any right to."

"You have come to his help with great munificence," said Josephine. "But I don't know why an allowance is better for being anonymous."

"I do," said Felix.

"I mean a father's allowance to a son."

"So do I," said Felix.

"It is not for me to say anything about it, one way or the other," said Jonathan.

"There is the reason illustrated," said Felix.

"Well, I did not see any reason for not admitting my quota," said Josephine. "I simply acknowledged it, as I do most of my actions. It seemed such a natural, inevitable thing."

"Then there was no reason for not admitting it," said Felix.

"An allowance from oneself hardly seems to me a natural thing," said Jonathan, with a laugh. "But we are talking about what has to be a mystery. I have been remembering, Josephine, that you will be alone after to-night. It goes to my heart to think of it."

"Alone? In a house of a hundred and eighty people?"

"Well, well, essentially alone."

"Well, actually alone very little. I hope I shall snatch a few moments to myself sometimes."

"I mean you will be alone at meals. That seems to me the dividing line."

"Well, I must try to get time for those, certainly. The interruptions get more and more continuous."

"I wonder Gabriel put up with it," said Felix.

"He did not put up with it. He guarded our tête-à-tête most jealously. But lately we have had the Giffards with us sometimes, and he seemed to think that a larger party justified intrusions. I shall have to cope with the precedent."

"Will you see much of Mrs. Giffard now?" said Jonathan.

"I shall see her daily. The running of the house depends on my seeing her."

"Can Gabriel love his wife as much as he loves us?" said Felix.

"She fulfils a relation to him that none of us can fulfil," said Josephine, with full concession. "It is not a question of comparative affection. That may be why we feel a faint resentment over people's marriages. Because I think there is no doubt that we do."

"Well, we must become more to each other," said Jonathan.

"We can hardly fail to become so in a way," said Josephine. "Gaps must close up; and any closing up involves a coming together."

"I think we are becoming more to each other already," said Felix.

CHAPTER XIV

"WELL," SAID JOSEPHINE, entering the housekeeper's room, where Miss Rosetti was sitting with Elizabeth, "here is my young gentleman already homesick! Already confessing to it, which is a further step! He wants to come home with Ruth to-morrow; is coming home, for he does not put it as a question. Home is the word that indicates that he is within his rights, I suppose. Is there any objection to it? The matter is more in your province than mine."

"And so sweet it is to have it there! Here is my dear companion letter! Such a funny round-off it is to our friendship, that we share the married pair! I almost feel that my share is the greater, as one of them is really mine. Any objection to their coming home? Ah, that is what we love them to say. Our two old heads are turned by the mere thought."

"It would take more than that to turn my head," said Josephine, smiling at Miss Rosetti whose eyes were on her face; "or it would be like a planet in a state of continual revolution. But in my life anything has to be reckoned with, to be managed. And it seems that we have to manage this: it is taken so very much as a matter of course."

"Ah, it is better sometimes to be the housekeeper than the head mistress," said Elizabeth, as Josephine left them.

"I would choose to be the head mistress," said her companion.

"Oh, I feel pity for my superior. I would rather welcome my own daughter than somebody else's son."

The next day Josephine listened for the sounds of arrival, held herself in check until they had advanced to the hall, and then came forth with a pleasant, casual welcome.

"Well, my punctual travellers! Home, sweet home to the moment! I hardly expected you quite on the stroke of the clock. A minute earlier, and I should have been engaged."

Gabriel approached to throw himself into her arms, but she held him gently back, and keeping her hand on his, turned to give the first welcome to his wife.

"Why, what a wan and weary-looking bride! I hope you are safe in your husband's charge. You did not look like that when you were in mine, but we must not expect old heads on green shoulders. We knew he was young to have the care of a wife. So, my boy!" She turned to give Gabriel a tranquil greeting. "It seems so natural to have you here, that I catch myself feeling surprised at having to celebrate such a normal condition of things. Now tell me where you both would like to sleep. The spare room is ready for Ruth; her own old room is occupied; but yours is just as it was."

"We are easy people, and only want one room or the other," said Ruth. "We always take our rest side by side."

"Do you, my dear? It is a short 'always', but it is even simpler to arrange, if you actually prefer it so. You will be able to stay in any kind of house, being easy, as you say. Here there will be a dressing room, to prevent the 'always' from becoming an oppression. We need not be the slaves of a word."

"We have never spent an hour apart," said Ruth.

"Have you not? Then you are not as I was in my early married days. I remember that I used to manœuvre separations, to come upon my husband afresh, and recapture the first fine, careless rapture, emotional young woman that I was!"

"It sounds as if your feelings required a stimulus," said Gabriel.

"Well, I could not have borne the full flood of them always: I should simply have been shattered."

"It would not do for them to be too violent to last."

"I certainly did not discern that possibility," said

Josephine, laughing. "It would not have occurred to me. You cynical, disillusioned young man!"

"It was the natural thing to say at the moment."

"It hardly seemed so to me, with my old-fashioned ideas. But we will not bear too hardly on a casual word. What does seem natural, is that Ruth should be impatient to see her mother, and be about to turn upon you for your pre-occupation with your own home-coming and oblivion of hers."

"We share our home-coming with other things," said Gabriel.

"Yes, we promised to rush to Mother's room," said Ruth. "We knew you would let us keep the promise."

Josephine walked to the bell and rang it.

"Now that will not do," she said. "The housekeeper's room is as honourable as any room in the house, perhaps the most honourable, as the workings of the house have their source in it; but it is not the recognised background for a welcome; and I think a welcome should be organised fittingly as an important thing."

She waited with her foot on the fender while Elizabeth was summoned, and then averted her eyes from her meeting with her daughter, but restored them as she turned to Gabriel.

"Such a rich woman I feel, with my son and daughter! Why should I mind the funny housekeeper's place? What better position could I wish, than the one that puts them in my care?"

"Well, for all that," said Josephine, "I do not extend the functions of the housekeeper's room beyond a point. It is a time-honoured custom to hasten to the hall to our guests; and if I have taken it upon myself to stage your reunion, I have done it according to my own taste, which is the only sincere method in judgement."

"Such a sweet reunion, such a thoughtfully staged welcome! Such a dear memory it will be, though it yields to the trivial round, the common task!" Elizabeth went to the door kissing her hand. "I will not attend to dear ones with half a mind, who have such a claim on the whole. The long, long talk will wait until the time is ripe—that is to say, free for it."

Josephine did not look after Elizabeth, but turned at once to Ruth, as to a personal charge.

"I do not think Ruth looks well, Gabriel, now she is out of my hands. Was it wise for her to travel to-day?"

"She has had a chill, and the alternative was to stay at home with servants who are foolish virgins. You will judge that she is better here than there."

"I always judged that she was well enough here. The suggestion of her making a change was a surprise to me. I hesitate to make much of her looks, as her mother was not struck by them, but I am going to take advantage of her absence and conduct her daughter to bed. Come, my dear." Josephine held out her hand to Ruth, as if to a child.

"Please let me be ungrateful and cling to the fire, Mrs. Napier."

Josephine resumed her seat.

"Such a peevish, poorly wife you have brought home, poor, dear Gabriel."

"We all keep saying the same thing in different words," said Josephine, laughing a little, and rocking herself without looking at either.

"Josephine, I think your advice was good," said Gabriel.

Josephine looked kindly but easily from one to the other.

"I shall have to unpack, I suppose," said Ruth.

"I will show myself a master of the accomplishment," said Gabriel. "You shall choose the better part, and sit at Josephine's feet."

"My dear boy, what are you saying?" said Josephine. "You cannot unpack for yourself, much less for anyone else."

"You have no conception of what I can do in these days. I am a qualified family man."

"I daresay you are," said Josephine, in a faintly

commiserating tone. "Well, go to the duties you have become qualified for, poor, toiling, moiling boy."

"Shall I leave your things on the sofa, my wife?"

"There, you see!" said Josephine, laughing and rising. "He has learnt how to unpack, hasn't he, when he does not suspect that putting things in their places is the foundation of it! Keep by the fire, my child, and I will go and superintend this newly learnt accomplishment. I do not expect to recognise the rudiments of it."

"We could not let you wait on us, Mrs. Napier."

"Well, we will go and face the herculean task, the three of us together. Not that there is much reason in that. There is hardly scope for a trio in a piece of work suitable for one." Josephine sat down, and Ruth and Gabriel left her.

"Your aunt wanted a talk with you alone, Gabriel. She gives the impression of a volcano on the verge of becoming active."

"It seems odd to hear Josephine called my aunt; she has always fulfilled such a different character. You know there is room for more than one person in my life."

"Only for one chief person. Mother saw that for herself. You can't put two people into one place."

"Gabriel's taste seems to be for several people in one place," said Josephine's voice at the door. "Three people can unpack, and three people will have to, if it is left to the third to supply the keys. These were in the hall, and there is reason in regarding them as a necessary preliminary to unpacking. The third person's contribution was indispensable."

"None of our things is locked, Mrs. Napier."

"Now, now, the third person really was indispensable. You will never be able to accompany Gabriel on further travels. This is the first time he has made a journey in that way."

"It is the first time he has been married, Mrs. Napier."

"Yes," said Josephine, in a tone of pleasant corroboration. "Both are for the first time."

"I always came down from Oxford with my baggage unlocked. I got quite used to it," said Gabriel.

"Yes, I was as indispensable as ever then. You never went back with it unlocked. I know that."

"No harm seems to have come of either method."

"The large one appears to be locked after all," said Ruth.

"Ah, you see the keys were necessary," said Josephine. Gabriel laughed.

"Gabriel could have fetched them, Mrs. Napier."

"Did he know where they were?" said Josephine.

Gabriel assumed a humorous expression of unconsciousness.

"Ah, you see, you needed me after all."

"Yes, but I asked you to come," said Gabriel. "I made no secret of my dependence upon you."

"Never make a secret of it," said Josephine, in a voice that suddenly defied his wife's presence; "and I will never fail you." She turned and left the room.

"Well, she is failing you over your marriage, Gabriel."

"Is she? Ah, my dear," said Josephine, looking back, "it is failing over a marriage, is it, to sacrifice both tangible and intangible things, to further it? Well, I think with you that it may be failing, that it is doing ill by people to deprive them of their sense of human justice."

"She must have known she was not meant to hear," said Ruth.

"No, I hardly knew it," said Josephine, causing Ruth to clench her hands. "I hardly understand this talking according to whether or no the talk is heard. It makes no difference in speaking the simple truth, as I speak it."

"Josephine, pray come in or go out," said Gabriel. "We hardly understand this talking to someone neither here nor elsewhere. It is an unbearable method of communication. Do make up your mind."

"It is made up for me, my dear. I have gathered—overheard, if you like—that there was some harm in my hearing what was said. Conversation is for me a thing that everyone within earshot may hear; but of course my principles may not be those of other people. I am not saying they should be. Every human being is one by himself in this world." She ended with a bitter lightness and closed the door.

"This is quite a false augury for the future," said Gabriel. "You will soon see the side of her that is super-human. You and I will end by vying for her favour."

"Well, we have not begun by doing that. I cannot face the next meeting without Mother's protection. I wonder if she has been asked to dinner. I suppose it goes without saying that she has."

At dinner, where Elizabeth was not present, Josephine appeared oblivious of the scene upstairs. When she caught Ruth's glance, she leaned towards her and laid her hand on hers.

"Suppose you give up regarding me as if I were a tigress, because I am not accustomed to having Gabriel belong to anyone but me! You don't take so very kindly to the idea that he can belong to anyone but you, do you? And you let me see it, as is natural. I am not slow to understand it. I never think it honest or desirable to hide too much of ourselves. You will find me charitable over the darker glimpses, if they are not too dark. And you and I are not dependent for our mutual feeling on our new relationship, are we?"

"No, Mrs. Napier," said Ruth, in a manner derived from the old relationship.

"It was as much my true self that you saw then, and your true self that I saw, as the selves that we see now; though, of course, my dear, I have my life as a woman, as well as a head mistress. It is because you had your life as a woman, as well as a junior mistress, that all this has come to pass, isn't it? And it is so bad for this boy to feel that two intelligent people are competing for him, that I for one withdraw from the competition; if I ever entered it, which

I doubt. And as I am sure you never entered it either, we are neither of us in it, are we?"

"No, Mrs. Napier."

"Are you always going to call Josephine Mrs. Napier?" said Gabriel. "She might as well call you Mrs. Swift."

"Well, hardly quite as well," said Josephine, laughing.

"She is a matron as much as you are."

"Well, a good many years less."

"I do not think of myself as Mrs. Swift," said Ruth.

"No, my dear, it is premature," said Josephine in a sympathetic tone. "You are Mrs. Gabriel Swift. My brother and I have several married relations senior to Gabriel. And you and I have known each other by settled names for a long time, haven't we?"

"Yes, we have, Mrs. Napier."

"Well now, your mother will be waiting in the drawing-room. I knew she was too busy to join us at dinner: I did not try to deceive myself about the amount of her work. This is a busy time in a busy house, and I am not one to deny what I have brought about myself. But her free hours have begun; so we will go and take advantage of them."

"It is dreadful that Mother should work, while we are free," said Ruth, crossing the hall with her arm in her husband's.

"No, why is it dreadful?" said Josephine. "I assure you I do not feel that about myself."

"You are such a powerful person, that it seems to be right that you should use your powers," said Gabriel.

"That is a good thing," said Josephine; "or a good deal would seem to be wrong."

"Well, Mother darling, free at last?" said Ruth.

"Free to take my real look at my boy and girl together. The girl looks as if it were time her mother's eyes were on her. Such a pale, pale face! The place for that head is on the pillow."

"I am giving a sad impression of myself," said Ruth,

lifting her arms above her head. "I can't be bright and entertaining when I am drooping with fatigue."

"You are a fortunate person, if you are bright and entertaining whenever you are not in that condition," said Josephine; "or rather other people are fortunate." She changed her tone. "I am sure they are, my dear."

"I feel a most unsatisfactory guest, Mrs. Napier."

"My child, you are in your mother's home. I do not forget that, if you do."

"Then I will betake myself with an easy mind to bed."

"Why not lie up on the sofa," said Josephine kindly, "and watch us all from there?"

"No, I would rather go upstairs and get away from human eyes."

"Be off, before you pay us further compliments," said her mother. "I will come up in an hour to see that you are asleep."

"She is paying me a compliment," said Josephine gravely. "I take it as such, when people in my house are enough at home to do as they like. And the poor child is simply doing what she must. It is easy to see that."

"I will follow you soon," said Gabriel to his wife.

"Now you sit down in your chair, and don't use your domestic gifts to keep her from her sleep." said Josephine. "We have had enough of those with your unpacking. There is a fire in her room, and a hot-water-bottle in her bed, and a hot drink on the way. I have not had my experience of young people, without becoming qualified to observe that such things would be needed by this young person, as soon as I received her into the house."

"My dear, those duties were not yours," said Elizabeth.

"They were of a kind to be anyone's who chanced to think of them. So as I chanced to do so, they were mine. As I did so, rather; there was not much chance about it."

There was silence for some moments, while Josephine seemed to be listening. At the closing of Ruth's door she turned to her friend.

"Now, as this is the cronies' chance of an evening together, shall we release you from the tedium of their sentimental intercourse? And postpone our general gathering until to-morrow night, when you will be free for dinner, and the child will be able to join us? I think I may say that she will be herself by then."

Elizabeth rose and went with running steps to the door.

"Yes, yes, I will not delay for a moment. A moment is a large proportion of the length of my sojourn. We know that all things are relative."

"They are a difficult pair," said Josephine, with a sigh.

"Do you mind if I smoke in your face?" said Gabriel, ignoring the words.

"I mind nothing you do, my boy."

"Even if the pipe burns your cheek?"

Josephine remained as she was, her eyes meeting the pipe as if in submission to his pleasure. Presently Gabriel started and moved aside, and a minute later his wife appeared in the door.

"I am a hopelessly harassing creature, Mrs. Napier. I am too restless to sleep, and I would fain have my husband sit at my side and soothe me. He need not disturb you by coming down again."

"Need not perhaps; but possibly he would wish to," said Josephine, mildly meeting her eyes. "He knows I should not be disturbed."

"He is as tired as I am; he will be better reposing at my side."

"Well, take him to his repose then, if repose is the word for what you were suggesting. I have yet to learn the effect on him of his new responsibilities; he has never been in need of repose at this hour. But I ought to be up for a while by myself; I have a good deal to get through. I must not forget the new drain on my resources."

"Good night, Josephine," said Gabriel, kissing her.

"Good night, my boy. I will try to make it up another

time," said Josephine, patting his shoulder and looking into his face.

Gabriel led the way from the room, and as he disappeared round the door, Josephine came up close to his wife.

"So, my dear, you listened from your room, and heard your mother come upstairs, and knew that Gabriel and I were alone? That was your method of finding it out, was it? Believe me, you were not dependent on it. I would have told you, will always tell you, when it is so, if it causes you uneasiness."

Ruth looked at her in silence.

"When you are alone with people, it is safe to leave you, is it not?" said Josephine, bending and speaking gently. "I am not so different from you, in that I thought a private conversation permissible. In fact, you tried to teach me that lesson yourself. And think of the number of times that Gabriel and I, or any other woman and her son or adopted son, must have been alone! If that did him harm, he would not be as you find him, would he; would not be the one man in the world to you? I hope that is how you feel to him? Suppose I could not leave him alone with you?"

"I am his wife," said Ruth.

"Well, no one will think it, if you go on as you are doing. They will take your marriage for some temporary, passing union. I would not force my worldly wisdom on you, but you must learn to be less afraid, must learn to be sure, or to seem so. Poor little one, you are young for all that. I knew that your time was not yet."

CHAPTER XV

THE NEXT DAY Ruth was unable to rise, and the doctor forbade her to leave her bed. From her pillow she held to her contest with Josephine, until something in Josephine rebelled against the unequal strife. As the morning went on, the latter came to Gabriel.

"I cannot feel easy about your poor little wife. She will never rest while you are with me, and you cannot live in a sick-room. Would it be wise for you to be called away to your work? She will be easy when you are out of the house, that is, outside my influence. And I shall not have this sense of taking advantage of her. It is a strange feeling to have, for spending an hour with the nephew, whom you have brought up from babyhood; but so things are just now. They will be better when health is better, and we all start again. I am prepared to start again myself; things were unfamiliar to me as well. But do you not think I am wise?"

The relief on Gabriel's face gave Josephine her answer.

"Ah, I know what is best for you. Trust me, and all will be well. Be wise in choosing the woman's hands into which you put your life."

"Mine not to reason why; mine just to do and die. At your word I will be dead to the house."

Josephine gave the word for the afternoon of that day. She sent her nephew for a walk in the morning, and letting his wife know he was out of the house, showed the girl a maternal kindness that conquered any reluctance to be left to her care. Her face was cheerful and her step light.

At the hour for Gabriel to leave, she led him herself to his wife, and stood smiling in the doorway over their farewell. Ruth lifted herself on her pillows and looked from one to the other, and Josephine, warning her back with a gesture, nodded and withdrew. In a few minutes, but not too few, her step was heard again, and her clear unhurried knock, and Gabriel rose from his kneeling position by the bed. Josephine followed him, shaking out her dress, and exchanging a smile with his wife over some need of repair.

Towards evening Ruth was greatly worse, and the doctor diagnosed inflammation of the lungs, and pronounced her condition to be grave. A nurse was established to attend her by day, and Josephine was to undertake the night, as Elizabeth's hands were full. Miss Rosetti, as Elizabeth's friend, was permitted to give her aid.

"No, I shall not be exhausted in trying to work day and night," said Josephine. "Trying to do it! Really doing it, or it would be less than no good; it would be criminal. No sleepy nursing for me! If I give up my usual work, I give it up. A mother is bound to make a nervous nurse. I can do a simple duty that is plain before me."

Josephine seemed impervious to weariness, and to be buoyed up by some inner strength. As Ruth's sickness drew her down into the depths of fear and suffering, she turned to her husband's adopted mother as much as to her own, seeming to recognise a greater force. When the crisis approached, and she cried out for her husband, who, though summoned, seemed to be delayed, Josephine moved as seldom as the mother from her side. It was imperative that she should remain covered in her bed; the slightest exposure might be fatal; and there was need for complete devotion. On the second evening, as Josephine watched in the dying light, her delirious murmurs became distinct, and Josephine's ear was alert.

"I knew he would belong to me when I saw his face, though he did not know. I cannot go to meet him now I am ill; but when I am well, I will go to him; and nobody shall watch us. We will tell her not to watch us. He is coming now!" The sick girl raised herself with all her strength, and seemed to be summoning it again to leave the bed.

Josephine sprang to prevent her, but stopped and stood with an arrested look, that seemed to creep across her face and gather to a purpose. She moved with a soft step to the bed, where Ruth had fallen.

"Do you want to get up, my child? Do you want my help?" Her tone seemed of itself to have become a whisper. "You know you may trust me."

"I think I can trust you in some things," said Ruth, meeting her eyes with a bright, clear gaze. "You are kind when I am ill. I must put on my things and go to Gabriel. He wants to see me by myself. You know we do not want anyone with us?" She turned her eyes again to Josephine. "You will not seem as if you did not know?"

"No, he shall see you by yourself. I have been too much with you: I will see it is never so again. Which dress would you like to wear? Which does he like to see you in? Come to the fire and tell me." Josephine lifted Ruth to her feet, and stood with her arm about her, but did not guide her forward. It was as if she felt some security in nearness to the bed. The girl leant against her, falling but for the support, and made no further movement. Josephine glanced from the open window to the door, and contracted her shoulders in the draught between them. Ruth's voice came again, steadied by the cold.

"I cannot be dressed to-day; Gabriel will know that I can't. He would not like me to be in the cold." She shuddered, and indeed the draught seemed stronger. "I will lie down and go to sleep; I am very tired. You will watch me, and wake me when Gabriel comes? If you listen, you will hear him coming. You know his step."

Josephine felt her body respond from head to foot, as the trust and weakness of the tones pierced something that bound her. Her face was that of another woman. She lifted the girl to the bed and covered her, bending to secure the clothes. As she raised her head, her eyes fell on the door, and set into a stare, while her body seemed to be fixed in its stooping posture. The door stood open; the reason of the draught flashed to her mind; the silent movements of sickness had escaped her ears. Miss Rosetti stood in the doorway, with something for the sick-room in her hand, her feet riveted to the floor, her eyes to Josephine's face.

"Oh, what a moment!" said Josephine, standing up straight. "I shall never forget it. She was out of bed in a second. I should not have thought she had the strength. I was not reckoning with it, and time got wasted. I could not lift her by myself. Oh, I wish someone had been here. I found myself counting the seconds through the horror of it."

The pause that followed seemed as full of effort as Josephine's words.

"It was a strange thing to happen," said Miss Rosetti, her glance going up and down Josephine's frame, as though measuring it against the task that had been beyond it. "One of those things that we cannot explain. Was she long in the cold?"

"It seemed hours to me," said Josephine, letting out her breath. "You must have seen us. I could not get her balanced, to help her forward. And she was hardly a yard from the bed; there seemed such irony in it. And the window was open, as the doctor said it must be. The draught was full on her; I felt it on myself. If only its being on her had mattered as little!"

"Yes," said Miss Rosetti, her eyes again covering Josephine's form. "But it does no good to talk about it. We may be in danger from our memories. And she seems to be sleeping now."

But Gabriel's wife did not sleep long. Her temperature went to a dangerous height, her breathing was ominously shallow and swift, and the doctor, summoned in haste, betrayed that his hope was gone. Josephine tended the girl with intense absorption, let no one but herself and the mother approach the bed, and seemed to feel it the object of her life that she should be saved. But the disease had gained ascendance, and they were losing hours. The crisis came with the expected force, and as it ebbed the life ebbed with it.

Josephine fell on her knees by the bed and broke into weeping. She and Elizabeth clung to each other, and Miss Rosetti went in silence about what had to be done.

Gabriel arrived in the small hours of the morning. The telegram sent to summon him had arrived too late, although Josephine had written and despatched it with her own hand. Josephine met him in open grief and weariness, but as she fell on his neck, her tones rang.

"My boy, you have what you have always had. You are not alone."

But after that moment Josephine herself gave way. She wept for her nephew's wife as she had never wept for her husband. There came no reaction from her despairing grief, and Gabriel, in his rather gentle sorrow, found himself consoling rather than consoled. She lamented her dealings with his wife, and held her own against herself.

"I do not need false comfort. I can face the truth. What are called the little things are the gravest human wrongs. No recognised wrong, even though it were injury or death, takes its place beside them in the scale of human harm."

"It is a good thing that you will never have a real wrong on your mind."

"It would be easier to bear; it would be a better thing. Better a murder than a meanness."

"A murder is the worst meanness. Yours were the least."

Gabriel's mood was readily in tune with a suffering that he saw as sympathy.

"A murder would never be done without an excuse: the things without excuse must remain the inexcusable things."

At last weariness had its way, and Josephine slept; and after the unconscious hours arose in her own strength. It had been assumed that she would not attend the burial, and she met the assumption with gentle surprise.

"I should not let anything keep me away. My place is with Gabriel."

"We thought you would not feel equal to it," said Miss Rosetti.

"I do not know that I do feel equal to it. But that has little to do with the matter."

"You did not go to your husband's funeral," said Miss Rosetti, her voice significant from its very lack of force.

"No," said Josephine, her hands trembling. "And you know that I know that, without your telling me."

"I suppose you see your own difference."

"And do you not see it? Then I will help you. Simon was a man and my husband, and this was an orphan girl. Then I had myself to consider; now I have Gabriel. Then my feelings were of personal loss; now they are of pity. Do you see the difference now? By the way"—Josephine spoke with a haste that precluded words from the other—"if you would find it too much for you, you will not go, will you?"

"I am not going, but not for that reason. I am remaining with Mrs. Giffard."

"I should have known if I had thought. It lifts a weight from my mind. I will not say that I am grateful."

Josephine stood with Gabriel at his wife's grave. Gabriel did not weep, but Josephine wept. A wreath inscribed with her name was laid on the coffin by his own.

On their return she parted from him as they entered the house.

"My son, we know what you have in your life. But to-day you must dwell on what you have not. I will leave you for a while alone."

There was a remembrance in both their minds of the day of Simon's burial.

"I have come to say a word of gratitude," said Josephine, as she sought the familiar common room. "I have not been blind to what I have not seen, your loyal carrying on of the school in your own anxiety and sorrow. I know that my feelings have been indulged, and yours conquered. If I

could have a pleasure, it would be one to make my acknow-
ledgement."

"We ought to say more than that to you, Mrs. Napier,"
said Mrs. Chattaway.

"No," said Josephine, her tone rising at this unconscious
testimony to Miss Rosetti's silence. "It does not apply to
me. I am the first to say it. That does not alter my recognition of a more sefless courage."

"You had a nearer anxiety than any of us," said Miss Luke.

"Nearer in that it was to me, that the child turned of all
people at the end?" said Josephine in a voice so low as only
just to be heard.

"I meant the anxiety for Gabriel," said Miss Luke, at
the same pitch.

"No feeling is nearer to me, than that I have for those
who work for and with me. In giving her that I gave her
what I could give."

"It is tragic that your nephew was not in time," said
Mrs. Chattaway.

"No," said Josephine gently; "not tragic. You must not
encourage me in making too much of what is in itself
indeed enough. The child was, as I have said, content; and
he could only be satisfied that it was so. And he was himself,
and let himself be satisfied."

"You have to attempt more for him than ever before,"
said Miss Luke. "And I know that is saying much."

"In trying to comfort him in a trouble that leaves him
myself? No, I have attempted that, and succeeded many
times. You must not make me feel that I am doing more
than I am."

"But never in such a trouble as this," said Mrs. Chattaway.

"Never in this trouble. But all the troubles have been
such as this, in, as I say, leaving him myself. And it has
already happened in the old way; and I am here with you,
feeling it has so happened. If it were not so, I confess I
should not be here."

"Then he did not—did not feel even to his wife, as he feels to you?" said Mrs. Chattaway.

"I have meant to say simply that I have left him comforted. I may say that simply, I think, among my friends."

"You may indeed," said Miss Luke.

"You have the anxiety and responsibility of Mrs. Giffard as well," said Mrs. Chattaway.

"The anxiety I have; the responsibility I have allowed to devolve upon Miss Rosetti. I have felt, rightly or wrongly, that a woman of her own will childless was the best comforter. And there must be other things in Miss Rosetti, that qualify her rather than me. Anyhow, it was to her rather than me, that my old friend turned." Josephine folded her hands and dropped her eyes upon them.

Miss Rosetti did not speak.

"Of course we look back in doubt on our dealings with the child," said Miss Luke. "We cannot expect to escape that burden."

"If there are burdens for all of us, does it not come to there being no burden for any?" said Josephine. "For some young natures—I say it in all tenderness, seeing in their youth their full excuse—tend to find grounds for unhappiness. It seems to satisfy some young need. The questions we have asked ourselves, for that we all ask them, lay themselves to rest."

"It is a great bond between you and Mrs. Giffard, that Gabriel must feel he is a son to you both," said Mrs. Chattaway.

"He is too much under the weight of things at the moment, to feel he is a son to more than one person. He has come creeping back to me like a little child. He can only feel that what has always supported him, is with him, and turn to it blindly, as the beginning and the end. I have simply to accept it, having no means of combating an instinct so deep and blind."

"It is terrible that he should be crushed on the threshold of life."

"It would be terrible. But he is young and brave. The young do not see courage in yielding. Forth they go on their different ways and in their different worlds!" Josephine moved her hand.

"And always together," said Mrs. Chattaway.

"And always apart. That is where the bravery lies for them. For us it lies in the truth, that the young in their eagerness and bewilderment ask so much, that we feel we have given little. And my own is perhaps the harder, the more humiliating. For I have to feel that Gabriel might have given more as a husband, if he had given less as a son. I have to let the truth close over me. And you with your little load of regret, come to me for comfort! Well, you may have the comfort of knowing that I am in comparison heavy laden."

During the silence that ensued, Josephine rose and moved to the door, stooping to Miss Rosetti as she passed her.

"May I ask you for a few moments of your time? I have taken so much, that I can claim no scruple in going further."

Miss Rosetti rose and followed, and at a distance along the corridor Josephine came to a pause.

"It is a strange place for setting on foot a discussion. But Gabriel is in the library, and we can hardly talk into youthful ears. And our friends seem to be established behind. I should have thought that this house was large enough for all its purposes, but we seem to be blocked up fore and aft. I wished to ask you if you are still available for me as a partner. If you are not, I must remind myself that I have given you time to change your mind, and not be surprised that you have used it. But now that I am harassed by personal troubles, I should be grateful for support in my working life. At one time it was not so. It is so now. Will you give me your answer, or do you desire me to wait? I need not say that I am in your hands."

Miss Rosetti looked at the ground, something like a smile creeping across her face.

"It is wise of you to make the offer. It is clever as well as wise. I do not say that it is not also kind. I will tell you that I would accept it, if the choice were mine. But the choice is no longer mine. If it were, I would be your partner, surprising though that may be both to you and to me. I will not give you the wrong reason for my refusal: I find that what I say is the truth."

"I am indeed sorry," said Josephine, in simply expressionless tones. "If things are ever different, I may rely on you to tell me?"

"I can tell you now that they will never be different. But I will remember the chance you have given me: I will remember both sides of you that I have seen, the many facets that go to make up the surface of a soul." Miss Rosetti spoke in her natural voice as she turned from Josephine. "Thank you very much, Mrs. Napier. I will not forget."

Josephine took a deep breath and stood as if bewildered, and then continued her way to the library.

Gabriel was turning the leaves of a book, and looked up and closed it, uneasy at betraying interest in it. Josephine went up to him and passed her hand over his head.

"Not equal to reading as yet, being as you are? Shall we lift the troubles off your mind, that I know are on it? What do you feel about returning to your work? Can you face the return alone? Ah, don't be afraid to break down, my boy; turn to me, and let me comfort you. You have it all left, a home and a woman in it. We will give up your house and make our life in this one, in yours and mine."

"What about my work?" said Gabriel.

"What could there be about it? Some other young man will take it, and be gladder to have it than you can be, because it fulfils his need. You are not a person who thinks himself indispensable in any little place?"

"Of course not. And this was a little place indeed. But there will be the money wasted."

"Not as much as will be saved."

"I shall give up both my allowances, when the bills are paid. My proper pocket-money, as a lad at home, will be five shillings a week."

"Well, have your proper pocket-money then," said Josephine, with easy tenderness, "and let the balance accumulate for the future."

"But you and Father will stop giving me help. Nothing else would be thinkable."

"No, why should I? Why should he? Why should an established plan be changed, when nothing has happened in direct relation to it?"

"Most people would see reasons."

"Well, perhaps I am a little different from most people."

"You certainly are," said Gabriel, a gleam of interest appearing on his face.

Josephine kept her eyes averted from it.

"My dear," she said, still in the manner of easy perplexity, "all that I have is simply yours, of course. You may as well see the stone gathering the moss. Your future is longer than mine, and I am concerned with nobody else's. I shall not leave my hard-earned savings to hospitals, whatever you may expect of me. You have by no means such a charitable aunt."

"A charitable aunt is what I have, if charity begins at home."

"It seems to me a good place for it to begin, if it does not to everyone. I will show you in a moment how our affairs stand." Josephine observed Gabriel's recoil, and sank back as if unconsciously. "I mean some time in the future, but I think in the near future. Nothing so helps to steady nerves and spirits as concentration on material things."

As the gleam of interest again appeared, Josephine left the subject and took up her sewing, her expression showing her own great weariness.

The cloud grew deeper on her face as her fingers worked. She felt no sense of comfort in her restored world. Something had not been returned to it; something was wanting.

A light seemed to dawn at the back of her mind, as she recognised a knock.

"I can hardly apologise for intruding," said Felix; "as I am a person who could not be felt to intrude. And I am not forgetting my position in the house. I simply thought that an outsider's influence might be wholesome."

"Come in, in whatever character you will," said Gabriel. "My present course is where madness lies."

Josephine seemed to herself to experience a familiar pang without feeling it. She sat in silence, her eyes going from one to the other, blinded by a flash of understanding. The pang she actually felt, was not for Gabriel, but for Felix! She rose and stumbled from the room, her face dazed and startled, as if from a shock. With her own power she faced the truth, and grappled with her knowledge of herself. Gabriel's place in her life had been filled by Felix! Gabriel had been snatched back to a world that was his no longer. If he remained away, it would have been better for him; it would have been better for her, as it would have left her Felix for her own.

Moving along, hardly knowing where she went, she came upon Helen, carrying some books.

"You are laden, my dear," she said.

"I am taking some books to the library, that Mr. Bacon has chosen for Gabriel—for your nephew, Mrs. Napier."

"Call him Gabriel, my child. I am glad for him to have friends of his own age. He must not lose youth and hope because one chapter of his life is closed. It is only a reason for his starting another. I hope you will cultivate a friendly feeling towards him?"

"We all have it already, Mrs. Napier."

"I meant you yourself, if you will let me say what I meant. You are of his age, of his tastes, of—may I say it? —his class and kind. I should be grateful for your companionship for him; and he would be grateful, if you would allow him the necessary time. May I ask you to join him sometimes when I have to leave him?"

"It would give me great pleasure, Mrs. Napier."

"It would give you a sense of duty done, of kindness accomplished, that would be a pleasure, I am sure. You may rely upon us to grant you the pleasure as often as we can persuade you to accept it."

CHAPTER XVI

"I would not say anything out of keeping with the circumstances of the house," said Felix, entering Josephine's library. "But this is quite in keeping. My father's health is failing, and he may not have long to live. I feel less ashamed of being alive myself, that I can offer you a death in my own family quite soon."

"That is sad hearing," said Josephine. "I think I am even sorrier for you than for him."

"Why? My health is good. You should be sorrier for my father."

"Well, your father's hold on life is light. He must be an old man."

"He is seventy-nine, and I am afraid his hold on life is confirmed. He is very used to living."

"Will you have to go and see him?" said Gabriel.

"Thank you for making it easy for me to ask for a holiday."

"I cannot refuse one for such a reason," said Josephine, moving in front of Gabriel.

"Would you refuse it for other reasons? I might enjoy a holiday more, if I were not in trouble."

"Are you really in trouble?" said Gabriel.

"The astonishing thing is, that I am. I thought I should have to face the absence of sorrow. And what I am facing, is just the ordinary presence of it. One thing about the sorrow is, that it is known not to be the sadder kind."

"Your mood seems to be one of complete unseemliness," said Gabriel.

"Surely you know what may be covered by a jesting exterior. You speak as if I had not just told you what is covered by mine."

"Is your father's health really failing?" said Gabriel.

"Do you think I would obtain a holiday under pretences?"

"Is your father becoming more resigned to your work?" said Josephine.

"He may be: he has always said it would shorten his life; and we must suppose that he is facing his end with resignation. Not that that seems to me a possible thing to do."

"Whom has he living with him?" said Gabriel.

"Some servants who are very attached to him. My father is never rude to a servant."

"Is he rude to you?" said Josephine.

"He has told me that he could not be rude to anyone. So I know he cannot be."

"There must be good in him, for his servants to be attached to him."

"Of course there is good in him. Did you think I would suggest there was no good in my father?"

"Well, you have often referred to his failings," said Josephine, smiling.

"I do not think it is time for remorse yet. It is the dead we do not speak evil of, and I shall treat my father as living for as long as I can. It is treating the old with more sympathy to speak evil of them."

"It is a change for you to feel sympathy with your father," said Gabriel.

"How can you say so? I have always spoken evil of him."

"What is wrong with his health?" said Josephine, in a gentle tone.

"His heart may fail at any moment, or he may live for years. It is very awkward for me. Behaviour is so different for years and for a moment. You have seen what mine has been for years. I think I must pay him a series of short visits."

"Won't he want you to stay?" said Gabriel.

"If I behave as I should for a moment, he can hardly

fail to. Unless it is almost too much for him. He would not like me really to shorten his life."

"I don't think your father has any great reason to be dissatisfied with his son," said Josephine.

"I hope you would never think such a thing. My father does not like anyone to criticise me but himself."

"I suppose he will leave you a great inheritance?" said Gabriel.

"Would your plans change, if he died?" said Josephine, almost at the same moment.

"I never talk about plans for after a person's death. And I never talk about inheritance at all. I cannot approve of your treatment of my father."

"You would go to live in your ancestral home," said Gabriel.

"He could not give up the life he has made for himself, for one simply handed down to him," said Josephine.

"That comparison might be made in another spirit," said Gabriel.

"Felix must do the right thing by his own life. That is a serious necessity in itself, apart from any reluctance of mine to make changes in the school."

"Were you reluctant when you changed to me? I did not suspect it. That makes me feel quite foolish."

"Well, I had my moments of anxiety. But while they are having their reward, I see no reason to complain."

'I will tell my father that I have given no cause for complaint. He sometimes asks me if I have, in a manner meant to wound me. I am glad now that I have so much to forgive. It will soothe me very much to forgive it."

"You will return to his house, when it becomes your own," said Gabriel.

"Well, if he returns," said Josephine, swinging her arms, "I shall give up being a slave to the school, that has only to be set on its proper basis, to get upset again. I have been getting tired for a long time of humdrumming along, and this shows that other people are in similar case. I had got so far a week or two ago, as arranging about a partner, but that has fallen through for the time. It will materialise in the end, and I shall be free to come and go with the rest."

"You don't mean that you will give up your work?" said Gabriel. "You have kept all this inner fermentation to yourself."

"People would not allow me to give it up. And I always keep things to myself until they come to pass. But I see that it does not do for me to be pegged down to one place, and make it a jumping-off ground for other people. So you will soon find yourself with a different aunt-sister, with part of her life in the school, and the rest of it elsewhere, wherever it takes its course."

"I hold my breath before coming events," said Gabriel. "And I see my father as the victim of one of them, rather than Felix's. My heart stands still before the thought of his future."

"Mine does not," said Josephine. "He will make his life for himself, as the rest of us do. We cannot check natural progress for people's dislike of it."

"I think my father would like us to in his case," said Felix.

There was a knock at the door, and Helen came into the room.

"My dear, this is kind," said Josephine. "People are not always so ready to confer a favour that is asked for. Gabriel, I have persuaded Miss Keats to spare us an hour sometimes. She is without contemporaries in her own sphere, and you are in the same plight. Shall Felix and I remain with you, or retire?"

"I think we have a touch with young people," said Felix.

"I should be badly off without that in one sense," said Josephine.

"I think I have it in the other sense."

"At what age does one cease to be young?" said Gabriel.

"I shall always be young in heart," said Felix.

"That may be when we cease to be young," said Helen.

"When we are really young, I think our hearts age with the rest of us."

Josephine turned and gave Helen a smile.

"Yes, we are talking about youth in years," said Felix; "I must face it."

"I never think about people's age," said Josephine.

"I often think about it," said Felix; "and hope they show it more than I do, and wonder if they can guess mine."

"I don't think it is a compliment to a man to be taken for less than his age," said Josephine.

"Is it a compliment to a woman?" said Helen.

"I don't think it is, my dear, though I believe I personally suffer from it. I seem never to be accorded the dignities of middle life."

"Surely no one is accorded more dignities than you are," said Gabriel.

"Oh, other dignities. I meant those that definitely pertain to middle age. I hardly take it as a compliment either though I have not given the matter much thought."

"You and I are so different," said Felix.

"Well, we both seem to have our trend towards youth," said Josephine.

"I think I will go home to Jonathan," said Felix. "I see that Gabriel shrinks from my company, because of my shallow experience. But I shall be able to take him on equal terms when I have lost my father."

"I have lost both father and mother," said Helen.

"Then I think you may take him on equal terms at once," said Josephine. "We will leave you to take advantage of it, leave him to do so rather. I also have lost both father and mother. We all seem to have a bond of that kind between us."

A few hours later Felix was greeting Sir Robert Bacon.

"Well, Felix, you have come to see me die?"

"You told me to come, if I wanted to see you alive," said Felix, sitting down by the invalid chair. "So I have come for that."

"Well, I am still breathing."

"I am glad I am in time; I am glad I am not too late. You must see how ill at ease I am in your presence."

"Ah, you may never live to be my age. It is not every man who lasts nine years beyond the three score and ten."

"No, I may miss the years of labour and sorrow. But it is not kind to remind me of it, when everyone wants them so much, and you have just had them. And I think you seem to think less of me for it."

"Ah, people may tell you that you are not equal to your father."

"Well, of course, they will not know that you have told me."

"I daresay you are imagining yourself in my place."

"No, it is you who are doing that. It is not a picture that I should choose to dwell upon."

"You will not escape hearing of the difference between us."

"I don't believe people will be as careless of my feelings as you think. When you came to the concert at the school, nobody let me hear a word of it."

"So it will take my death to get you out of that position?"

"Well, I could not tender my resignation on any trivial ground."

"Well, that will not be trivial."

"No, no, that will do," said Felix.

"My son, we may get to know each other better in my very last days."

"I am sure we shall. I know you better in the very last minute."

"Felix, would you keep a promise to a dying man?"

"Yes. I am one of the very few people who would. Now do you think you know me a little better?"

"Will you promise me to marry and carry on the place?"

"Do you feel that that would be fair to a woman, when your opinion of me is so low?"

"You will be able to offer your wife a good deal."

"I don't think you have a high opinion of my wife, either. As you feel we are so suited, of course we will marry. I am glad that she will accept me, even though it is not for myself."

CHAPTER XVII

"Well, my only child," said Elizabeth, as Gabriel entered the housekeeper's room, "so you have remembered again that we are going on with our lives under the same roof? I am not to feel that I am left with nothing of my own?"

"I hope you do not feel that I am nothing. I meant to come to you earlier, but empty lives are always so full. Tell me how you have spent your day."

"I have done my work as usual. Josephine thought it was better for me to do it, or anyhow better for the work that it should be done. And between whiles I sit and call up my courage: I do not let it go. It has held through so much of my life, that it ought not to fail now. But if yours fails, I shall not love you less; I confess that I shall not. No, I know it is Josephine who will take thought that it does not fail."

"Josephine is not the arbiter of my happiness."

"Not, my love?" said Elizabeth, putting back her head in a faint peal of mirth.

"She acquired the habit of doing without me with most unlooked-for ease. We are apart now for hours in the day."

"But those are the hours she takes thought for."

"She disposes of them as a duty. I can give you as many as you like. I am flattered to feel that I am not superfluous in the house."

"Well, of course I should like them, my son. You are all I have; and I gave you all I had. You represent my life to me. And Josephine has had so much that was mine: I feel I must tell you of all she has taken: I cannot carry the burden of bitterness alone."

Elizabeth told the story of herself and Josephine, believing that she knew it to the end.

"Josephine is built on a large scale," said Gabriel. "She is powerful for both good and bad."

"Yes, she is destiny, and we are her sport."

"I should not describe myself as that."

"No, no. It was foolish to use the words. We are only talking of the wind and the way it blows: it must carry the young and tender with it."

"I married in the teeth of it, and it is not such a blast as it used to be. My life is my own."

Gabriel went downstairs at the hour when he expected to be joined by Helen, and Felix overtook him in the hall.

"I have come to keep you company."

"So have I," said Helen. "I hope it will not become more general."

"I don't feel a very fit companion."

"Do you want to feel your loneliness?" said Felix. "Then why not remember that the truest loneliness is amongst numbers? When my father dies, I shall at once seek society."

"Mrs. Napier did not mean us both to be here together," said Helen. "You may do her that justice."

"Which of us would you like to go?" said Felix.

"I will go myself. I am going to sit with my wife's mother, and dispose of loneliness for both of us, now that there is no question of it for either of you."

As Gabriel left the room, Felix came up to Helen.

"Do you feel a faint admiration for Gabriel, for not being embarrassed that his mother-in-law is the housekeeper?"

"Yes, a very faint one."

"Mine is very faint, too. We are much more alike than most people."

"Then we may as well keep each other company."

"I think we had better just keep company. I think my father would wish it. Would you be disconcerted if Mrs. Napier came into the room?"

"Yes, just a little; she would expect Gabriel to be with us."

"That shows I am keeping my promise to my father," said Felix.

CHAPTER XVIII

"I HAVE TOLD your father that we will bring Miss Keats, when we go to dinner," said Josephine to Gabriel.

"She must be tired of being involved in our family life. We have not concerned ourselves with hers."

"She has no family life. You told me yourself that she was an orphan. So do not pretend to be more ignorant than you are; it is a thing that is seldom advisable. Your father wants to give you a companion of your own age, and to set me free for companions of mine. The older men want a word at times with a mature, feminine fellow-creature. And why should I always be the only woman in the company?"

"You must be inured to it by now. I don't know what has come over you of late. You seem to have your being in the clouds."

"Well, we all seem to have our being in some such wise. So I am only in the fashion if I do. And I daresay the clouds will break."

"You are of the wrong age to become unsettled in your life. At once too old and too young."

"Oh, too old and too young, am I? At once too old and too young for a good many things. Other people have noticed it."

Jonathan came into the hall to meet his guests, walking with an old man's step, which had suddenly come upon him, and of which he seemed to be aware.

"My dear sister, my dear son; ah, my dear, you are very kind to us; I should not have ventured to ask you for myself. You are all three doubly welcome. We need a tonic more than you know. You have not heard what has come to us, Josephine? We are at a parting of the ways. You know that Felix's father died last week?"

"Yes, we have heard. May I offer you my sympathy?" said Josephine, giving her hand to Felix. "You must have had a full and exacting time since I saw you."

"Do you not generally feel that my time is that? But it is especially so, when you atone for forty-one years in a few weeks. That is so different from a day's duty for each day."

"You feel you have atoned?" said Josephine in a low tone.

"No; I have found how impossible it is to undo the past. It is odd that people should ever think it is possible."

"Your father was content to die?"

"No. So little content that he could not be told he was really going to."

"Did he not suspect that his end was near?"

"Yes. It made things very difficult for everyone, and of course unbearable for him."

"Content to die?" said Jonathan. "Ah, I must try to be content."

"Well, people are so under the influence of some religions," said Fane.

"That is a different content," said Helen. "Provision is made for its being the opposite."

"I suppose your father did not hold any dogma?" said Fane.

"I should have supposed that he held the dogma of the Church, as he did."

"His religion was of no help to him?" said Fane.

"None at all. He died," said Felix.

"Had he hope for the future?" said Josephine gently.

"No. He had certainty. He told me. But I think he must have been living in the present."

"People never do live much in the future they are certain of," said Helen. "They live more in the nearer future, that is known to be uncertain."

"Well, his place will know him no more," said Fane.

"That was just it," said Felix.

"Ah, another place is to know its possessor no more,

Josephine," said Jonathan. "Felix is to succeed his father in his home. I am an old man to remodel my life."

"That is really your decision?" said Josephine to Felix.

"It was my father's."

"Was it his last wish?"

"That was that he should live to fill it himself. It was one of his last commands."

"There was an element of real pathos in it," said Josephine.

"It sounds to me to have been all pathos," said Gabriel; "to have had no element of anything else."

"Well, he would have been eighty on his next birthday," said Fane.

"Yes, but he was probably not going to have the birthday," said Felix.

"People are often hardly responsible on their deathbeds," said Jonathan.

"I promised not to be influenced by people who said that. I did not know that I was promising not to be influenced by you."

"No one would try to influence you."

"My father did not know that."

"Of course Felix will spend his life where his forebears lived before him," said Gabriel. "It is what he was born and bred for."

"My father said those very words. He must have been responsible."

"How does it feel to be called 'Sir Felix'?" said Josephine.

"It makes me feel rather inclined to give a faint smile, and inwardly to admire my father for taking it as a matter of course."

"I suppose you will give me a certain amount of notice about your work?" said Josephine in an almost rallying tone.

"He told me to tell you, that I must give it up on his

death. But he hoped it would be a good deal of notice. You will do him justice?"

"I was not prepared for quite such arbitrary dealings."

"And I have so often told you things about him, that might have prepared you."

"I thought I was dealing with you, and not with your father."

"It seems extraordinary now, that you should have thought that."

"You are not a man of an independent mind," said Fane.

"I know that people are often taunted for attending to a death-bed wish."

"Now I must have justice as well as your father," said Josephine. "You must allow for my moment of anxiety for my own plans. Your place will have to be filled; but that can be done with all places: I daresay mine could be filled to-morrow. Life has to be a succession of changes. It may be well to recognise that change is good."

"You think that change is good in itself, Mrs. Napier?" said Fane. "Well, I daresay I allow myself to sink somewhat into a groove."

"I sometimes think I have allowed myself to do the same," said Josephine. "It might be salutary to be rooted out."

"How soon shall we come to visit you, Felix?" said Gabriel.

"As soon as it is possible for me to entertain, without disrespect to my father's memory."

"You appear to show more respect for his memory than you showed for himself," said Fane.

"Not more than is always shown to people's memories, compared with themselves. And of course I did not show enough respect for himself. Is not my remorse sacred to you?"

"Yes, yes, we have to be on our guard in our dealings with the dead," said Fane.

"And we may do as we like about the living," said Helen. "It never seems a practical arrangement."

"Well, the dead cannot retaliate," said Fane.

"That is what I was thinking of," said Helen.

"I never feel I have to be on my guard in my dealings with people, alive or dead," said Josephine in a quiet, distinct tone.

"Well, that is a great tribute to you, Mrs. Napier," said Fane.

"You can have us to stay with you, one by one, Felix," said Gabriel.

"Wouldn't that seem like trying to fill my father's place?"

"You will be in your father's place yourself."

"If it will be only trying to fill my place, of course I can have you."

"You are already changed by your position," said Gabriel.

"I do not at all mind your saying it. I promised my father to let it change me at once."

"Most people lose their fathers," said Fane.

"That does seem to me astonishing," said Felix.

"Your pupils will miss you very much," said Josephine to Felix.

"I am so much changed, that I feel it odd that I should have pupils. Of course they will feel it a come-down to be taught by a woman."

"I am sure you do not think that."

"I am talking about what my pupils will think."

"Why do you assume that they will have a woman to teach them?"

"My father told me that no man but me would do it. And what do my personal opinions matter, compared with his?"

"Our personal opinions always matter, if they are honest."

"I don't know that my personal opinion about teaching

drawing to girls was honest. It was just in keeping with my whimsical side. It was my father's opinion about it that was honest."

"It is natural that you should feel in that way about him just now," said Josephine.

"You think the feeling will pass? Of course you have had more trouble than I have, and know about it better."

"I know about it only too well."

"You do seem to, rather," said Felix.

Josephine laughed and rose from the table, and stood with her hand on Gabriel's shoulder, courteously waiting for Helen to pass.

"My dear, you are my brother's guest to-night, and hold only that relation towards me. Not that I should not welcome you in any other."

The four men followed the women, Jonathan leading the way, with a gesture of relinquishing on this occasion the talk of his own sex.

"Will you still have a home for me, Swift?" said Fane.

"No, neither for you nor myself, Fane. My evil days have come. But I shall be doing something for my sister's life by joining her; and I have enough for that, without being a burden. And I shall see more of my son. I have little to complain of. No one is less alone."

He went forward into the drawing-room, blinking his eyes.

"This is great news!" said Gabriel. "It atones for the loss of Felix. Have you told Josephine that you do not propose to continue in neglect of your family?"

"No, my boy. You might do that for me, might just say a word," said Jonathan, edging up to him. "I have a hesitation, if you understand me. I have a claim; I know I am claimed. It is enough; and yet I do not deny the feeling. But I will not yield to it. Josephine, you have a place in your home for an old man?"

"For an old man, or a young man, or any kind of man at all. That there is a place for any kind of woman, I have given proof. My house would not be mine, if it could not expand at need. And I welcome a deputy to leave behind, in the event of my visiting pastures new. It will give me a large part of my life for my own, which has been my ambition for some time."

"I hope you will appreciate your post among the ladies, Swift," said Fane.

"He cannot fail to," said Felix. "I know what such a post is like."

"I shall not be among the ladies," said Jonathan. "I shall share my sister's family life."

"I am glad of that," said Felix. "I want my tradition to be something quite by itself. Do you ever have former members of your staff to stay with you, Mrs. Napier?"

"Very often," said Josephine.

"Because if you did not, I could not come. I am going to be more conventional now my father is dead."

"And now it is of no good to him," said Fane.

"I see you cannot understand loyalty to the dead," said Felix. "I should hate to die, if I belonged to you. I begin to understand my father's uneasiness."

"You were never unconventional," said Gabriel.

"No, never: I quite agree. I think it was wonderful how beneath everything I really conformed."

"You have the funeral and everything safely behind you?" said Josephine in a low tone.

"Yes, but I have not used the word, 'safely'."

"You are free to look forward?"

"Yes, but I have not used the word, 'free'."

"No, no, a funeral is a great landmark in our path."

"Especially in my father's!" said Felix.

"Yes, yes. But your father would not wish you to look back."

"He said he hoped I always should. On our last days together."

"But you will not, I hope?"

"You and he never seem to agree," said Felix.

"I suppose you are really looking forward in your heart?"

"Why do you suppose that, after what I have said? And the heart would be a shocking place to look forward in."

"I mean, you must be making plans for the future."

"No, I am still making plans for the past, and imagining myself my father's comfort and companion."

"That will not have much result, will it?"

"No, but sometimes one likes people better for doing foolish things."

"Are you not indulging in a little self-deception?"

"Yes, and I am finding it an indulgence, and almost feeling that my father is, too."

"Well, you are honest with yourself, anyhow."

"I think you are contradicting yourself."

"Well, that is better than contradicting somebody else," said Fane.

"When the first alternative is Mrs. Napier?" said Felix.

"No, no, well, perhaps not then," said Fane.

"You are both very kind to me," said Josephine.

"Will you walk home or drive, Josephine?" said Jonathan.

"Well, I think we will drive," said Josephine, in a deliberate tone. "Having given up a good many years to economy, I think it is time we adapted ourselves to a different routine. I am a great believer in adaptability."

"It is Felix who will have to show that virtue," said Gabriel.

"Or has he already been showing it?" said Josephine, with an arch expression. "Has his part in the school been the most subtle exercise of it? Ah, there have been times when I have had suspicions. I am not a person whose mind is bounded by the walls of a school."

"Stone walls do not a prison make," said Fane.

"No, I have freedom—in my soul am free," said Josephine.

"Our world is tumbling about our ears," said Gabriel, as they drove home.

"No, it is only building itself up after a shock," said Josephine. "The death of a man in the position of Felix's father was bound to have its reverberations. We must be able to turn our eyes to the future. I am sure Miss Keats is of that mind."

CHAPTER XIX

"Well, Jonathan," said Josephine, entering her brother's study, "it is a new experience to me to be despatched on errands; but I am too much against becoming set in any one character, to be disturbed by it. The truth is, though I would not say it to anyone; the truth is, Jonathan, that I have got over Simon's death, and find myself anchorless and rudderless. Well, we must not be restive under the hand of time. It may have further changes for the future." .

"For those of us who have a future," said Jonathan, who was rummaging in his desk in a purposeless manner. "I am glad you are over your trouble; I would not ask to get over mine. My miss of Felix will be my life."

"You are busy very early," said Josephine, looking at her brother, who seemed to be restless and uncontrolled.

"Yes, you find me preparing for my last journey. Naked we come into the world; naked we go out of it. I am not planning to go with more than I came. I do not feel I can carry my treasures in my hands; I have not quite so much in me of the ordinary man. I am preparing for my last two flittings at the same time. It is the last thing I have to do for my friend."

"You have not come to the end of things with the end of one chapter. We must not set ourselves against the advance of our lives."

"That has to stop some time, or go in the wrong direction. I have no part in the future. You have come to talk of what has nothing to do with your brother."

"I have come with a message from Gabriel. He insists on giving up that allowance. You know he found out it came from you. It has been generous of you, Jonathan; I have never known how you spared it; and you cannot spare it in the future. He is right to save you the move in the matter. Shall I tell him that you make a virtue of necessity?"

Jonathan stared at his sister, with his hands still, and suddenly threw himself back in a fit of laughter.

"My dear Josephine, I never gave Gabriel an allowance! I give people nothing. I only take from them. I thought you knew that."

"Why did you say you did, then?" said Josephine in a bewildered tone.

"I did not say so. He insisted on it. The poor boy wanted to have something from his father; and I wanted, wretched old man, that he should have it. I have not been able to give much to him; it seemed I could give him this; and what was the meaning of it from no one, the good of it from nowhere? The giver would never have made herself known, made himself known—he, she, it—what a silly thing secrets are! They make us solve them somehow. Well, I gave my solution of this." Jonathan went into further laughter, this time it seemed as a cover for his feelings.

"It was an extraordinary thing to do."

"Why was it extraordinary? It served a purpose for two people."

"Did you mean it for a sort of joke?"

"No, it was not a joke; it was a temptation. Why was it a joke to give my son an illusion, that his father had done something for him, one little thing in all his life? You don't understand the pathos of never being able to give."

"Well, what are we to do now? You know who the giver is? It is a woman, did you say?"

"No, I did not; I say nothing," almost shouted her brother. "I do not speak the truth, so of what use to tell you? Of what use to speak at all? You would not be any wiser. When I told Gabriel, he was not any wiser, was he?"

"I am afraid he was not. But what are we to tell him now? He must know that the money does not come from you, as he insists on returning it."

"You would not like me to have it, as it comes in?" said Jonathan, with an openly crafty expression. "To tell him to send it back to me? Was it fair to take me by surprise? To behave as if you did not know me?"

"Come, pull yourself together. Tell me what you wish me to say."

"Oh, say that the money comes from you. Say that I began to give it and stopped, and that you continued it. That sounds true to life and character. Or say that you always gave it, and did not like to seem to give so much. That saves my face, and ends my concern with the matter."

"We must say something. We can hardly admit either the truth or the mystery. Gabriel might talk about it to Felix and his other friends."

"Well, say that then. Have the credit for yourself, and understand how I felt in trying to get it."

"It is a funny person I have for a brother, to be sure. What are you doing, making that mess and muddle? Are you stirring up your papers or sorting them?"

"Stirring them up, stirring them up!" cried Jonathan, sweeping the pile together, and causing some to flutter to the ground. "Stirring them up for the bonfire! The past may have what is its own. Let my dead things go before me."

"You are not in a mood to make a decision. So we may as well give your account for the moment," said Josephine, picking up a paper and toying with it, her eyes down. "One story is as good as another, when neither can be true. This is a familiar writing, Miss Rosetti's, from a long time ago. A hand does not change any more than a face; or it changes like a face, becomes older and remains the same. Gabriel will have no need to speak of this, Jonathan. I will explain our joint thought of him, and he will be grateful."

"I shall have his gratitude after all, shall I? We shall both have it, you more out of proportion than I." Jonathan spoke in a harsh manner, glancing at the paper.

"Miss Rosetti might have been my partner by now,"

continued Josephine in the same conversational tone; "but she had some reason against it; some question of money, I suppose. I may offer to give her a partnership; why should we go through life doing nothing for our friends? This note has no beginning or end." Jonathan moved his hand towards it, but withdrew it and gazed at the ground. "The writing is clearer than her writing now. The words stand out apart. 'Gabriel is safe for life, and I will no longer see him as mine. That is best for all of us. This is my very last word. Maria'—Maria! Maria Rosetti! What is this Jonathan? Had Miss Rosetti anything to do with Gabriel when he was young? Did she know him then? Tell me it all."

"Of course she knew him then. She is my old friend, as you know. She had some thoughts of adopting him, and changed her mind."

"Did she ever adopt him? This sounds as if he had belonged to her. Tell me the truth." Jonathan was sitting with his shoulders hunched, his eyes looking straight before him, his body still. "He was only a few months old when I took him; and she came to me soon afterwards. Is this what it seems to be?"

"I know nothing; I say nothing. As you know my words mean nothing, why ask me?" Jonathan plunged his hands about on his desk, drumming his feet on the ground.

"Your wife never existed?"

"You have never believed she did exist. To pose as knowing less than you do, is not the way to get to know everything."

"You pretended to be a widower for Gabriel's sake?"

"And for my own sake, and your sake, and the sake of your girls' school. You did not want me to do anything else, did you? If you had an alternative, why did you not offer it?"

"I see you could do nothing else," said Josephine, in a quiet, charged tone. "But you could do something else than put Maria Rosetti into my house; to watch me in my life with Gabriel; to spy on my dealings with him; to satisfy herself that he was safe; while I, your sister, went on my way, unwarned, watched, in danger. You could have done something other than this, Jonathan."

"No, I could not, to serve my double-purpose. It was the only thing that could serve it. Why should I not put them both in your house for you to look after?" Jonathan laughed and drew with a pencil on his desk. "You have served yourself and Gabriel and her and me. Surely it was a good thing that you should serve us? And if you had made her your partner, it would have been a good finish up. It is a pity that you did not see your way to it, before her position changed, before she changed her mind."

"Oh, that is it!" cried Josephine. "I see it all. Miss Rosetti gave the money to Gabriel! She saw the chance at long last of doing something for his future. And I think it was time. If you want a finish up, this does very well."

"I am glad it satisfies you; I should have preferred the other myself. It would have been better for her, and through her better for me; and Gabriel would have got as much from you in the end." Jonathan's voice fell away again into laughter. "Well, you know all my story now. I can be at ease in your house. If I want a word with Maria, I shan't have to hide it." He moved his fingers as though he were playing the piano, and moved his lips as if in song.

"Tell me about your earlier life with her."

"No, I will not," said Jonathan, shutting his lips. "When have you asked me about my life with Gabriel's mother? I was a widower to you, wasn't I? It is not worth while to change my habits now. I will prepare myself for the long silence."

"Why did you not marry her? I suppose Gabriel is really your son?"

"Oh, know it all, know it all," said Jonathan, banging down his hands. "Gabriel is Maria's son and mine. She did not want to marry me. She wanted to support herself; and I did not want to support her. I put her in your school to work for herself, and as you have said—it seemed to me a natural thing—to watch over her son. She has not watched over him. She saw he was safe, as you say, or she saw nothing. If she did not look, she would not see. I don't know why she came to his help over his marriage. When I asked her for money, she did not often give it to me."

"She has lived in my house, as Gabriel's mother, deceiving me, letting me give her my trust, treat her as my friend——"

"She has never lived in your house as Gabriel's mother. You have never treated her as a friend. She has worked in your school and earned your trust."

"I must see her," said Josephine, drawing herself up. "I must tell her simply, that there are some things on which I cannot turn my eyes."

"Yes, tell her that simply. Turn her out and keep her son. I don't mind what you do. She has not cared for Gabriel; we have agreed never to speak of him; I could not bear her words of my son. She can have my money to live on, and I will live on you; I don't mind living on a woman." Jonathan moved his hands and feet together, adding the pedals to his performance.

"What are we to say about the allowance? Gabriel can never know the truth."

"Keep to the account we settled on. Take something else from his mother."

"I have borne that from her, which no woman should bear from another," said Josephine, in slow, recitative tones. "I do not speak of her having a child; I would not speak of her in that matter, except as another woman should speak." Jonathan raised his eyes, with a movement of snapping his fingers. "I have my own understanding. I could sympathise with her there."

"Well, sympathise then; because I could not; she has repelled my sympathy all along the line. Well, who comes here?" Jonathan turned to the door with his pipe set jauntily between his teeth. "So, Felix, it has come on me at

193

last! It has come out at the end. We need never think to escape the end, of life or anything else. This is an end indeed." He made a motion towards the paper, and Felix took it up and turned to Josephine.

"You have had an experience that comes to very few," he said.

"Yes—yes, I have. I have to do my best with it. It is a revelation to me, something new. Well, I must try to do my best." Josephine suddenly spoke to her brother.

"So Felix has always known the truth?"

"Of course he has known. We could not have lived on the terms we have, with our tongues tied on our memories," said Jonathan, with simple testiness. "He has not known what we were talking of before, what you know now." His voice grew loud and hard. "I mean about the boy's money! But he may know. Another thing between us won't make much difference."

Josephine laid her hand on her brother's shoulder.

"He will not want to know. He will leave it between the brother and sister. He knows that that relation goes back to the beginning; that it is the longest, if not the deepest. He will leave its own silences." She paused and turned to Felix with an uncertain smile. "I find myself in a difficult position, in a hard place. I cannot at the moment see my way."

"I could see mine in your position, the position of knowing something against someone who knew nothing against me. I should enjoy showing a quiet freedom from superiority. That has no point when you are really free from it. I have a great respect for you."

"I must do my best. It is a real experience. I must remember that it is real for someone else. Yes, there must have been much reality. There may be temptations to which I would not yield. I trust I shall not betray any littleness, any inclination to the use of power."

"I trust not: it would kill my respect."

"Well, my brother, I will leave you for to-day. The times of our separations will soon be of the past."

"Until the long separation," said Jonathan in a deep tone, giving his sister his hand without raising his eyes.

"Until death do you part," said Felix. "Those words remind me of something to do with myself. May I come and see you later in the day, Mrs. Napier? People are so much easier to deal with, when their own lives are disturbed. We have to watch for the time and take advantage of it."

Josephine stood as if arrested for a moment, and then rather blindly gave him her hand and left the house.

"Your influence over my sister is good, Felix," said Jonathan, speaking on the instant.

"But it does not seem to have had much effect on you. What is this about Gabriel's money? I don't claim not to be curious: I beg you to tell me."

"Maria gives it," said Jonathan in a nonchalant tone, his lips twitching. "I knew I was safe. If she had heard that it came from me, she would not have betrayed me, or been surprised. But it is a good thing that you are leaving me, Felix; you want a fitter companion."

"We all come round to my father's views in the end. What will Gabriel say when he knows?"

"He is to think that Josephine gives it; that I came to her rescue over her giving too much," said Jonathan, his smile broadening. "We can make quite a useful world out of our imagination. I don't know why falsehood does not do as well as truth."

"It often does better; that is why it is used instead." Felix broke off, and the two friends went into laughter. "I always wondered how you got the money. I like to think I have been the intimate of a bad man."

"Well, you have a future of innocence before you. It is not for me to disparage any kind of future; I have none."

"I wonder if I can be innocent without becoming ordinary. I see you think it is impossible."

"You are bound to become more ordinary. Your father wins in the end. I must not grudge him his victory."

"Indeed you must. I do want to feel that I leave empty hearts behind."

"Well, we will make the most of our last days. I will not cloud your looking forward with my looking back."

"How do you know I have been looking forward? I thought I had concealed it."

Felix locked his arm in Jonathan's and danced across the room. The old man fell out in a moment, stiff and breathless.

"Ah, there is a parable! I have gone far enough at your side. I can go no further."

CHAPTER XX

JOSEPHINE WENT HOME, walking rapidly, seeming excited and upheld. She reached the library and remained for a while by herself, and then sent a summons to Miss Rosetti. As she unfastened her bonnet and cast it on a chair, she saw it with a new sense of its significance. She took it in her hand, and perceived Miss Rosetti coming towards her, with her eyes upon it, as though she guessed her train of thought. Something resolute and braced in her bearing revealed her sense that the moment had its meaning.

"My dear," said Josephine, hesitating after the phrase, as though she had hardly brought herself to use it, and moving her hand towards the other woman's shoulder; "I have sent for you to tell you that I know it all; the meaning of your life with me; the meaning of my life with you, under your scrutiny. My poor brother betrayed it; in innocence; do not blame him. I came to understanding in innocence; do not blame me, more than you have had cause to blame me during my twenty-four years before your judgement."

The other met her eyes with an almost humorous expression, that implied she had not herself rehearsed a speech.

"Will you now tell me your story of your own life?" said Josephine.

"There is nothing left to tell. My early years I have described to you; my later ones you have seen; the few in between have been betrayed in innocence—that is, completely betrayed. Few of us should reveal the whole of our history, and you and I are not of the few. It is not through the fault of either of us that ours has been revealed." There was a pause, and then Miss Rosetti continued in quick, almost careless tones. "I have said that there is nothing to tell of my life, but there is one thing that I will tell.

I have not cared for Gabriel; I have cared in my way for the women whom one by one I have tried to care for; and I have come without trying and almost without knowing to care the most for you."

"There is the money you gave to Gabriel," said Josephine, with almost a threat in her tones.

"I hardly know why I gave it. I suppose from some sense of pity, duty—some sense of atonement." Miss Rosetti made a gesture as if perplexed at herself. "It is given: I will not take it back."

"I would not ask you to do that; I would not so far violate your human feeling. I am wondering what else to ask you, what to ask of myself that some solution may be found for us. Have you enough affection to give to me"— Josephine showed no surprise at the other's admission—"to take the partnership in return for what is given to Gabriel, and so given to me? Because, although he is your son, he is mine. Will you give me your answer? On that matter you must know your mind."

"Yes, I have enough feeling," said Miss Rosetti in a slow tone. "I see that the money is in a way given to you. I refuse to be even a name to Gabriel. And you and I have each looked at the other's hidden side, and looked away; and that is much." She paused, and as Josephine was silent, resumed in her usual manner. "I shall be grateful to have my share of the school, interested to use it. It will satisfy my ambition, satisfy my human side; for I have come to love it. It would seem to some people a small ambition; but I am content with it; it is mine."

"Then you are my partner, and I am yours; and we will live our partnership in our lives, observing it in thought and word and deed." Miss Rosetti knew that on some things there would be silence. "We begin our new life from this moment."

"It will easily cease to be new to me; it is my natural life; my happiness depends on women."

"I think with me it has been the other way round," said

Josephine, causing the other to give her low, deep laugh before she knew it.

The two women seemed to be easy with one another, with their permanent ease.

The younger voices were heard in the hall, and Josephine seemed to brace herself to sustain a shock.

"Here are some of our young companions! Well, two of them young, and one approaching our own age. We will say a word to them as the partners that we are. I am glad of this practice in going into partnership; I have seldom met an experience that has not been grist to my mill."

Miss Rosetti stared at Josephine, several expressions succeeding each other on her face; and shrank back as Helen and Gabriel and Felix entered, as though in recoil from the coming scene.

"Let me introduce you to my partner," said Josephine, in an almost triumphant voice. "In every capacity but that, you already know her. It is to her that you should address yourselves; there is no reason to turn your attention to me. Not that I also do not accept congratulation. Both for my partner and for the coming freedom of my life I accept, nay, demand it. I am almost disposed to become a sleeping partner, and establish Miss Rosetti in my place. So you see it is indeed to her that your words are due."

"Words are also due to my partner," said Felix. "I also accept, nay demand congratulation. And I also am disposed to become a sleeping partner, and establish her in my place. I am sorry that your satisfaction cannot equal mine; but I am in that foolish state when we think that no one's experience can compare with our own."

Josephine looked from him to Helen, as if she hardly followed his words. Afterwards she seemed to remember hearing her own voice, coming after a crash and through the ensuing din.

"Why, what an interesting piece of news! Did we expect it, or did we not? I can hardly say for myself: I have been too much occupied with my own partner to think about other people's. How egotistic that sounds, when it is the first time I have had an engagement in the school! It quite marks a stage in its development. And I am in a position to give a recommendation to you both. That is one happy side of it for me."

"I am not sure that the development is on the right lines," said Miss Rosetti, with a natural liveliness. "We shall have the school meeting the fate of over-developed things, and neutralising itself."

"What can Felix have been thinking of, when his thoughts should have been on his work?" said Gabriel.

"And what have you been thinking of, to let him get the better of you?" said Josephine in a sudden, startling manner, which she at once controlled. "Well, I am glad I have a partner, who can take a firm line about such proceedings."

"It is too early for Miss Rosetti to take lines," said Felix. "It will be a long time before I behave to Helen as her husband. And I don't think I shall ever behave as my father's son. He said I should not. I can hardly tell you how sensitive and gradual I shall be."

"Well, I can tell you what I shall be, and that is far less idle than I thought, in the future," said Josephine. "With two of the people I depend on deserting me, I shall have to put my energies back into the school. Miss Rosetti will be justified in insisting upon it."

"I don't think Miss Rosetti is behaving well," said Felix.

Josephine turned a smile upon Miss Rosetti, who was regarding her with a look of simple admiration.

"Do you think of being married soon?" Miss Rosetti said to Felix, pushing the truth at once to its extreme for Josephine.

"Well, it is hardly worth while to learn to manage my house, when I shall so soon endow Helen with it."

"You take your marriage vows literally," said Josephine.

"There is no other way of showing that you are keeping

them. When people have kept them in other ways, I should never have guessed it."

"Well, tell me the worst about your intentions."

"The worst is that Helen has to wait, until a relative's house is free for her to be married from. She has no settled home."

"I should have remembered that: I blame myself that you have had to tell me. I cannot claim that this house is her home, as she has been here so short a while; but if she will be married from it, I shall appreciate the feeling it will prove. She will not be the first or the second, and I have always appreciated the feeling."

"I should be most grateful, Mrs. Napier," said Helen.

"Grateful? My dear, why?"

"I hope I did not seem to be hinting," said Felix. "Not that I am a person who cannot be under an obligation."

"There is no obligation here. And if there were, I should be too used to it to reckon with it."

"Did your father know of your intentions, Felix?" said Gabriel.

"He told me he wished me to marry, and I am sure he did not think I should disobey him."

"He gets more and more fortunate in his son."

"And I in my father. He simply thought of everything."

"I think we are all fortunate in each other," said Josephine, taking a step away from the group, as if feeling her presence were due elsewhere.

Helen and the men withdrew, and Miss Rosetti came up to Josephine.

"Do you still want me as a partner?" she said in a blunt, rather ruthless voice.

"Why, what a question! I want you more than ever. And you are already my partner; so the question cannot arise. With yet another vacancy on the staff to fill, we shall indeed be dependent on each other. I cannot have you talking so out of the spirit of your place. And you know Miss Keats better than I do, and will be able to tell me her youthful desires. She may hesitate to impart them to me: I make no claim to your gifts with young women." Josephine's tones seemed to fail through some lack in the feeling behind behind them. She caught the eyes of her companion, and, starting forward, fell into her arms, and the two women stood locked in their first embrace.

Josephine freed herself and hastened from the room, to be met and checked by Gabriel.

"My boy?" she said, with something of her old tone.

"Did you give my message to Father? Have you his message for me?"

"Yes, I gave it: I did not fail you. His answer is, that the money never came from him. I was to tell you that, as his message; and I can tell you myself that I fully sympathise with what he did. You may assume that the money comes whence you will; or you will be wiser and assume nothing."

"Tell me the truth," said Gabriel.

"There has been no change in the arrangement, peremptory young man."

"You always gave it! As well as the other! You did well to be ashamed. So that was the mystery. And Father—Well, poor old Father!"

"Yes, your poor old father, my boy! My poor old brother!"

CHAPTER XXI

"It is a rule that women should not appear on similar occasions in the same clothes," said Miss Luke, coming downstairs dressed for the wedding. "Well, someone must play the part of the exception that proves it."

"I have a varied wardrobe," said Miss Munday.

"Well, I have been brought nearer to that state than for some time," said Josephine. "I am not forgetting my last *faux pas* in the matter of wedding garments."

"It is a pleasure to see you out of your widow's dress, Mrs. Napier," said Mrs. Chattaway.

"Then I am glad I am out of it on this occasion; though it will be a pleasure to me, or a relief rather, to be back in the habiliments in which I am at peace with myself, in so far as a sense of what I am wearing has any effect upon me."

"You are not going back to them?" said Mrs. Chattaway.

"My poor, suitable, useful garments! What a tone to take! I am living in other people's lives to-day, and not in my own. As I said, I have had a lesson on indifference to the bridal mood of others."

"You are that rare thing, Mrs. Napier, a truly considerate person," said Miss Luke.

"Yes, I am completely considerate, in this one small matter, on this one small occasion; great occasion rather, as it is great to other people. That is not much to do for my friends. And as I am to give the bride away—Sir Felix was clear that that was my prerogative; he seemed to think the position nearly as important as her own—I want to look as fully in sympathy with the moment as I shall be feeling. No doubt I made that demand on others when I was a bride."

"It is something to have been less exacting in one's life," said Miss Luke.

"I think that romance must have passed me over," said Miss Munday.

"It is sad that Miss Keats has no parents," said Mrs. Chattaway.

"Now that was not at all the speech to make at that juncture," said Josephine. "Yes, I have felt it sad; but I think less so on this occasion than on others."

"Do you think that the pair are suited to each other?" said Mrs. Chattaway.

"I trust so; indeed I trust so. I don't know why I should use such vehemence, except that my connection with the occasion hardly requires the enhancement of remorse."

"Ah, it was you who brought about the marriage?" said Miss Luke.

"I wonder if we have prompted things as often as we think we have," said Josephine, almost in soliloquy. "It may be that we are carried with them. Well, these things are as they are."

"They no doubt have the impression that they have been independent agents."

"Yes, yes, surely," said Josephine, putting a touch of anxiety into her tone.

"The wedding will bring back the other wedding to us all."

"Now," said Josephine, "you must not let it. You must yield yourself to the moment. Believe me, I shall not find that effort harder, that I have friends making it with me."

"Mrs. Giffard and Gabriel are in the heroic place," said Miss Luke; "play the heroic part."

"Mrs. Giffard is not playing any part at all; I thought it better that she should not. Especially when I found that Gabriel was willing to attend the wedding; glad indeed to do his duty by his friend, but glad also, poor boy, of the break for himself. That perception might have given her an heroic part; but I thought of it in time for her."

"Ah, we must not forget the difference between maturity and youth," said Miss Luke.

"Well, I think my friend must, on this occasion. I hope I have contrived that she will. And here is our bride, coming downstairs with Miss Rosetti! I wonder which of them looks nicer in her way, and which way is the better? She does Miss Rosetti great credit! I see I was wise in not offering my own help. I admit I felt rather maternal and interfering, but I controlled my impulses. Well, my dear, this is the first and last time in your life that you will look like that. And I have an odd confession to make, one that will seem to you very odd. You bring back to me my own wedding day and wedding dress, though I was much older than you when I became involved in such things. That must be my excuse for the insistence of the memory."

"I have never imagined myself a bride," said Miss Munday.

"Oh, I have; oh yes," said Miss Luke, looking straight about her. "It took me some time to set into myself. Mrs. Chattaway did not leave the matter to imagination. So, Miss Rosetti, we have only to await your confession."

"I have never imagined myself a bride. I tried to, and found that I could not. Your carriage is waiting, Mrs. Napier."

"Now, my dear," said Josephine to Helen, in an almost regretful voice. "It is time for you to offer yourself up as a sacrifice. Yes, there must be something of that in it for the woman; but we do not regret it; no, we do not. No, you lead the way, and I follow: I am in the man's place, and must not fail in chivalry. And I don't think any feeling is more suitable"—Josephine looked back to the other women—"in an elderly woman toward a young bride."

"No, it is not, it is not," said Miss Luke, looking after Helen. "Well, we must soon be following. We are able for the part of spectators."

"Of course, Mrs. Napier is not elderly," said Mrs. Chattaway; "but she does look older than usual, which is odd, as she is in lighter clothes. No doubt the other wedding is in her mind."

"The other weddings, yes," said Miss Luke.

"The gift from the girls has come after all," said Miss Munday. "Perhaps it can be presented after the service."

In the course of the reception in the concert hall, this token was carried by the youngest girl to the bridal pair.

"Is this for my wife and me?" said Felix. "We really feel it is too much, but, of course, we can do nothing but simply accept it. I will make the speech of thanks myself, because I feel I shall make it better, and not because I think the man should take the lead."

"We are the more delighted with the gift and the inscription, that we were beginning to be afraid we should not have them. We knew that you would not offer us wishes by themselves, would not ask us to accept only empty words, would not say that it was feeling that counted, and not material things. It would be absurd to say that a thing like this does not count. We are only sorry that we almost misjudged you; we feel we should have known you better, and now, of course, we do.

"And am I to make the mistresses a separate speech, or have they joined in the same gift? I knew there was some explanation of its being so good; I saw at once that it was no ordinary gift; that is why I was curious about it.

"Now I know that my worldly goods belong to my wife, but surely this does not belong only to her. A thing with this inscription cannot possibly be called worldly; and I will keep my share for myself.

"We have both been very happy amongst you, doing our daily work for the best kind of reward; not that we mean any disparagement of the gift. And I hope that you will never forget your old drawing master, and that when a different one comes, you will never feel he is the same.

"You know you have taken us quite by surprise, and so you have proof that I speak on the spur of the moment; and I feel that is a good thing, as it does need proof."

As applause ensued, and Felix left his place, Miss Luke ran up to him.

"There is a small token coming from us by ourselves, Mr. Bacon. You need not fear we have forgotten you."

"I did not really fear it. I should not be clever at others' expense, especially at yours. I have only been clever at expense to myself."

"We are sorry that our small remembrance is so late."

"I hope it was not an afterthought?"

"No, no. We claim for it all the value that comes from thought and feeling; though not much of any other kind."

"We will try not to mind," said Felix.

"May I congratulate you on a charming speech?" said Josephine.

"I was afraid you were going to congratulate me on my marriage, and opinions differ so much more on speeches. I am sorry for the hint of effort about mine; I had no time to make it spontaneous."

"Do you know, I find it odd to think of you as a family man?"

"I don't think the words quite give me."

"You came to the family state yourself, Mrs. Napier," said Miss Luke.

"Yes, I did. I have admitted to-day that the occasion has stirred my own memories."

"Are you dressed like this in sympathy with them, or with us?" said Felix.

"With you. In sympathy with them, I dress as I generally do. I fear it shows that we live for ourselves more than for other people."

"I don't think that needs showing," said Felix.

"Well, anyhow, you will not see me in these clothes again."

"Why not?" said Gabriel. "They will surely wear for longer than Felix's wedding day."

"They will wear for several years, as the best garments of the woman to whom I propose to send them. At least I am afraid they will."

"What will you wear when you come to visit Helen and me?" said Felix.

"The things you generally see me in, or replicas of them."

"Oh, I am sure they would be replicas. But it is getting out of sympathy with us very soon."

"Well, I cannot live always in other people's lives. I shall not expect you to live in mine, and assume a sable array."

"Well, you are safely married, Miss Keats, I should say Lady Bacon," said Fane. "No one can take that from you now."

"Do you believe in one standard for the man and another for the woman?" said Felix.

"No, no. But it is the lady we think of on these occasions. There are more on which the men have to be reckoned with."

"That is so untrue," said Felix.

"Yes, I think that on the whole women are accorded the human interest," said Josephine.

"Now I wonder if there is a difference," said Miss Luke.

"I have been wondering why people are supposed not to enjoy their wedding day," said Felix.

"I was very happy on mine," said Josephine.

"Yes, yes, I think it would be a happy day," said Miss Luke.

"Well, I daresay you chose your life of your own free will, Miss Luke," said Fane.

"I was helped a little towards it by poverty," said Miss Luke, giving no further account.

"Well, that is not so much of an admission," said Fane.

"I am enjoying my wedding day more than I thought," said Felix.

"Well, Miss Rosetti, we can give you congratulations of your own kind," said Fane. "The partnership is what has come to be important to you. And it is important in itself. Oh, yes it is."

"Now, if you want to catch your train," said Josephine, in a mellow tone.

"Good-bye; good luck; long life; health, happiness!" said Fane.

"All those things and more," said Miss Luke.

"Good-bye," said Miss Munday.

"We are glad that you are not as sorry to go, as we are to lose you," said Mrs. Chattaway.

"I think they are a little sorry to go," said Josephine, looking gently from Felix to Helen. "I mean in the midst of their other feelings."

"It is not in the midst of them," said Felix. "It has ousted them: I am afraid it will overcome us."

"Then we will not prolong the moment. Good-bye, my dear; I am not going to say anything of all that goes without saying. But as I have been in the position I have, you will treat me accordingly and let me hear."

"We will write to-night, Mrs. Napier."

"Oh, no, you will not: I have no intention of being such a burden. If you write in a week, that will be about what I ask. I am not anxious about you in safe hands."

"Well, we have had our vicarious glimpse of romance," said Miss Luke.

"Yes, we have lived through it, Josephine," said Jonathan. "Ah, I do many things for my friend. You have not had to put the force upon yourself that I have. Well, I shall soon be coming to your house to die."

"No, I have been able to give myself a free rein, certainly. But the pleasant occasion will be spoiled, if you choose it for talk of that kind. And we have not been so entirely out of sympathy with you; we have our own little regrets."

"Yes. Things will never be so amusing again," said Mrs. Chattaway.

"No, I do not think they will. Not just that," said Josephine.

"Well, I suppose the next thing will be the christening," said Mrs. Chattaway.

"Well, I hope not quite the next thing," said Josephine, with a laugh. "And I am always a little sorry when the first deflection of feeling comes."

"Poor child, she has all the future before her," said Miss Luke.

"She would pity us for having so much less of it," said Miss Rosetti.

"Yes, yes, but I know," said Josephine to Miss Luke. "The compassion of maturity for youth."

"It is quite nice to hear your cynical view, Miss Rosetti," said Mrs. Chattaway. "You have been silent to-day."

"A wedding strikes no chords in my heart."

"Oh, it does in mine. Oh, yes, it does," said Miss Luke.

"I cannot think of a pair more suited to each other," said Mrs. Chattaway.

"No, neither can I," said Josephine, "in the sense of striking, as it were, the same note. We certainly must not pin our faith to the attraction of opposites."

"I can just imagine their conversation," said Mrs. Chattaway.

"Now I don't know," said Miss Luke, with her head slightly on one side. "Does Mr. Bacon like an audience?"

"He will have the audience he likes best," said Mrs. Chattaway.

"Now that is too pretty to dispute," said Miss Luke.

"Which of the two do you regard as the more attractive, Mrs. Napier?" said Mrs. Chattaway.

"Well, on a wedding day the bride surely carries all before her."

"You are looking tired, Mrs. Napier," said Miss Rosetti. "You have been filling too many characters, even for you."

"I am ashamed to say that I have been filling one character, and that my own. I have already made the admission that the day's proceedings have raked up my own past. Well, I will go and divest myself of these trappings, that no doubt do make an odd set-off to my experienced phiz. You are accustomed to seeing me attired in harmony with it. I promise you that when we next meet, it will not suffer from the force of the contrast. Well, it has been my sacrifice to the occasion."

"It had not struck me," said Miss Luke; "had it struck any of you—that Mrs. Napier is a tragic figure?"

"Yes, it had struck me," said Miss Rosetti, idly.

"She would be, if she were not so strong and masculine," said Mrs. Chattaway.

"I should not call her masculine," said Miss Rosetti.

"No, perhaps she is too maternal," said Mrs. Chattaway. "But the feminine type is often quite as strong."

"Yes," said Miss Rosetti.

"I think we might call you masculine, Miss Rosetti," said Mrs. Chattaway.

Miss Rosetti was silent.

"Miss Munday and I can only claim to be neuter," said Miss Luke.

CHAPTER XXII

"WHAT TIME DOES our late employer arrive, Helen?"
said Felix, entering the drawing-room in his own house.
"As I do not keep my least thought from you, I confess
that I hope she will be impressed by what she sees. That is
really my least thought. I have no other quite so small."

"I have one smaller. I hope she will suffer a personal
pang."

"Must you have one as small as that?"

"Yes, I must, because of the thought you do keep from
me. You can't pretend that you did not suspect the
truth."

"Of course I pretend that I did not suspect it. Would
you have me behave in a natural manner?"

"You need not improve on yourself when you are with
me."

"I meant that for the height of sensitive chivalry."

"It was anyhow the height of self-esteem."

"The very height. I could only just attain to it. But
chivalry rises out of esteem for others, even less than other
virtues."

"I almost admired Mrs. Napier, when she proved that
the truth did not exist," said Helen.

"I am going on with my chivalry," said Felix. "What
could she do more than give us proof? The odd thing is
that none of the other women gave us any truth to suspect.
Eligible bachelors are not prepared for life as it is. They
ought to be trained quite differently."

"Most of them were older than you."

"Yes, but that was not their reason. They did not need
any reasons. Their attitude to me was the same as mine to
them; and that was much less natural than it sounds."

"I am not the person to explain it. I showed the natural attitude."

"I should not mind, if they had not been sensible of my charm. But they were sensible of it, and yet they did not want to spend their lives with me. I think they must have thought that charm was not everything. So they were content with their lives as they were, though the neighbours here would never believe it."

"I was not so content."

"It will be wiser to give the impression that you were. Doing something derogatory is better if you enjoy it. It is a mistake to think it would be worse. Of course it would be best to have done nothing at all."

"Neighbours don't seem to hold the Greek view of the nobility of suffering."

"Neighbours are English," said Felix.

"There is no disgrace in honest poverty."

"You can't really think that. There is no point in being too Greek."

"Well, there is none in useful work."

"You can't separate the two things," said Felix.

"No. No one calls wealth honest, though its honesty is above the average. It is like talking about the dignity of grey hairs."

"You put me in mind of Jonathan, though his grey hairs have no dignity. I hope we shall be able to carry off his visit. It is more awkward to meet the person you have lived with for twenty-three years, than it sounds as if it would be."

"He knows your feeling for him will never change."

"He knows it is changing. Things are easier for us, for being put into words. And I daresay they are easier for him than we think. They so often are."

"Did he feel your leaving him less than you expected?"

"Yes; I almost thought it would kill him. I suppose I was just going to let it. Engaged people are supposed to be selfish, and I think this shows that they are. But he is still looking forward. He has a wonderful hold on life."

"People have. What kills them is their own death, and not the loss of anyone else at all."

"Yes. My desertion never killed my father. What killed him was his own heart at seventy-nine."

"There is the carriage!" said Helen. "We must hasten to the hall. If we let Johnson announce them, it will look as if we were conscious of our new position."

"As if we thought living in a family home with family servants different from teaching Latin and drawing in a school. It would never do to seem to think that. And I really do not think it, as much as many people."

"I wonder what difference we may be conscious of?"

"Of being everything to each other. It does not seem suitable, when we greet our guests; but it is what they will expect of us."

"Well, my bride and bridegroom!" said Josephine, coming up the steps in full and fresh garb of widowhood. "I have managed to get away to pay my visit. It has not the most spontaneous sound, but 'managed' is the word. With this house on your hands, you will understand the demands of mine."

"My boy, we see you in your proper surroundings at last. We do not grudge you to them," said Jonathan.

"That is shallow of you, after only five weeks. My father comes out better and better."

"Ah, well, your father was your father," said Jonathan, moving forward with a steady, deliberate tread and a roving eye.

"You never used to think that," said Felix. "I used to wonder that you did not see it."

"Ah, blood is thicker than water," said Fane.

"I used to think water was thicker," said Felix. "And I am sure Jonathan did. But if he has changed his mind, so have I."

"Well, you will both have new duties to take the place of the old," said Josephine, allowing herself to glance round for the first time.

"And it won't be all duty, if I can judge by the look of it," said Fane, having already judged by this means.

"You don't any of you understand the value of leisure," said Gabriel.

"Oh, do I not understand it?" said Josephine. "I had been making plans to get a little more of it; but they have met the fate of the majority of human plans. I have been sucked back into the vortex. I need not have thought I could extricate myself."

"Does not Miss Rosetti make a difference?" said Felix.

"Indeed she does. Indeed she must, being as she is, being as you remember her. But the difference seems to be absorbed somehow in the oncoming force of things, in the flood of progress. In a word, the school is growing."

"But it was not put in a word," said Helen to Felix.

"You are getting accustomed to your new form of address, Bacon?" said Fane.

"Yes, but I find it is not true that pleasure is blunted by custom."

"It is after all a superficial difference."

"I seem as if it were no difference at all."

"Well, I should not like to change my appellation," said Josephine. "I have found doing so once quite enough."

"I have no prospect of changing mine, as I happen not to be heir to a title," said Fane.

"Is the temporary drawing mistress as popular as I was, Mrs. Napier?" said Felix.

"No, I think she is not," said Josephine, meeting a question with the simple truth.

"Are the men generally more popular than the women?" said Gabriel.

"I think women in life are more popular," said Felix. "I often hold unusual opinions."

"Do you know, I think they are?" said Josephine.

"It is not an unusual opinion," said Gabriel.

"Well, I still hold it," said Felix. "I do not change it.

Mrs. Napier, we are a little hurt that our places have to be filled."

"Your places will not be filled," said Josephine. "No one who makes a place of his own, leaves it without leaving also his own void. And you must remember that you neither of you went at my request."

"Oh, of course we were not dismissed," said Felix.

"I did not tell you at the time quite how much I regretted you."

"Ordinary people would have chosen that time to tell it," said Helen.

"I thought it might cloud your going forth," said Josephine simply. "But I am prepared to admit it was unimaginative to fancy you would give a thought to it."

"We always give thought to things," said Helen. "People always do, really."

"Why not leave the wedded pair to their mutual regard, Mrs. Napier?" said Fane.

"I never mind telling people my good opinion of them."

"I have never met another case of it," said Felix. "I don't wonder at Fane's surprise."

"You have not had all the praise you could do with, in your life?" said Fane.

"I did not know people ever had praise, except from Mrs. Napier."

"Well, I have had very kind things said to me on occasions," said Fane.

"I have met great generosity in thought, word and deed," said Josephine.

"I have met it in deed," said Gabriel.

"You have, young man," said Fane, moving towards him and lowering his voice. "I should have offered my congratulations, if I had felt that the matter came within the bounds of comment. In my mind I have done so each time an instalment of your dues has left our office."

"It is a roundabout way for them to come, when their source is in the house."

"Oh, you know it now, do you? The mystery is out?"

"Yes, it is out. And I am betraying no scruple in benefiting by a woman's toil."

"Now I think that is wise. I congratulate you both upon your good sense and your good fortune. A man must have his own views about being the slave of convention. You have come to the decision that gratifies both yourself and your benefactress. Though she is no relation of yours, she is an old friend of your father's, and your aunt's partner. She has not many claims upon her resources. To my mind you have nothing to be sensitive about."

Gabriel was silent, suppressing the words that sprang to his lips.

"Her business affairs are in our hands, in common with those of most of the people in the neighbourhood. Not every woman is as capable of being her own lawyer as your aunt."

"Of course the fact that I am aware of this truth, does not mean it is to be public property."

"My dear young man, you are talking to a partner in a reputable legal firm," said Fane.

"Do you get on well with your household?" said Josephine to Helen. "A new mistress is the object of a critical regard."

"Helen passes every test," said Felix.

"Well, I should find it go rather against the grain to face all the responsibility under the cloak of ease. I would rather have the responsibility naked and unashamed, as I am used to it."

"People despise responsibility less under a cloak of ease," said Felix.

"That seems to me a strange view," said Josephine.

"And yet it is almost universal," said Felix. "How long can you all stay with us?"

"I must go back to-night, as I have told you. I go because I am needed, and for no other reason."

"We did not expect that you would go because you

could not bear to be here," said Felix. "You have not made things any better."

"Things are bad, as I have explained. I hoped for more ease and leisure, and see no prospect of them. You, who are more fortunate, ought to pity me."

"Ought we to pity people who have less leisure than we have? I used to be rather annoyed with people who did that. When my father warned me that I should be an object of pity, I think he meant me to be annoyed."

"Well, I am content with my lot in life," said Fane, "though I also am called back to-night by my duties. May I offer you my escort, Mrs. Napier?"

"You are feeling settled in your new surroundings, my dear?" said Josephine to Helen, as she adjusted her cloak. "I should be so glad to feel that, before I leave you."

"I am not feeling so very settled yet."

"It will come, it will come," said Josephine, letting go her cloak to place her hands on Helen's shoulders. "I remember my early restless time. Believe me, it will pass, and the other time will come."

She embraced Helen with simple affection, and took her leave of Felix with almost indifferent friendliness.

"We were too homesick to be at our best, Helen," said Felix.

"Yes. Seeing Mrs. Napier made us feel terribly out of it all."

"We ought to ask the mistresses to visit us."

"But it might bring on the first feelings. It will be braver to settle down into our new life, and remember it is all we have."

CHAPTER XXIII

Gᴀʙʀɪᴇʟ sᴏᴜɢʜᴛ ʜɪs father as soon as the guests had gone.

"The truth is out about Miss Rosetti. I am not going to tell you how. I am tired of being helplessly involved in mystery. But I ask an explanation from the beginning. It is clear that you and Josephine must know."

"My boy, you have had a shock," said Jonathan, looking at his son with simple compassion. "I never meant you to have it. I thought the truth would never come out. At one time I hardly could think it, but when it had been hidden for twenty years I saw it as safe." Gabriel stared at his father, closing his hands. "I don't know how it has come to you now."

"It is time it all came to me. Whatever is to be known, I demand to know."

"My son, I owe you complete confidence. But is there anything I need to say? You ask for an explanation from the beginning. But there is only the beginning. Soon after you were born, your mother gave you up to me. There was nothing further between her and me, or between her and you. She offered nothing to either of us, would have taken nothing. I had my friends, and my sister gave you a mother's care. I did, as your father, what it was in me to do. You have seen that that too was almost nothing. But things have worked out as well for us, as for many fathers and sons. I have not lost your affection: I have never deserved it, perhaps never had it: but I have not lost it. And I hope I have had it in a measure; I have had much for you."

"And the allowance comes from my mother, from Miss Rosetti? That is as I have been told?"

"Yes, yes, the allowance. Oh, the allowance! Yes, that

came from your mother, my boy; I was at a loss to explain it. Josephine came to my help at last. Ah, well, you have an odd old man for a father."

"Father, I am not going to say or listen to another word of the past. I can hear it all from Josephine. But there is the future to be thought of, both for you and for me. We cannot live, either of us, in Josephine's house. Things would be too much for all of us, when ignorance had given place to silence. There would be too much silence, and too much underneath. The relation between you and me is anyhow open to the world. We will set up a home, and ask Ruth's mother to manage it. I will get some work, and we shall have enough between us. I could not face a life with my adopted mother, and my actual mother, and my mother-in-law, all under the same roof."

"My boy," said Jonathan, in a broken voice, standing with his hand on his son's arm, looking almost childishly into his face, "this is a great release from hopelessness. I could not face it even with courage, the life with the women. I should not have had human happiness enough for self-respect, for human dignity. A man's dignity must have gone beyond hope. I should have lost it; I was losing it. Some of the consequences have fallen on you. And that poor creature, your wife's mother, is sadly placed in Josephine's house, with her daughter dead, and Maria gone over to Josephine. I have known what it is to lose a friend. It is I who should help her; I have not lost my child. I will ask Felix and his wife to keep me until my house is found. I shall not burden them for long. I have my plans for my future."

He seemed to push his way from the room, his head bent forward in eager purpose.

"My dears, I have come to beg a favour, to ask you to shelter me for a time. I know it is what you have looked for, but it is not asked in that spirit. I am at a loose end only for the moment. My plans are made. My son and I are to set up a house together, and I want a roof over my head until I have my own."

"What is your reason for the plan?" said Felix. "Please tell me exactly."

"Oh, there was a reason that started it. But we feel we shall be in our right place in a home together."

"We might have come to the conclusion before," said Gabriel. "The real reason is, that I have stumbled on the truth about my mother. I suppose you have always known it, Felix?"

"Well, you have always known about my parents. I am not a person to avoid the subject of parents. So pray do not let us avoid it now."

"It is less embarrassing to lose a parent than to gain one."

"Yes, I quite agree. I gained my father at the last, and it was much more embarrassing than losing him. Does Mrs. Napier know the truth?"

"She knew just before she made Miss Rosetti a partner," said Jonathan. "Ah, she is a noble creature, my sister."

"It does not trouble me that my parents were not married," said Gabriel.

"Well, I should think not, my boy. That would be a silly thing," said Jonathan. "It might have happened to any one of us."

"Not to me," said Felix. "I must do justice to my father's memory. Will you speak of it to Miss Rosetti, Gabriel? I would not ask that, if I could bear not to know."

"I shall speak of it once, and then never again," said Gabriel.

"I am upset that you are thinking of the future, Jonathan," said Felix, turning quickly from Gabriel. "I took it for granted that you would always think of the past. I thought I should break up your life, and I seem to have done nothing to it at all."

"Ah, healthy lives pull up. They have their resilience, like all healthy things."

"I did not know that your life was healthy; I thought you had a morbid attachment to me."

"Ah, I have been attached to you. But you have filled my place, and I must even fill yours. And I shall rejoice to fill it with my son. Ah, that is the natural tie."

"Of course it is. But you wanted an unnatural one. And I have kept your place for you, and carefully put Helen in another."

"Ah, well, words of that kind are words."

"But it is kinder to say them. Mrs. Napier said she could never fill my place, though she had filled it even temporarily. She said that Helen and I would leave our voids. And I had kept a void for you. I don't think you ought to neglect voids. My father was always talking about mine. And to think that I gave you preference!"

"Ah, well, it was your own choice. I did nothing about it."

"You always did everything about it. I wish my father were here to support me. There is a saying that marriage alters friendship, but I never knew its real meaning."

"Mrs. Napier will miss you, Gabriel," said Helen.

"No, not so much. Ours was a case where marriage altered friendship."

Gabriel returned the next day to Josephine's house, and went at once to the library, where she and her partner were together. Miss Rosetti's presence on the scene of so much of his experience seemed suddenly to weld itself into the material of his life. As he stood in the doorway, she lifted her eyes and gave a startled glance from him to Josephine.

"I think my position is unique," said Gabriel, striving for his usual manner. "But I do not find that any assistance in dealing with it."

"It may be unique," said Miss Rosetti, looking at him with a faint smile. "It is certainly an unusual position, both for you and for me."

"I have come to say that I know it all," said Gabriel, his mood broken, and his eyes swerving from Miss Rosetti's face to Josephine's; "the whole story of my life from the beginning. I should have been glad if I had never known; but as the knowledge has come, I must do my best with it."

"I hardly know what that need be," said Miss Rosetti. "I too wish you had never known, and I too must do my best with your knowledge. That will be to do nothing. It will make no difference to you or to me. You seem as if you had suffered harm, but you have had great kindness in your life. Many people have done their utmost for you. I have done it, and will do it now. My utmost is to tell you that I am glad that you cannot see me as your mother. When I gave you money, it was to your wife that I gave it: I cannot bear the thought of hardship for a girl. When she died, I could not see how to withdraw it; but you need not fear; it is withdrawn. Mrs. Napier discovered the truth, and offered me the partnership in payment. She felt it was given to her, as it was given to you. So it comes from her, as you have understood. You see how matters are between us."

"If you say that my knowing the truth will make no difference, it must make none," said Gabriel.

His mother did not speak.

"I shall give up the money, of course, both for the future and the past."

"Yes, I suppose you will give it up. I shall be glad enough to have it, and put it to my own use; for one thing a share of the school on normal terms. I thought you would never come on the truth: there was no reason why you should come on it. I do not care if you pay back what you have spent; it will not count more with you than with me."

"I stumbled on the truth. No one has betrayed a trust."

"No, no. I am sure the standard of human behaviour has been high. I do not see myself as a person who need doubt it."

"How are we to meet in the future? I have not said what I should have thought it natural to say; but I must just ask that."

"We seem to be quarrelling already," said his mother, with a smile. "But we shall not have much more chance. We shall meet as we have always met. And we have not met, have we?"

"You have done much for me," began Gabriel.

"That is enough," said his mother. "Surely you have understood?"

"It was hard on Josephine," said Gabriel, in tones of forced lightness, "to be compelled to shoulder my peculiar liabilities."

"It may have been hard. She did not seem to find it so."

"Well, curious young man, have you finished your inquisition?" said Josephine. "If so, run away and sort your thoughts, and leave two experienced women to do the same by theirs. We can meet again later, with all the questions to be asked and answered."

"Josephine, I cannot live at home," said Gabriel, looking at Josephine as if Miss Rosetti were not present. "It would be too much on me, with all this underneath. I could not know it, and not know it; I could not live one life, and live another, hidden by it. We should all be defeated by our common effort in the end. We should be enduring the strain of a double life; and we are people who find a single strain enough. And my father cannot live his last years with all the complications of his youth. He and I are going to take a house, and ask Mrs. Giffard to manage it. That will solve another problem that is not solved here."

There was silence, while Josephine faced the alternative future; a future with Gabriel and Gabriel's mother living and knowing each other under her roof.

"My boy, you must do your best for yourself; your best for those whom you have taken into your life. I know from experience that that is a long, long duty. You have not found me fail in it. You may go and follow my example, if it comes to you that that is to be the final form for the bond between us."

As Gabriel left the room, Miss Rosetti turned to Josephine.

"Well, you have heard me speak as a mother, and you will understand that I shall never speak as one again."

CHAPTER XXIV

"I HOPE I AM not presuming on your friendship in assuming that I am still welcome?" said Josephine, coming with some hesitation round the door of the common room. "I am ashamed of being so tardy in expressing my gratitude for my partner; but between making the partner of one of you, and a bride of another, my time has hardly been my own."

"The rest of us you have left as we were," said Miss Munday.

"Yes, and I am glad I have. I must have some of my friends in their old relation to me: I have not altered mine to them."

"We are proud of supplying the partner," said Miss Luke; "and of supplying the bride, too. Oh, yes, we are proud of that."

"Yes, I have altered it to that extent," agreed Josephine. "My debt is greater."

"Is Miss Rosetti happy in her higher sphere?" said Miss Luke.

"Higher? In what way is it higher?" said Josephine.

"Oh, I only meant in the spiritual sense."

"I should say that teaching is spiritually a higher work than organising. You meant perhaps in a conventional sense?"

"Yes, perhaps I did. Well, that is a very real sense."

"I don't think 'real' is the word," said Josephine, with a slight frown.

"But organising is what you do yourself, Mrs. Napier," objected Mrs. Chattaway.

"Yes," said Josephine.

"It is Miss Keats who has moved to a higher sphere," said Mrs. Chattaway.

"And in what sense?" said Josephine.

Mrs. Chattaway did not say.

"You are losing your nephew again, Mrs. Napier?" said Miss Luke. "This time deliberately allowing him out of your care?"

"I could not help it," said Josephine, putting out her hand as if to repudiate criticism. "I had to teach him at last to recognise my brother's claim. I have always had that duty in front of me. They say that things are never as bad as we expect; but I can't say I found it in this case. Well, it is over now."

"Mr. Swift will not join you here?" said Miss Munday.

"Yes, he will, if I am not careful. That is what he will do, unless I provide for him elsewhere. It seems a natural arrangement; but there are reasons why I feel it is not suitable for him, and perhaps for others. My brother is, if you will not misunderstand me, very much of a man."

"We will not misunderstand you," said Miss Munday.

"You saw Sir Felix and Lady Bacon happy and settled in their new home?" said Miss Luke, breaking in rather hurriedly.

"Well, I flashed upon them, and flashed back again. I saw them happy, I think, but hardly settled. You are right that it seems a new home for him as well as for her. They still seem to be looking out of the haze that envelops the newly wed. I remember too well being obscured by it myself, to feel disposed towards criticism."

"It must have been hard for your nephew to see the married happiness."

"Yes—yes, it must have had its element of hardness. I thought of it for him when I felt the call on my own memories."

There was a silence.

"We miss Mr. Bacon's and Miss Keats' bright retorts," said Mrs. Chattaway, as though explaining some want felt in the atmosphere.

"Yes," said Josephine, "there was a great element of

brightness about both. That is what I meant by saying that there was a haze about them just now. The brightness is somehow a little dimmed. Unless it is that their new atmosphere is less fostering to it."

"Do you mean that they are less happy than they were?"

"No, I do not mean that at all. I should not have chosen that way of stating it; if it had struck me, which, I am glad to say, it had not."

"Do you know that someone once said," said Mrs. Chattaway; "of course you do not, it is too foolish a piece of gossip for your ears, but someone said that you—you and Mr. Bacon—that Mr. Bacon and you wanted to marry."

Josephine looked at her with a courteous expression and made no reply.

"You are surprised at my repeating it?"

"Yes, I am a little surprised at that."

"Of course I should not have done so. But it seemed such an idle rumour, so utterly meaningless, that it seemed hardly to matter."

"In short, its sole point was that it could be repeated," said Josephine, smiling. "It does not matter in the least."

"There was nothing to prevent Mr. Bacon's proposing to any or all of us," said Miss Luke.

"Well, there were things to prevent it," said Josephine. "Our ages, our being settled in professions, other things."

"I wonder which it was," said Miss Munday.

"Whichever it was, it did its work," said Mrs. Chattaway, her eyes on Josephine.

"We were talking about Sir Felix and Lady Bacon's surroundings," said Josephine. "They are beautiful, and they struck me as suitable to both. If my personal feeling is for something more tonic, more productive, it may be that I am influenced by my own prosaic history."

"Would you like to marry a man shorter than yourself, Mrs. Napier?" said Mrs. Chattaway.

"I liked to marry a man taller than myself, as you know.

I am not polygamous, polyandrous, whatever the word may be."

"Mr. Bacon was very much moulded by his background, considering how long he had lived away from it," said Miss Luke.

"I think the moulding was a little conscious," said Josephine, drawing in her brows. "Did you not think so? That it would have been a freer, a more spontaneous development, if it had come about of itself?"

"I always thought it was wonderful how he adapted himself," said Mrs. Chattaway. "Of course we cannot know how far it went."

"I am in need of your advice," said Josephine, in a detached manner. "Do you think that Sir Felix's post would be better filled by a man or a woman?"

"Would you be able to get another man?" said Mrs. Chattaway at once.

"With the growth of the school, the post would be suitable for anyone suited to it," said Josephine, gravely answering her true meaning.

"Oh, yes, of course; I know. I only meant——"

"You are mistaken in what you meant," said Josephine.

"I suppose you would not consider a man for Miss Keats' post?" said Mrs. Chattaway, attending simply to her own position.

"As it is a resident post, there is hardly a question of that," said Josephine, scarcely accepting the improvement.

"Dear, dear, the days pass, and our places are filled," said Miss Luke; "and we feel that they are particularly ours."

"I feel I have been using words vaguely," said Josephine. "My feelings are the opposite of value. Two different people will take places that will be determined by themselves."

"And you will have Mrs. Giffard's place to fill as well," said Mrs. Chattaway. "I don't mean, of course, that you can fill it. You will have it on your hands, to cope with in whatever way you decide."

"Well, I think I shall fill that place," said Josephine, causing Mrs. Chattaway's face finally to fall. "I don't see anything about the way in which it has been discharged, to preclude the measure. I am not going to claim that I regard all places as equally well filled; I have too much respect for due apportionment of credit."

"Mrs. Giffard has had to meet many demands from her own life," said Miss Luke.

"She has," said Josephine, "and she has met them fully. And I have met the result with the understanding of one who has felt similar temptation, and all but yielded. But I am not going to exalt the yielding; I can only sympathise with it."

"It will be an ideal solution of her life to keep house for your nephew," said Miss Luke. "It will seem in a way to give her daughter back to her."

"Yes, I think it will in a way seem to do that. There was a moment when I think she rather felt he was taking her from her. But he is in the rapid, youthful stage, and would be about on the point when he should yield her back. The experiment should work."

"She will not expect him to have sent down deep roots in so short a time," said Mrs. Chattaway.

"He is too young a plant for deep roots," said Josephine.

"Will his living with his mother-in-law prevent his marrying again?" said Miss Luke, in a tone of by no means repudiating life.

"Yes," said Josephine; "I think it may for a time. But time is plentiful in youth."

"Is it wise for Mrs. Giffard to give up her work, if she may need it again?" said Mrs. Chattaway.

"She will never need it again: I have seen that she is not fit for work."

"You are a wonderful friend, Mrs. Napier."

"If I am told that so often, I shall begin to believe it. And it surely is not good for us to think we are wonderful."

"Ah, it is a great privilege to give," said Miss Luke, laughing as she ended. "It must be, I mean."

"Is it?" said Josephine. "I believe I have not found it anything but a rather prosaic matter of course."

"Your life will be lonely in the future, Mrs. Napier," said Mrs. Chattaway.

"Yes," said Josephine; "as it has been since my husband died. But I shall be glad to spare the people the sight of the loneliness, who believed they prevented it, dear ones that they were. The effort not to show it made my life something of a strain. It will be a relief to be free from it."

"Now, we shall resent your stealing Miss Rosetti, if she does not cure those feelings," said Miss Luke.

"Yes, that is healthy," said Josephine, not missing the intention. "And do you know, I believe she may cure them? I have even felt myself that she may. I assure you that I have found myself turning my eyes to the future."

"We have not realised all you have been through, Mrs. Napier," said Mrs. Chattaway, perhaps feeling more contrition than she deserved.

"Well, I hope not. The heart on the sleeve is not correct, is it? And I am doing my best to convince you that much of it, that some of it, is behind."

"Have you engaged successors to Miss Keats and Miss Rosetti?" said Mrs. Chattaway.

"I have offered the posts to two women, who have accepted them."

"Oh, that is exciting," said Mrs. Chattaway, receiving the impression of a simple affirmative. "We shall have two new companions. It will almost make up for our loss."

"Yes, I think in a way it will," said Josephine; "I think it should. We should give people every chance in a new life. Those who are leaving us have it, I hope, in theirs. They too are succeeding others."

"Would you say that the newly-married couple are very devoted?" said Mrs. Chattaway.

"Yes, very devoted in their way," said Josephine, rising.

"But there seems to me something hard and bright about them, something hard and bright about their relation. I hardly know how to put it. They are like agate, beautiful and bright and hard."

"Agate is a beautiful material," said Mrs. Chattaway, uncertainly.

"You will not use words upon what we have dealt with without words?" said Josephine, in a low, very rapid tone, going to the door.

"No, indeed we will not, Mrs. Napier," said Mrs. Chattaway, hastening after her with politeness as prompt as her comprehension.

Josephine returned to the library, and encountered a maid coming out of it.

"A gentleman waiting to see me in the drawing-room, Adela? I am quite innocent in causing him to wait: I proceed from one claim to another with all the despatch I can."

"Someone come about the post of drawing master," said Miss Rosetti. "Shall I see him for you?"

"No, I must even do my own business. If I fail to keep my drawing master, I must submit myself to the onus of getting a new one. I hope this one will not be frightened by my sombre figure. He can see, anyhow, that I have no husband to protect me; people are hardly prepared for the masculine element when they come to a girls' school. Not that it is reasonable to object to it, when they are masculine themselves. Well, I will go and do my best with this male aspirant to my post."